### "Hello, Lindsey."

That was it. Two simple words. Years had come and gone since she'd last seen Graham. Ten long years, and now it all came down to a simple hello.

"Hello, Graham," she answered, her shaky voice little more than a whisper. A thousand sleepless nights she'd wondered if her memories had been accurate. If his smile had really been that captivating, if his hair actually fell in lush, dark waves, framing his classic features. Now she knew just how deceptive memories could be. They hadn't done him justice.

"Detective Graham Dufour, Homicide," he announced, flashing his badge for everyone to see. His voice had almost broken on the first hello, but it was all business now. Whatever they had once shared had died a long time ago. At least for him.

"Do I understand, *Miss* Latham, that you think you saw someone murdered in the crowd last night?" he asked doubtfully.

"I don't *think* anything. I *know* what I saw," she snapped. "And if you don't look into this matter, I'll call your supervisor, the district attorney, the governor—"

"And if that doesn't work, *Miss* Latham, you can always call Da

# SAFE HAVEN

# JOANNA WAYNE

*Behind the Mask*

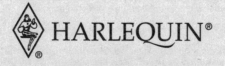

## HARLEQUIN®

TORONTO • NEW YORK • LONDON
AMSTERDAM • PARIS • SYDNEY • HAMBURG
STOCKHOLM • ATHENS • TOKYO • MILAN • MADRID
PRAGUE • WARSAW • BUDAPEST • AUCKLAND

ISBN-13: 978-0-373-36175-5
ISBN-10:    0-373-36175-0

BEHIND THE MASK

This edition published by arrangement with Harlequin Books S.A.

® and TM are trademarks of the publisher. Trademarks indicated with ® are registered in the United States Patent and Trademark Office, the Canadian Trade Marks Office and in other countries.

www.eHarlequin.com

**Printed in U.S.A.**

## JOANNA WAYNE

Joanna Wayne was born and raised in Shreveport, Louisiana, and received her undergraduate and graduate degrees from LSU-Shreveport. She moved to New Orleans in 1984, and it was there that she attended her first writing class and joined her first professional writing organization. Her first novel, *Deep in the Bayou*, was published in 1994.

Now, dozens of published books later, Joanna has made a name for herself as being on the cutting edge of romantic suspense in both series and single-title novels. She has been on the Waldens Bestselling List for romance and won many industry awards. She is a popular speaker at writing organizations and local community functions, and has taught creative writing at the University of New Orleans Metropolitan College.

She currently resides in a small community forty miles north of Houston, Texas, with her husband. Though she still has family and emotional ties to Louisiana, she loves living in the Lone Star state. You may write to Joanna at P.O. Box 265, Montgomery, Texas 77356.

# Chapter One

Lindsey Latham lunged for the support rail as the jerky movements of the Mardi Gras float propelled her forward. She breathed deeply, determined to ward off a persistent bout of queasiness, and stared out into the never-ending sea of faces. They were all one now, a voluminous cloud of eyes and mouths floating in space. And hands. Thousands of hands, all waving wildly and begging for the baubles that glittered in the moonlight like precious jewels.

"Hey, lady, throw me something—for the baby!"

Lindsey adjusted her feathered mask for the umpteenth time and looked down at the demanding man, and at the small boy he lifted toward her like some heathen sacrifice. He was weaving dangerously close to the slow-moving float, throwing caution to the winds to get his share of the carnival bounty. But the child was adorable, no more than a toddler, grinning through lips coated with the sugary remains of cotton candy.

Lindsey reached into the box at her feet and took out a small stuffed alligator. The crowd around the man surged forward at the appearance of the cheap toy, all with hands outstretched, pleading for their chance at one of the prized throws. Prized, at least, for the duration of the parade.

She dropped it into the child's chubby hands and then quickly threw a handful of doubloons to the crowd waiting patiently on the walk. She threw another one of the alligators, too, far into the crowd, to reward those who were heeding the safety warnings and staying clear of the unwieldy floats.

"I can't believe this is your first time to ride on a Mardi Gras float, Lindsey. Don't you just love it?" Brigit asked, her voice bubbly with excitement.

"It's different," Lindsey admitted. "The verdict is still out on the fun part."

Lindsey watched as Brigit dangled a long strand of silvery beads, taunting the spectators so that they clamored around her, begging for the sparkling throw. She twirled the necklace in the air flippantly and then leaned over to drop it into the hands of an eager teenage girl.

"Wow, get a look at that!" Brigit yelled above the din of the crowd. "Just the guy I need to keep me warm at night."

"Which guy? There's only a few thousand out there," Lindsey quipped good-naturedly.

"The hunk. Over there, in the LSU shirt." She pointed with one hand and dug around in the overflowing box at her feet with the other. "I've got to throw him something good. Like my phone number," she said teasingly as she caught his eye and tossed him a long string of imitation pearls.

He snagged them in his outstretched hands and blew her a kiss before adding them to the multitude already draped about the shoulders of the blonde who stood at his side.

"Glad you only threw the beads," Angela offered, leaning over from her spot on the other side of Lindsey.

"Yeah," Lindsey said, "I'd hate for you to waste a perfectly good phone number on a guy who probably has his own phone book."

The procession of brightly lit and elaborately decorated floats made its way slowly down St. Charles Avenue as police on horseback tried in vain to keep the crowds pushed back. They were good citizens who'd never think of crossing an officer of the law at any other time, but carnival fever had hit. Fun was the supreme ruler from now until Fat Tuesday.

The float jerked and then came to an abrupt standstill. Lindsey clung to the side. "I hate these sudden stops," she lamented. Even the most reserved parade viewers left their places on the walks and the neutral grounds that bordered the parade route to swarm around them. She backed away from the edge as the noisy crowd pushed closer, climbing atop friends' and parents' shoulders to shove hands and even faces into her space.

"Just relax, Lindsey. Have fun. This is the best part. The rough part comes later, when we hit Canal Street," Angela said, the thrill of the night adding a lilt to her Uptown accent. She tossed a large supply of beads and doubloons into the street below them, clearly taking her own advice.

"Enjoy it. This is the best part," Lindsey repeated to herself. She should be having a ball. The other seven girls on her float were.

But they were native New Orleanians, she reminded herself. Even in high school, they had been far more practiced at carnival revelry than she. Not that she hadn't loved the Mardi Gras season. It was just that her tendency to order and organize had always made it a little more difficult for her to dissolve into a state of total chaos.

But here she was, back in New Orleans with her high school classmates, partying as if it hadn't been ten years since they were young and eager seniors at Dominican High. She was here, and she had followed their urging, joining in all the Mardi Gras festivities. Parties, masked balls, coronations…

And the krewe's big parade.

The float jerked forward, bucking like a nervous horse. The motion sickness Lindsey had been fighting all evening attacked again, this time with a vengeance. She held on to the sides of the float and silently ordered her stomach to cooperate.

She knew better than to ride in the parade. But saying no to this bunch of party animals had been about as useless as that last order she had given her stomach. Especially with Grace Ann resorting to her infamous pleading look. The one that had been known to topple powerful men like matchsticks.

Grace Ann had been one of her best friends in school. Sweet, pretty, incredibly rich and generous to a fault. And now she was Queen Grace Ann, of the Krewe of Minerva, a regal monarch who wasn't willing to take no for an answer. What was the good of being queen, she had argued quite persuasively, if your friends wouldn't help you celebrate?

So here she was, Lindsey mused, atop a tractor-pulled contraption of brightly painted papier-mâché figures, her costume slipping off her shoulders and her mask riding her nose like a loose saddle. And she was trying not to even think what her stomach was doing while the float snaked along at the pace of an aged snail.

Brigit leaned over the edge, dropping toys and decorated plastic cups to a group of youngsters who were all but climbing in with them. "Come on, get with it," she told Lindsey playfully. "Your adoring public is begging for treats."

Lindsey tossed a supply of beads into the crowd, high above the heads of those who swarmed around her. She tossed more toward a balcony full of gray-haired women hanging over the rails. Brigit was probably right about this being the best part of the route. Huge oaks and massive old homes lined the wide streets. And the crowd, though rowdy by her standards, was mostly families, out to enjoy a beautiful evening and all the excitement of Mardi Gras.

She reached for more beads, but the float jerked to a stop, sending her swaying against the rail.

"I think I'm going to be sick."

"Here? Now? You can't be." Brigit offered a reassuring pat. "But, if you must, aim for that tall guy with the stupid hat. He grabs everything I try to throw to anyone else," she suggested, only half joking.

Lindsey smiled in spite of herself, although Brigit would never see her expression beneath the stiff masks all the float riders were forced to wear. "I'm serious. I may have to bail out. I could signal one of the policemen to get me a ride."

"Sure, there are plenty of medical people around," Danielle threw in, stepping from the back corner to join in the conversation, "although it's usually the marchers that pass out, not the riders. But you'd miss all the fun."

"But I don't know how much more fun I can handle," Lindsey countered. "The two hours of serious toasting before we even started rolling is a tad more than I'm used to." She leaned back, resting her head against the float's center frame. "I'll try to make it a while longer, though," she conceded. ''Who knows? I might get the hang of this, if I last long enough.''

The band that marched in front of the float swung into a popular rock tune, and the fun-loving spectators broke into applause. The faces in the crowd were shifting now, moving and swaying to the music as the float inched forward. Lindsey stood between her two friends and strived to adopt their carefree manner. She stared into the night, trying to focus on eyes, mouths and noses that appeared and then disappeared, like Alice's Cheshire cat. Now you see them, now you don't.

She flung a multitude of colored beads into the distance. Patterns of purple, green and gold swirled magically through the night sky, falling like manna from heaven into the upstretched hands.

A beam of light caught Lindsey's attention and held it. A tiny sliver of illumination in an otherwise darkened house. There were no people on this balcony, just a lit window in the middle of a rounded turret. The curved French window was pushed open, and the night breeze caught the wispy curtain, billowing it like a sail.

A couple danced into view. The girl was dressed in flowing velvet, her long blond hair encircling her face like an ethereal halo. The man held her close, and she rested her head on his broad shoulder.

They were dressed for the evening. She was the traditional Southern belle, he the dashing uniformed soldier. But they were obviously in no hurry to leave the privacy of home for a costume ball.

Young and in love. Lindsey remembered the feeling well. Too well. Especially here in this town, where it had all begun for her. Begun and ended. Squeezing her hands into fists, she smiled determinedly. She was here for fun, not to be tortured by old memories.

Mesmerized, she watched the young lovers, ignoring the chanting crowds around her. She sighed as he tipped his face toward the girl's and slowly lowered his mouth to hers. Framed in the golden light, they were as clear as a motion picture, acting out their roles, celebrating carnival in their own intimate way.

He ran his hand along her arm, down to the sheath at his side. His lips never leaving hers, he pulled a shiny dagger from the sheath. He was a picture, all right, the brave young soldier, ready to protect his woman.

No, not to protect. Lindsey's heart leaped to her throat. Oh, God! It couldn't be!

She watched, a scream stuck in her throat, suffocated by the terror that washed over her, bringing with it bone-chilling paralysis. Watched as the dashing soldier raised the weapon high above his head and plunged it deep in his lover's heart.

Lindsey blinked and shook her head to clear it of the warped confusion. The images couldn't be what they seemed. A deception, a cruel joke, but not what they seemed.

Yet the woman was slumping to the floor, the green velvet pooling around her, drinking up the crimson river that flowed from her chest. The man turned, for an instant, for an eternity. Then his eyes bored into Lindsey's. For a moment, they were as one—the cold, hard perpetrator and the silent witness.

Her body began to shake, spinning as the float jerked forward, but still she couldn't scream. And she couldn't look away, couldn't tear her face from the nightmare that had begun with a kiss.

Then, suddenly, the sliver of light went black. Lindsey fell forward, and her whole world was bathed in darkness.

## Chapter Two

Detective Graham Dufour dragged himself into head-quarters at half past two in the morning and poured himself a mug of old and mercifully strong coffee before plopping down in his swivel chair. He rubbed tired fingers across his brow and lifted the mug to his lips. No need to worry about caffeine overload tonight. As tired as he was, he'd drop off to sleep in two seconds flat. With luck, he could persuade his body to wait until he got home and into bed first.

Another one down, he reminded himself, with the smallest inkling of satisfaction. The first big weekend of this year's Mardi Gras season was half-over, and there had been no major incidents reported. Now, if that record could just hold until the big day…

He picked up the computer printout of the night's routine complaints. It was a bad habit of his. Minor infractions weren't his responsibility anymore, not since he'd been promoted to homicide. Nothing but the big stuff for him, except during Mardi Gras, of course. For two weeks a year, everybody pulled a few extra duties. It was the only way the good old NOPD could stretch its manpower to safe levels.

Lack of sleep blurred the names as he skimmed the

list. A few drunks arrested in the Quarter. Nothing serious, just tourists satisfying appetites they didn't give in to at home. Several fights, a mugging on Esplanade, a parade watcher hit in the stomach with a cymbal. And some woman claiming she'd witnessed a murder.

Instinctively his mind jumped into working gear. Female on Minerva float, slightly inebriated, passed out and came to in Touro Infirmary mumbling something about seeing a murder.

"Yeah, yeah, sure, sure. A few drinks and those rich society babes in the Minerva parade are liable to see anything," he mumbled to nobody in particular.

Lindsey Latham.

The name jumped out at him like a striking snake. He took a deep breath and tried to ignore the pain that settled in his gut. Old memories died hard. And some never quite made it to oblivion.

Lindsey Latham was one of those. The vivacious sweetheart of Dominican High. Daddy's girl. She'd been the prime example of what brains, looks and money could produce. She'd had it all, including Graham's young and impressionable heart. But what was the heart of a poor jock worth? Evidently nothing, judging from the way she'd dropped him when it was time to move on to greener pastures.

Graham reached for the mug and swallowed another gulp of the black coffee. The bitter taste was suddenly a good match for his mood. It was stupid to let a mere name from his past have such a devastating effect on his ego.

Besides, Lindsey hadn't been back to New Orleans in ten years. No reason to think she'd returned now. No, the Lindsey Latham hallucinating at Touro was probably some party-loving young debutante, hell-bent on creating her own excitement.

"Are you still here? It's almost 3:00 a.m. I thought you'd be home and in bed now, especially on a night as quiet as this one."

Graham nodded at the young detective who had stuck his head in the open door. "I'm on my way. But if I had a sweet little thing on the string like you do, I would've been out of here long ago. In fact, if I'd known you weren't taking care of her tonight, I might've been entertaining her myself," Graham joked.

"You would've wasted your time trying. My woman never settles for second best."

Graham managed a smile. Rooster was a good man. One of the best young ones to come along in a while. He'd worked with him on several cases, and he was always thankful to have him as a backup when the going got rough.

"Did you work the Minerva parade?" Graham asked, trying to sound only mildly interested.

"Yeah, matter of fact, I did. Why?"

"I was just looking over this report. It says one of the float riders passed out and ended up in the hospital. She claims she saw someone murdered."

"We checked it out. The streets were packed, and not one other report came in to substantiate her story."

"So you think it was a false alarm."

"No doubt about it. There was lots to see out there tonight, believe me, but fortunately, there were no dead bodies."

Rooster started to leave, then turned around and lounged in the doorway. "You know, it's amazing what body parts some girls will show for a string of cheap beads."

Graham drained the last drop of coffee from his cup and rose to go. "Not all women settle for cheap beads, old boy. Some want it all. Power, prestige and lots of cash. Especially cash." Flicking off the light, he headed for the front door.

"Don't tell me you're back on that old gripe again. You need a good woman, Graham. That's what's wrong with you."

"I need sleep. And I'm on my way to get some, right now. You'd better do the same. Anything might happen during the next week and a half, and probably will."

Graham toyed with the keys in his pocket as he took the steps to street level. He was tired, but there was only one way he'd get any sleep tonight.

He'd have to make a quick stop at Touro first.

LINDSEY TRIED to catch her breath. She'd been running for hours, looking everywhere for something…someone. She couldn't remember.

"Lindsey, are you all right?"

The voice seemed to come from nowhere. She tried to move, but her body wouldn't cooperate. A strong hand wrapped around hers, stroking tenderly.

"That's okay. Don't try to wake up. The nurse says you need to sleep. I'll be back in the morning, and you can tell me everything."

She breathed deeply. It was Graham. He'd come to help her find…something, but what? It didn't matter. Graham was here now. Everything would be all right. She closed her eyes and rested.

"HEY, Sleeping Beauty, welcome back to the land of the living. Or are you just passing through again?"

Lindsey blinked her eyes repeatedly, trying to bring

the unfamiliar surroundings into focus. She was flat on her back in a single bed that was as hard as a rock, definitely not her own. The dimly lit room smelled of antiseptic and rubbing alcohol.

"I thought you'd never wake up. I've been sitting right here in this dreadful place for over two hours."

"Brigit? What's going on? Are you all right?" Lindsey reached out and grasped the hand of her friend, grateful for contact with warm flesh and blood and a semblance of normality.

"I'm fine. It's you who passed out on us. You mumbled something about a soldier. Next thing we knew, you were lying on the floor of the float in a lifeless heap. Nearly scared us all to death."

A soldier. The dashing man in uniform. The long dagger. The gush of red on the green velvet. It was coming back now. All of it. In living color. She squeezed Brigit's hand as a frightening chill inundated her body.

"It was awful, Brigit. He murdered her in cold blood!"

With determined movements, she rose to a sitting position, throwing her bare feet over the side of the bed.

"Hey, take it easy. You're not going anywhere. Not yet, anyway," Brigit insisted, placing a hand on her shoulder.

"Get the police, Brigit. I have to talk to them. Now. While they still have time to catch the murderer."

"You don't need the police. You need a doctor, and you have one of the best. Dr. Benson, a friend of my dad's. He says you're suffering from a case of pure exhaustion. And an overdose of partying, of course."

"Nonsense," Lindsey protested. She maneuvered past Brigit's well-meaning attempt to restrain her and pushed to her feet. Her resolve was short-lived. The room began to spin like a carousel. She sank back to the bed.

"The doctor said you'd be a little dizzy when you woke up. It's the drugs. Aspe… Oh, I don't remember. Something with a long name."

The doctor was right. Now even the bed was spinning beneath her. And her mind was playing cruel tricks. She could have sworn it was Graham and not Brigit who had sat at her side during the night.

But of course it hadn't been Graham. He didn't even know she was in town. And even if he did, he wouldn't be interested. It was just the drugs that were reviving thoughts she'd carefully tucked away, deep in her subconscious.

"I don't understand it, Lindsey. What do you do up at that university that's so important you don't even take time to eat or sleep?"

Lindsey massaged her brow with shaking fingers. She had to clear her mind, put foolish dreams of Graham aside and remember all the details of the gruesome scene she'd witnessed. The drugs were not making it any easier. And as for working too hard, that was a way of life for her. A situation that wasn't likely to change anytime soon.

"I don't know what you or the doctor are talking about. I'm fine. But I need to see a policeman. We've wasted too much time already."

"Good. I'm glad you're ready for them, because after the way you talked to that old buzzard that was on duty when we arrived last night, I don't think they're going to be too friendly."

Lindsey took a deep breath. A few hazy recollections were churning about in her mind, but none of them made much sense.

"You do remember talking to the cop, don't you?" Brigit asked patiently. "I'm sure he remembers you. You were pretty much out of it, though. Mostly mumbling incoherently. You were a frightful—''

"So the police already know about the murder?"

"Now just stay calm, Lindsey. Dr. Benson says you shouldn't get all choked up."

"I have no intention of staying calm. A girl was brutally murdered. Now answer my question. Do the police know what I saw?"

"They know you were mumbling about some guy with a dagger, thanks to our benevolent head nurse. She couldn't wait to report your so-called murder. I told her you were out of your head, but she didn't budge from her position. Hospital policy, you know." Brigit mimicked the nurse's haughty manner, but Lindsey ignored her attempt at humor.

She traced the folds in her hospital sheet, then stared out the window. Even through closed blinds, it was obvious the sun was high in the sky.

"What time is it?"

Brigit studied the jeweled timepiece that adorned her wrist. "Exactly 11:36 a.m."

"Oh, no… All night and half the day wasted." Taking a deep breath, she pulled her drugged body up to a sitting position again. She shivered. The room felt cold, and no wonder. The only thing covering her was a thin hospital gown, and it wasn't covering much.

"Get my clothes, Brigit. I'm not exhausted, and I'm not ill. You know me. I've always had trouble with motion sickness. And I probably had a little too much champagne." She rocked forward, cradling her spinning head in her hands. "Maybe way too much champagne."

"It's probably not the liquor, Lindsey. The doc gave you a shot. He said it would make you sleep. And it did, too. Right through the policeman's questioning." She suppressed a giggle. "Except when you told him to get his fat, lazy self out of here and catch murderers. Only you didn't put it quite that nicely."

Lindsey groaned and crawled out of the bed, bending over to look for her shoes. They weren't to be seen, and a quick glance around the sparsely furnished room didn't reveal any sign of her clothes, either. She stumbled toward the small closet, grabbing the back of a chair for support when her knees proved more the consistency of Jell-O than bone.

"Your clothes aren't here. Grace Ann took care of that. You're the victim of a Dominican Daredevils conspiracy. You need rest. Doctor's orders. We plan to see that you follow them."

The Dominican Daredevils. Funny, she hadn't thought of that nickname in years. So much had happened since her days at old Dominican High. But for Grace Ann, Brigit and the others, life was just one long extension of the friendships and habits begun so long ago. Like so many others in New Orleans, they had never moved away, had even attended colleges that let them remain close to home.

She eased back to the bed to contemplate her next move. Her friends meant well, but obviously they were convinced she'd imagined the whole stabbing incident. And apparently the doctors and the police were just as certain. A cold shiver shook her body as the scene replayed in her mind. They were wrong. Somehow, she had to prove that to them.

"Ah, Miss Latham, I see you're awake. And feeling a lot better than you were last night, I trust."

Lindsey looked up and into the bluest eyes she'd ever seen, playful and twinkly, peering from behind a multitude of wrinkles. The graying gentleman stepped closer and stuck a steady hand in her direction.

"Dr. Matthew Benson," he offered, grasping her outstretched hand and shaking it firmly. "How's the head feel? Still a little dizzy?"

"Yes," she admitted, reluctantly. She didn't want to argue with the doctor, but she was getting out of here. Now. Or at least as soon as she located some clothes.

"The drugs appear to be wearing off fast, but I think you'll feel a lot better for the night's rest. You gave your young friends quite a scare when you started hallucinating."

Brigit smiled at the doctor in conspiratorial fashion as she backed away from the bed.

"But I told them we'd see what some sleep would do for you," the doctor continued. "I'm glad I gave you the shot before the officer showed up. If I hadn't, I'm afraid our determined man in blue would have harassed you half the night. And you weren't ready for that."

Harassed? What was it with these people? Did she look like a basket case, or were murders just so commonplace in the Big Easy that nobody even bothered to report them anymore?

"I appreciate your concern, Dr. Benson, but I must talk to the police at once. Coherently. A young woman was murdered last night, and I may well be the only witness." She turned to Brigit for support, but she had conveniently disappeared through the open door. "For all I know, the killer is still on the loose, doing who knows what," Lindsey continued. "Running for his life. Maybe even killing again."

The doctor flashed a patronizing smile, but his words were stopped short by a strident voice from the hall.

"You'll have to wait. Dr. Benson would have my hide

if he knew I'd let you in last night after he specified no visitors. Though personally I don't see why he's so worried about just another girl who overpartied. Mardi Gras! I'll be glad when it's over.''

Two sets of footsteps, one heavy, one barely discernible, moved closer to the door.

"I have to agree with you on that. But I'm just doing my job, ma'am. Just like you're doing yours.''

A man's voice. Strong and husky. And familiar, like an old love song. Lindsey struggled for air. It couldn't be Graham. She was losing it, imagining things. Maybe the doctor was right. If her mind was playing tricks on her now, how could she be sure it had been any different last night on the float?

She waited, her body tense, as the heavy footsteps grew closer. Waited until a tall figure stepped inside, smiling uncertainly, his eyes riveted on her.

Her breath caught, settling in her throat like hot coals. She'd known this day would come eventually, but not now. Not like this.

"Hello, Lindsey.''

That was it. Two simple words. Years had come and gone since their last meeting. Ten long years, and now it all came down to a simple hello.

"Hello, Graham,'' she answered, her shaky voice little more than a whisper. A thousand sleepless nights she'd wondered if her memories were accurate. If his smile was really that captivating, if his hair actually fell in lush, dark waves about his high forehead, framing his classic features. Now she knew just how deceptive memories could be. They hadn't done him justice.

"Detective Graham Dufour, homicide,'' he announced, flashing his badge for her and the others to see. His voice had almost broken on the simple hello, but it was all business now—and that was a message she needed to heed. Whatever they had once shared had died a long time ago. At least it had for him.

"I'm Dr. Benson." The doctor broke the painful silence. He extended his hand, but the warmth he'd flashed at Lindsey was missing in his greeting to Graham. "It appears you've already met Miss Latham."

"Yes. Lindsey and I are…old friends."

Suspicion pulled at the lines of the doctor's smile. "I'm going to let you have a few minutes with my patient. If she's ready to see you, that is. But I want you out of here in ten minutes. She needs rest. So ask your questions fast and be on your way."

"I'll be fine, Doctor." Somehow Lindsey managed a reassuring smile.

Graham's gaze traveled over her, scrutinizing her face, her eyes, the outline of her body beneath the revealing covers of the hospital bedding. She pulled the sheet higher and raked her fingers through her long brown hair, pushing the wispy curls away from her face.

The doctor stepped to the door, then stopped. "When you've had enough, Miss Latham, just push that button on the edge of your bed. We'll escort your young detective out of here."

He pulled the door to, leaving behind a cloud of silence that threatened to suffocate her. She struggled for composure. She didn't dare sit up, didn't want to deal with Graham in her weakened condition. He'd surely notice the dizziness that once again had the room spinning unmercifully. He'd seen her weak and vulnerable before. He wouldn't get that chance again.

She turned to slide the pillow higher, needing the added support.

"Here, let me help you with that."

He stepped beside her. The smell of him assaulted her senses. A clean smell, soap and after-shave, and something more. That unmistakable musk that had always clung to him like a personal aura, a permanent badge of his masculinity.

"No, that's okay. I can get it."

"Of course. You always could take care of yourself, couldn't you?"

"I manage." At least she had been managing. Suddenly all her independence was going up in smoke. Her body longed to reach out to Graham, to bury itself in his strong arms, the way it had done last night in her dreams.

"So, what brings the famous Nashville research doctor back to old New Orleans? Surely not Mardi Gras. You were never one to mingle with the poor masses. This was always your week for skiing in the Alps."

Sarcasm edged his voice and hardened the lines in his face. Nothing had changed in the ten years since she'd seen him. Nothing ever would. Those were the facts she needed to keep in front of her, not some romantic fantasy from her dreams.

"This isn't about me, Graham. Things will go better for both of us if we just keep to the reason you're here."

"You're right. So tell me what happened, before the good doctor runs me out."

"I witnessed a murder last night. A young woman."

"And where were you when this happened?" he asked, his expression cold and stony, successfully masking all feeling.

"I was on a float, in the Minerva parade." The words came slowly, rolling off a tongue that felt too big for her mouth. No doubt another side effect of the drugs. "We had stopped. The crowds were pushing closer and closer.

I backed away, against the support frame. I was just staring into the horde of spectators.''

Graham pulled up a chair and straddled it, his long legs stretching to the edge of her bed. ''And you think you saw someone murdered in the crowd?'' he asked, doubt clearly written in his face. ''But no one else saw it?''

''No. I don't *think* anything. I *saw* a murder.''

''Point made. And taken.'' He settled in his chair.

Lindsey chose her words carefully. She needed to be as accurate as possible, in spite of the drugs. ''I'm not sure where we were exactly, the route was so long. But it was somewhere in the Uptown section.''

''Was it near the beginning of the route?''

''We were about an hour into the parade, but we were moving slowly. I know we were on one of the avenues. There was a grassy neutral ground separating the two sides of the street. Almost all of the houses were huge, and they had balconies loaded with people,'' she continued. ''But not this one. It was dark as night, except for a sliver of light from an upstairs window. The window and room were rounded, like a turret, jutting out from the rest of the house.''

Lindsey tried hard to concentrate on her story. But everything seemed hazy. She wished she could blame it solely on the drugs, but she couldn't deny the effect seeing Graham again was having on her senses. And the way he was staring at her now was definitely not helpful.

Detective Graham Dufour. He'd always talked of joining the police force, and she'd thought his aspirations far too limiting. But she'd been only seventeen. What had she known then of life…or love?

''And you saw something in this window,'' he offered, keeping her on track like a good detective.

"Yes. A young couple, in costume."

"A soldier and a Southern belle?"

"That's right. How did you know?"

"It was in the report from the hospital. A patient named Lindsey Latham admitted for treatment. Slightly inebriated and talking out of her head, mumbling incoherently about the dashing soldier who'd stabbed the beautiful Southern belle."

"So you knew it was me?"

"Let's just say I thought it might be. I wasn't sure you still were *Miss* Latham."

No. He wouldn't be. Not when *he* had been so distraught over their breaking up that he'd managed to stay single a whole three months.

"Did you come here last night?"

"As soon as I read the report. You were out of it."

"But you stayed for a while?"

"Yeah. I stayed, until one of the nurses threw me out."

Lindsey met his gaze, for just an instant, and once again pain pierced her heart. She stared at the muted pattern in the wallpaper, determined not to let Graham invade her life again.

"Are you all right, Lindsey? You look so pale."

No, she wasn't all right. She wouldn't be all right as long as Graham was around, but she would never let him know it.

"I'm fine. And you're wasting a lot of time sitting here, when you should be out catching the murderer."

"If there's a murderer, I'll catch him. Now, exactly what did you see through that window, Lindsey, besides a soldier and his girlfriend?" he questioned, Sergeant Friday–style.

"They were dancing, close together. His hands were around her waist. Hers were wrapped about his neck."

"And you were able to pick up all these details?"

"Yes, I was on one of the tall floats, above the crowd. The street was narrow, and the house sat close to the sidewalk. Besides, like I told you, the round room jutted out, putting them even closer. It was almost as if I could reach out and touch them."

"Okay. You had a perfect view, and they were dancing. Then what?"

"It was beautiful. She looked so happy, so much in love. The soldier lowered his lips and kissed her. It seemed to go on forever. His lips on hers, his arms wrapped around her. But then he dropped one hand to his side and began to run his hand along the sheath there."

Lindsey paused. The room seemed so cold. And the memories so vibrant. "It happened so fast. No one could have stopped it. He just yanked the dagger from out of the sheath and plunged it into her heart." She fought to steady her voice. "One minute she was lost in his kiss. The next she was crumpling to the floor."

"It's Mardi Gras, Lindsey. You remember how it is. The people go crazy. What you saw was probably just an act, a performance for the enjoyment of the crowds outside their window."

"No!" She wanted to scream. Why wouldn't people listen? Why wouldn't they believe her? She'd seen a woman murdered, and all anyone could do was question her story. "It wasn't an act. The blood was everywhere, gushing, covering the bodice of her green velvet dress."

"And what was the soldier doing while you watched the woman die?"

"I don't know. I only remember her. When I noticed him again, he had started to walk away."

"Started to walk away? What stopped him?"

"I'm not sure. Perhaps me. He paused and stared out the window. I was too far away to see his eyes, of course, but his face was turned, as if he were looking straight at me. As if I were part of his deadly conspiracy."

Her throat was dry now, like cotton. She reached for the glass of water on her table.

Graham beat her to it. He handed it to her, his fingers lightly brushing against her own. She jerked away, frightened by the feelings that accompanied something so meaningless as an incidental touch. She sipped the water slowly, struggling to keep her mind on the task, to keep feelings from the past at bay. She had to concentrate, to remember everything that might lead to the killer's arrest.

"The float jerked forward then." She shook her head again, to clear the haze from her thoughts. "I'm not too sure about what happened next. Just that I lost my balance, slid to the side and into Brigit. When I looked up again, there was nothing where the window had been. Nothing but blackness. That's the last thing I remember."

Graham stepped closer. "Rounded window on the Minerva route. Neutral ground and ancient oaks," he muttered, as if to himself. "Uptown. Maybe St. Charles or Napoleon. We'll check it out, see what we can find. We'll probably need to get back to you on this, though, when you're feeling stronger."

Lindsey jerked to a sitting position, temporarily forgetting her state of undress. She couldn't believe his lack of concern. She had seen a murder, and she was not going to just stand by while the murderer walked away.

"What do you mean, you'll get back to me?" she demanded. "No wonder the crime rate's rising so fast around here! I'm the only one who can recognize that house." She swung her feet over the side of the bed. "And I'm going with you to look for it!"

"Don't be ridiculous. You know what the doctor said. You need your rest." He moved toward the door. "Besides, your description is adequate. I'm sure I can find the house even without your personal assistance."

She pushed the call button and slid to the floor, careful to keep her back and the open hospital gown toward the wall.

The voice on the intercom wasted no time in responding. "What can we get for you, Miss Latham?"

"Clothes. And I need them now."

"But the doctor said you needed rest, and your friend Brigit—"

"It doesn't matter what the doctor or my friend Brigit said. I'm telling you that I'm walking out of here in the next five minutes with this police officer. It would look a whole lot better for everyone concerned if I did it with my clothes on."

"Yes, Miss Latham. We'll bring them at once."

Graham's eyes captured her, his dark eyes flashing threateningly. "Clothes or not, Lindsey, you are not going with me."

"Listen, Graham. I'm not any more excited about spending time with you than you are with me, but we don't have a choice. I can find that house. You can't turn down my help. If you do, I'll call your supervisor, the district attorney, the governor if I have to."

"And if that doesn't work, you can always call Daddy."

Anger fueled Lindsey's resolve. Daddy. Ten years, and the argument was still the same. "It doesn't matter what you think of me, Graham. I'm the one who can recognize that house, and one way or another, I *am* going with you."

"Suit yourself. I won't spoil your chance of playing policewoman. But just remember," he said, stepping out of the way as the nurse entered with her clothes. "Murderers don't always listen to Daddy."

## Chapter Three

Lindsey stared out the window as she'd done for the past two hours, studying each house, each identifying detail, with the eye of a practiced researcher. She'd been so sure she would recognize the house and the window. But her memories were clouded by the sights and sounds of a Mardi Gras parade.

Everything looked different in the stark light of day. Houses that had appeared magical in the soft glow of artificial lighting now showed signs of cracked and fading paint. Cozy porches and balconies alive with eager spectators were now lonely and imposing. Except for the few stray beads that dangled haphazardly from barren tree limbs and whitewashed porch railings, there was no way to tell that the Krewe of Minerva had ever passed this way.

Maybe she wouldn't know the house at all. They had passed several with turrets and rounded windows that swung open, but nothing about them had reached out to her. There was always something missing. The problem was, she wasn't sure what that something was. Only that it had been in the picture last night and wasn't there today.

Graham pulled the unmarked police car to the curb and

slowed to a dead stop. He reached for the parade guide and opened it again to the map of the route Minerva had followed last night.

"We've been down St. Charles twice, Lindsey. I say we break for lunch. We're getting nowhere with this. Besides, that last police report confirmed the earlier one. No bodies of blondes found. No young women admitted to the hospital with dagger wounds. Not even a missing-persons report that fits your description."

Stuffing her hands in her jacket pockets, she glared out the window. There was nothing to back up her claim, and now she couldn't even locate the house. A truce of sorts had existed between Graham and her ever since they had left the hospital, but she could tell his patience was wearing thin.

"So, do you want to stop for lunch, or can I drop you off somewhere?"

"Not yet, Graham," she insisted. "Let's try once more. And drive slowly. The neutral ground, the trees, even the houses, look right. But something's different."

He shook his head in annoyance and spun the car around, heading back up the street.

Lindsey resumed her searching. The house couldn't have moved overnight. She tried to peer through the tree branches, imagining how things had looked from her perch above the crowd.

"Stop here! In front of the brown brick!"

Graham pulled off the street and parked at the beginning of the driveway. "We studied this house earlier. You said it couldn't be, that it wasn't quite right," he reminded her, his irritation no longer masked.

She jumped from the car, letting the door slam behind her. Graham followed.

"Where do you think you're going?"

She ignored him, walking under and past a towering tree, her eyes following the lines of the house, beyond the wraparound balcony on the second floor, to the third-level turret. Her breath caught. This was the image haunting her mind. The perfect couple in an imperfect frame.

"This is the house."

"You're sure?"

"Dead sure." She shuddered at her choice of words. "It was the angle. That's why I didn't recognize it before. See? The top of the right shutter is broken off. It was hidden by the tree when we were riding in the car, but from here you can see it clearly, just like I saw it last night."

"You never mentioned a shutter before."

"No, I'd forgotten about it. Or maybe it had never registered, except in my mind's eye."

"Of course. How could I forget? That photographic memory of yours let you ace every test in high school, while I struggled for *C*s."

Lindsey walked ahead of him, scrutinizing every detail of the house. It stretched out in all directions, almost Gothic in appearance. Vines of ivy climbed the steep walls, and untrimmed branches hung low around the windows.

A sudden gust of wind stirred, chilling her to the bone. But it was more than the temperature that raised goose bumps on her flesh. It was the cold feeling of doom. She took a deep breath and started up the walk.

"Hold on, Lindsey. Where do you think you're going? We can't just knock on the door and ask them if they happened to notice any bodies lying around. I'm a detective. These people have rights."

"Fine. You're a cop. I'm not. So just get back in your

car and you won't have to worry about your little policeman rules.''

Lindsey took a deep breath and glanced over her shoulder. Graham was a few feet behind her, glaring threateningly. But this was the house. She was sure of it. She
walked to the door and pressed her finger firmly against
the cold bronze button. By the time the melodic chimes
finished their performance, Graham was right behind her.

''Looks like no one's home,'' he offered in the long
silence that followed.

Lindsey eyed him suspiciously. ''Your relief is obvious. So why did you come to the hospital to question me
in the first place, if you had no intention of following up
on my story?''

Stepping back, he leaned his muscular frame against
the brick column that bordered the steps. He smiled, the
same devastating smile she remembered. But something
was different. Something she couldn't quite put her finger
on.

''Oh, I intend to follow up, all right. And if there is a
murderer, I'll catch him. You can count on it. But when
I get started, I'll do it the right way.''

She turned back to the door and gave the bell a final
attempt. All was quiet. But not still. The curtain at the
front window inched sideways.

''And it looks like you're about to get started,'' she
quipped.

Graham shot a penetrating look in her direction and
stepped in front of her. ''Lucky me.''

The door opened slowly, and a tall, thin woman peeked
around the edge. She wasn't old, no more than forty-five
or so, but streaks of gray dulled her dark hair, and deep
lines had already formed around her mouth and beneath

her eyes. The furrows in her brow deepened when Graham presented his badge and an introduction.

"I hope we're not disturbing you too much, ma'am. I just need to talk to you a minute."

"What is it, Officer?"

"Just a couple of questions. Someone reported a disturbance in this area last night."

"You can come in, for a minute. But I doubt if I can be much help. I work here five days a week, but I wasn't here last night." A New Orleans accent flavored the woman's voice.

She motioned them into the massive foyer with a wave of her hand. "My name's Ruby Oleander. Most people just call me Miss Ruby."

Graham stepped back to let Lindsey enter in front of him. "And how about the owners of the house? Are they in?" he asked, closing the door behind him.

"No. They're out of the country. In Rome. They have been for three weeks," she explained, ushering them into the formal living room.

Lindsey took a seat beside the window and listened as Graham proceeded with the questioning, his easy manner quickly putting the suspicious housekeeper at ease.

She had worked for the LeBlancs for twenty years, Miss Ruby explained. And no doubt the LeBlancs could afford to pay her well for her services, Lindsey noted as she studied the opulent surroundings. It was no wonder Miss Ruby took her job as caretaker of the estate so seriously.

The house was furnished in antiques. Authentic, unless she missed her guess. Lindsey's gaze followed the lines of the marble fireplace down to the hardwood floors that were covered with well-worn but exquisite Persian rugs.

It was like visiting a living museum, even down to the smells of age and lingering cigarette smoke.

The place screamed money. No, not screamed, bespoke—elegantly. Apparently old money. Uptown at its finest. The same type of homes many of her high school friends had lived in. But not the way she had lived. Her dad epitomized the flashiness of new wealth. He liked life on the cutting edge, everything new and thoroughly modern.

Lindsey shifted her weight and tried to get comfortable on a period chair designed for women who had nothing more stressful to do than needlepoint.

"This must have been a great place to watch the Minerva parade from," Graham commented, his tone as relaxed and friendly as if he were chatting with an old friend. "I heard it was impressive for a new krewe. What did you think of it?"

He was pretty smooth. Lindsey would have to give him that. She would have just plunged in herself, demanding to know who was in the house last night. Of course, Miss Ruby would probably have shut up like a clam.

"I didn't see the parade."

Miss Ruby's tone cooled considerably as she responded curtly to Graham's question and then shut up like a clam. So much for smooth.

Graham flashed her his most dazzling smile. "I didn't see it, either. Not much of a paradegoer myself. I heard it was nice, though."

"There's really nothing I can tell you about last night," Miss Ruby offered, regaining her composure quickly and sliding back into her friendly-housekeeper role. "You'll have to ask one of the other neighbors. This house was empty last night, locked up tight."

Lindsey squirmed about in the chair, determined to

keep her mouth shut, even if it killed her. Her agitation did not go unnoticed.

"Could I get you some coffee? Or perhaps a cup of tea, Miss—?"

"Yes, some coffee would be nice." Lindsey nodded appreciatively at the woman, but decided against providing her name. Especially with Graham intensifying that "keep quiet" look he'd been shooting her way ever since they'd stepped inside the door.

"And you, Detective Dufour?"

"No, nothing for me."

Lindsey waited until Miss Ruby left the room, then moved over to the couch beside Graham. "The woman's an expert liar," she whispered. "That story about no one being here last night. Pure fabrication. And she told it with a straight face."

"Maybe."

"Not maybe. There were people here. At least two, and one of them didn't leave the house alive."

"Try to stay calm, Lindsey. I'll handle this. I don't want you getting all upset."

His eyes bored into hers, and for a second she could have sworn there was more there than just casual concern. She pulled away and moved back to her chair.

"Doctor's orders," he added. "Benson said he was holding me personally responsible for your well-being today. And I don't need any more trouble."

"You don't need to worry about me," Lindsey answered. "I can take care of myself, remember?" But she smothered any further protests. Miss Ruby's feet were already padding back down the carpeted hallway.

The woman reentered the room slowly, bearing an impressive silver tray laden with two delicate china cups and saucers and a pot of steaming coffee.

"I brought sugar and cream, but I have artificial sweetener in the kitchen, if you prefer. You don't look as if you need it, though," the housekeeper offered, easing the tray onto the marble-topped table by Lindsey's chair. She filled one cup and then looked Lindsey in the eye. "And I'm sorry, but I don't believe I caught your name."

"Green. Officer Green," Graham supplied quickly.

Lindsey stirred the lump of sugar she had dropped into her coffee with renewed vigor, attempting to hide her surprise. As far as she could see, there was no possible reason to lie about her identity or to hide the fact that she'd witnessed a murder. She was perfectly willing to testify, to do whatever it took to bring the ruthless killer to justice.

"Are you sure you won't change your mind, Detective?" Miss Ruby asked, lifting the other cup and tipping it in his direction. "It's fresh."

"No, none for me, but I was wondering if you'd mind if Officer Green and I took a walk through the house. You know, check things out for you."

"I'm sure that's not necessary, Detective."

"Probably not, but like I told you earlier, there was a report by one of the parade watchers of some kind of unusual disturbance around here last night. Of course, it could be a mistake, but if someone did break in here… Well, you know, you just can't be too careful these days."

"They were mistaken," Miss Ruby retorted indignantly. "If someone had been in the house last night, I would know it. You can be sure of that."

For once, Lindsey believed her. The housekeeper didn't miss much. It was a safe bet the woman knew that someone had been in the house. And she probably knew a lot more. Like who and why. But Graham wasn't going to get it out of her. Not with that polite little questioning method he was using. It probably worked on some people, but Miss Ruby was far too astute for that.

"Nonetheless, we'd like to look around," Lindsey insisted, ignoring Graham's warning look. "What possible harm could it do? Unless, of course, you have something to hide."

She regretted those last words as soon as they left her mouth, especially when she watched Miss Ruby's guarded smile cool to a frigid frown.

"Do you have a search warrant?"

The words were issued as a challenge. Lindsey stiffened her back and silently returned the woman's stare. She wasn't sure what game Miss Ruby was playing, but she wasn't about to be intimidated. Not by someone heartless enough to hide information about a murder. With a slow, deliberate movement, she placed her cup on the tray.

"No, no warrant," Graham was assuring the housekeeper. "And there's no reason for me to get one at this time. It was just my concern for your safety that prompted my request to check out the house."

"I understand, and I appreciate it. But I don't think Mr. LeBlanc would like for anyone, even a nice detective like yourself, to go wandering through his home. He values his privacy."

"And exactly when did you say the LeBlancs would be returning from Rome?" Lindsey asked, not willing to give up without foraging out every detail she could.

"On Monday. At least Mrs. LeBlanc will. In time for the Mardi Gras hoopla. Hordes of people crowding into the streets, blocking the drives, trashing the yards. I can't imagine why anyone would want to come back for that, but Mrs. LeBlanc loves it. Her costume ball is one of the highlights of the social calendar.''

Graham stood up and walked toward the window, his gaze traveling about the room as he moved, seeming to look at everything at once. "That balcony out there... It looks like the perfect place to catch a parade or two. Your friends and family must pester you all the time to bring them over during Mardi Gras. Especially when the LeBlancs are out of town.''

"No. Not at all. My friends know that I would *never* violate my employers' trust by invading their property.''

There it was again, Lindsey noted. The same iciness that had edged her tone when she asked about the warrant. There were two sides to this woman. And one was coolly calculating.

"Sounds like the LeBlancs are pretty lucky to have you taking care of things for them. And I appreciate your taking time out to talk with us,'' Graham answered.

Lindsey seethed silently. A murder had taken place in this very house, probably just above where they were sitting right now. And all Graham planned to do was waste time in meaningless conversation.

He left his post at the window and made his way back to the door. Reluctantly Lindsey followed his lead. She didn't have a lot of choice. As much as she'd like to butt in, to pursue the questioning further, she'd seen enough movies to know that Graham was right. Improper search and questioning could blow a case right out of the courts. And she wanted the murderous soldier caught and punished, not freed on a technicality.

"Thank you for talking with us, Miss Ruby. If we have any further questions, we'll get back to you. Or to the LeBlancs, when they return.''

"And thanks for the coffee,'' Lindsey added, trying to

manage some of the fake friendliness Graham seemed so good at.

"I'm just sorry I couldn't be of more help."

"You've helped more than you know," Graham assured her pleasantly.

You will be a lot more help, Lindsey wanted to add, as soon as we return with the search warrant.

Graham stepped outside and all but pulled Lindsey out with him. His stride was long and purposeful, and she had to run to keep up with him.

"'Unless you have something to hide,'" he muttered, opening the car door on the passenger side. "For heaven's sake, why didn't you just ask her if she had a dead body upstairs? It would have been about as obvious!"

"Oh, I'm sure there's no body upstairs. Not now. But there would have been if you and your fellow officers had investigated the crime hours ago, when I first tried to report it."

"Don't change the subject. You were out of line in there, Lindsey, and you damn well know it. I'm the police officer in charge. I'm the one who's supposed to do the talking."

Lindsey pulled herself into the car and slammed the door behind her. Could she help it if she was more efficient than the cops? "So while you're doing the talking, how about explaining that 'Officer Green' routine?" she demanded as Graham opened the door and climbed behind the wheel.

"I'll explain it, all right. It was a *mistake,* a big one. But it was the best excuse for having you tagging along with me I could think of on the spur of the moment. I had to do something to shut you up before you blurted out the whole story about why you were really there."

"So what if I had? I have nothing to hide. I'm the witness, not the criminal."

Graham reached for the black notebook stashed behind the visor. He scribbled furiously for a few minutes, then placed the notebook on the seat beside him as he started the car.

"Okay, Lindsey," he offered, pulling the gear into reverse and backing out into the heavy traffic. "For the sake of argument, let's say everything happened exactly the way you say."

"Okay, for the sake of argument."

"This is my case, and you're my number one witness."

"Your *only* witness."

"All right. My only witness. So I say we make a bargain. I'm willing to buy your story, even though there's no body, no motive and no suspect. We can't even prove we're at the right house."

"You have my word."

"Exactly. That's why I'm climbing out on a dead limb. But now you've got to trust me to handle the investigation. My way. Without your help, unless I ask for it."

Lindsey stared straight ahead. Graham's way or no way. Like it had always been. Why should she expect anything different? She'd trusted him once before. Ten years ago. He'd repaid her trust with betrayal. But matters of the heart were quite different from police work. Besides, she didn't have any alternative now. She'd be catching a Sunday-night flight back to Nashville.

"Okay, Graham. We'll do it your way."

"Great."

He eased up to a red light and slowed to a stop. He turned to face her, and Lindsey could all but feel his nearness. She looked away. There was nothing between them, and it had to stay that way. He hadn't changed in any way that mattered.

"I don't want to frighten you, Lins."

*Lins.* The nickname rolled off his tongue like an endearment. Just the way it used to. Oh, God, was it always going to be like this? One minute, she had the past buried away where it belonged, the next, something as simple as a nickname turned her insides to a quivering mass. She directed her gaze straight ahead, at the bumper of the blue Buick in front of them.

"I'm sorry I got so rough with you back there." His voice was smooth, but insistent. "But this is not a game we're playing. I'm not sure what's going on here, but until I am, I don't want you to tell anyone else what you saw."

The light turned green, but still he didn't move.

"Promise me, Lins. No one else is to know that you're the one who witnessed the crime. You've told too many people already."

His hand squeezed hers, and behind them a horn honked impatiently.

"I promise," she answered, "at least for now. But I'm willing to testify, Graham. I'm not afraid."

He dropped her hand and eased his unmarked car across the intersection. "No, I'm sure you're not," he answered huskily. "But I am."

THE FRENCH QUARTER on Sunday morning. Lindsey stopped for a minute, letting its magic wash over her. It was exactly as she remembered it, a wonderland of sights, sounds and tantalizing odors. She slowed her pace to a crawl as she neared the entrance to St. Louis Cathedral, marveling at the white structure that watched over Jackson Square like a kingly ruler.

It would have been only a short walk from her hotel to the Court of Two Sisters, where she was meeting the gang for brunch. Too short. That was why she'd taken the long way around, through the street musicians, mimes and sidewalk artists who breathed life into Jackson Square.

It was early for this part of the city, not quite eleven, but the tourists in town for the carnival were already out in droves.

"Paint your face, miss? Only five dollars. A special price for a pretty lady."

Lindsey smiled at the thin young man who'd spoken, but declined his offer. A little lipstick and a touch of blush were plenty of paint for her. She crossed over the narrow street to peek in the window of La Madeleine.

She couldn't resist a glimpse of the fresh-baked breads and pastries that filled the shelves at the bakery. The door opened, and a group of laughing tourists walked out, holding the door open long enough for Lindsey to catch the aroma of strong French coffee.

New Orleans, the Crescent City, the town where anything goes. Friday night, she'd had a taste of everything bad about the city. Today, she was experiencing the excitement of everything good. She stopped for a minute and watched a laughing clown bend and twist a couple of balloons into a floppy-eared puppy and hand it to a wide-eyed tyke. Smiling, she hurried on to meet her friends. God, she'd missed this city.

She'd loved New Orleans from the day they moved into town, just a week before her fifteenth birthday. She'd hoped against hope that for once her dad would resist the urge to open a new branch of his mining and drilling company in some foreign country. Prayed that for once he would stay in one location long enough for her to make real friends.

And she'd gotten her wish. They'd stayed four years. Long enough for her to graduate from Dominican High. Long enough for her to meet, and fall head over heels for, the handsome and popular Graham Dufour.

Graham was a big part of the reason she'd loved the city. And he was the real reason she'd stayed away for so long. She might not admit it to anyone else, but she could at least be honest with herself. Coming back to New Orleans always meant the possibility of running into Graham. And now that she had, she knew she'd been wise in staying away.

Lindsey stepped around a crack in the sidewalk and then walked through the open door into the busy restaurant. Strains of a lively jazz tune floated down the brick hallway as she squeezed past groups of patrons waiting for a table. Stretching her neck to see over the balloons that decorated the patio, she spotted Danielle and Brigit at a table near the fountain.

"About time you made it. We're already on our second mimosa," Brigit said.

"Good. You two have all the champagne you want, but I'm taking my orange juice straight. After Friday night, I don't mind if I never have champagne again."

"Party pooper," Brigit said mockingly, scooting over to another chair and motioning Lindsey into the chair between them. "You need to sit by Danielle. Maybe you can talk some sense into her. She's letting that rat of a husband move back in."

Lindsey took the chair between the two, but not because she was in any shape to do marriage counseling. She'd already had more than enough emotional upheaval for one weekend. Fortunately Grace Ann and the rest of the entourage rounded the corner, and a new series of hugs and excited chatter began.

Finally they managed to halt the gossip long enough to help themselves to plates of steaming seafood omelets, oversize portions of grits and grillades and mouth-watering eggs Benedict.

"How do you people stay so thin?" Lindsey asked, finishing the last boiled shrimp on her plate.

"Who's thin?" Emily asked, patting her stomach, which now had stretched to support the new life growing inside it.

"Chasing kids will keep you from getting fat," Grace Ann added, pulling out pictures of her latest.

"Oh, how adorable!" Brigit exclaimed, oohing and aahing over the photographs.

"So, when are you taking the plunge?" Angela asked Brigit teasingly. "If you'd settle down with one man, you could have one of those adorable babies of your own."

"As soon as I meet the right man."

"What about that hunk you were with at the Minerva Ball?" Emily asked. "The man looked like a keeper to me."

"He's nice, but the bells didn't ring. Besides, he can't afford me."

"Money isn't everything, Brigit. But hang in there for the bells. Love may not make the world go around, but it sure makes the bedroom a lot more fun."

"Tell me about it, Grace Ann. You and Michael looked like brand-new lovers at the ball the other night," Angela said. "It was hard to believe you're the parents of two toddlers."

"I have news, too," Beth announced, breaking into the banter. "But not in the kids or lovers department. I'm going back to the university next year. I've decided to work on my Ph.D.''

A round of exuberant cheers and hugs followed her announcement. Lindsey sat back and listened, letting the warmth of camaraderie wash over her. Ten years without a reunion with her friends had been much too long. Everyone had so much to share.

She smiled as Danielle set a bowl of bread pudding drenched in rum sauce and a cup of café au lait in front of her.

''Eat up. The lady over there said it was delicious.''

Lindsey looked in the direction Danielle had pointed. The woman was petite and young, and long blond curls framed her heart-shaped face. A shudder climbed Lindsey's spine as memories of Friday night attacked her senses. She spooned a mouthful of the rich dessert, but the delectable sweetness couldn't lift her spirits. Not now.

A minute ago she had been one of the relaxed and carefree crowd enjoying Sunday-morning brunch. But seeing the blonde, so alive and happy, had plunged her back into reality. And the reality for Lindsey was that another woman, one much like the friends around her table, had been murdered two nights ago.

The scene had never been far from her mind, even though Brigit and the others were carefully avoiding any mention of her passing out during the parade. And they hadn't brought up the subject of Graham Dufour. Bless them for that.

She sat quietly, watching the others. The Dominican Daredevils. They were just a group of girls who'd gone to high school together. But something had happened between them. They'd formed a special bond that nothing could separate. Not heartbreak and not good fortune. Nothing but…

The noonday sun shone down on the open patio, causing most of the diners to shed their sweaters and light jackets. Lindsey pulled hers tighter. A strange chill coursed through her veins. They were all together today. Good friends, young, energetic. The best years of their lives should still lie ahead of them.

So why was this ominous feeling weighing her down? She couldn't explain it, couldn't even understand it herself, but somehow she knew the truth, felt it in some secret place inside her soul. They would never all be together this way again.

*THE MAN INHALED SLOWLY, taking a shred of solace from the half-smoked cigarette. This was no way to live, a one-room apartment with nothing in it that belonged to him except a few changes of clothing.*

*He should be flying to some exotic port by now. And he would have been if things had gone as planned. But they hadn't.*

*He took a last puff on the cigarette and then ground it into the ashtray. With trembling hands, he picked up a half-empty bottle of pills and shook several into his hand. Deliberately, he placed them between his dry lips, chasing them down with a swig of whiskey.*

*But he knew the headache wouldn't go away, not until the whiskey did its job. Until it let him pass out and block the memories from his mind.*

*He hadn't wanted to kill. He'd loved Roxy. But she'd double-crossed him, left him no choice. Still, there wouldn't have been any problems if he'd only noticed that she had pushed back the heavy drapes and opened the window, leaving nothing but the sheer curtains to hide them from view.*

*Damn. The pounding in his head was growing*

*stronger. He picked up the glass and gulped down the rest of the whiskey before letting out a string of curses. He was feeling the liquor now. It wouldn't be long until he got some blessed relief.*

# Chapter Four

Graham paced the floor of the narrow office. This was just what he needed, the return of Lindsey Latham, so damn close there was no escaping her. She had been planted in that same chair for over an hour, futilely poring over photographs of every hood who plagued the streets of New Orleans.

He shoved his fists deeper into his pockets. She was cool and collected, sitting there in designer jeans that fit in all the right places and a crisp tailored blouse that opened at the neck, revealing tempting glimpses of soft flesh.

Damn, he should have known enough to run like hell when he first saw her name on the police files. She had been out of his league ten years ago, and becoming a cop sure hadn't improved his social standing.

"Your plane leaves in little more than an hour, Lindsey. You need to get out of here if you're going to be on it."

She looked up, but made no move to go. "Just a few more minutes." She bent back over the mug book, her brows wrinkled into serious furrows.

Graham dropped to his chair and lifted his loafer-clad feet to the top of his cluttered desk. He'd warned her that the chances were next to nil that she'd find a suspect this way. For the most part she was skimming through shots of common street hoods. The guy she was looking for was probably a different breed altogether.

He'd already checked out the LeBlancs. High society, filthy rich. The kind of people Lindsey had grown up with. The kind that had always made it clear Graham Dufour was a few rungs below them, not fit to date their daughters.

He picked up an almost empty mug of coffee from his desk and downed the last drops, trying to swallow with it the bitter memories that gnawed at his gut.

He'd spent years trying to forget Lindsey Latham, determined to block every thought of her from his mind. Most of the time he'd been successful. But not always. In weak moments, the traitorous memories had crept back in.

How many nights had he lain awake, wondering what it would be like to see her again? Wondering if the relentless heartache would still wring the life from him, the way it had in the first painful weeks and months after she packed up and headed off for a new life that didn't include him.

Well, now he knew. It wasn't a damn bit easier today than it had been then. If anything, it was worse. And even now he didn't have the good sense to stay away from her.

He walked over and stood behind her. She still smelled of honeysuckle and summer mornings. So many things about her were the same. The soft, wispy hair that fell in dark cascades about her slender shoulders. The same dancing eyes beneath lush lashes.

But there were changes, too. Some were almost imperceptible, like the deepening of her voice, which was sexier, more self-assured than ever. Some differences were strikingly visible, like the full breasts, the sensuous curves of a woman's hips.

At eighteen, she'd been cute and vivacious, a girl with lots of promise. At twenty-eight, the promises had all been fulfilled. He stepped away from her. The promises were for somebody else. And somebody else was welcome to them, he reminded himself.

Finally Lindsey reached the last page and closed the book. "I hate to leave like this, with nothing settled, not even a suspect for you to look for."

"You told us everything you could."

"I know, but it doesn't make sense. I can see the girl as clear as day, every detail, down to the way her blond hair was swept up on top of her head, loose curls tumbling down around her cheeks."

"It happens that way sometimes. The trauma of seeing a murder leaves you too shaken to focus on the perp."

"But that's not it. I *do* remember him. I watched him take her in his arms and kiss her. I remember the way his uniform fit his broad shoulders. I remember thinking how dashing and handsome he looked." Her shoulders fell dejectedly. "But his face…it's as if it didn't exist. There were so many faces that night."

"Maybe his back was to you."

"No. I saw his profile. They were framed in the window. Two beautiful lovers." She stood up and walked over to the coatrack. "I don't understand why I can't picture the facial features. I've always been so good with details. I make my living making observations."

Funny, he knew Lindsey was a researcher, but somehow he'd never actually pictured her going to a real job. One thing was for sure. It wasn't working so you could eat and put a roof over your head, like it was for him and his colleagues. Her father could buy and sell most people with his pocket change.

No one knew that better than Graham. Good old Frederick Latham had even tried to buy him. He hadn't been for sale. Of course, as it turned out, he might as well have been. He walked across the room and waited for Lindsey by the office door.

"Police work is a little different, Lins. So why don't you leave this one to us? We'll find the killer. It may take a while, but sooner or later, he'll slip up. When he does, we'll nab him."

"I hope so. But I can't get it out of my mind. She was so pretty, so alive—"

Her voice broke on the painful words, and Graham clenched his hands into fists. What was it with him? One minute he wanted to wring Lindsey's pretty neck for bringing old memories home to roost. The next, he was struggling with his hands just to keep them from pulling her into his arms.

Keep cool, he reminded himself. Keep everything in perspective. She is here strictly to identify a murderer. The woman has no more need of you now than she did ten years ago.

She reached for her coat, and he moved closer, helping her with it as he would any other woman who happened to be in his office. Strands of satiny hair brushed across his skin, and his hand tightened on her shoulder.

Lindsey didn't pull away, and he couldn't. Instead, he eased her around to face him. Her eyes stared into his, dark and moist, and her full lips curved into a half smile.

"Thanks, Graham, for believing me when no one else did."

"No problem." She was doing it again, making him purr, when it would be much safer to stick to his usual growl. He slid his hands down her arms and took both her hands in his. "Are you sure you don't want me to drive you to the airport?"

"No, I still have Grace Ann's car. She said to leave it in the parking garage. She'll send someone for it." Lindsey turned and studied the wall clock. "If I'm going to make my flight, I'll have to leave now."

"I know." Reluctantly he let go of her hands and walked to the door. "Remember what I said, Lins. Don't talk about what you saw. And if anything unusual happens, anything at all, I want you to call me at once."

"I remember, Detective." She gave a tiny salute. "Now you get busy and find the killer."

"I'll do that."

I could do it a lot more easily if I just knew where to begin, he thought as he forced himself to turn away from the door. He had to turn away. Letting Lindsey walk out of his life again was more painful than a strong right to the gut. Watching her do it would be much worse.

LINDSEY SKIPPED hurriedly down the steps of the crumbling brick building that housed Graham's precinct station. She had to have air, had to put some heart-saving space between herself and Detective Graham Dufour.

Her fingers shook as she reached into the compact leather bag that hung from her waist. The car keys had slipped below her wallet, and she worked her fingers down to retrieve them, scraping across the gold mask pin Grace Ann had given her as a souvenir of the krewe's parade.

She grimaced. Fate had been unbelievably cruel the past few days. It had ruined her visit with Grace Ann, Brigit and the rest of her high school friends with a senseless crime. And as if that weren't enough, it had struck the crowning blow, reuniting her with the one man she had hoped never to see again.

Everything had ended between them long ago. He'd told her that if she left him to go away to college, he'd be out of her life forever. She'd thought he was only bluffing. She should have known better. His threats had never been idle. Three months later, he'd forgotten her so completely he married someone else.

She shook her head to clear it and slipped the key into the Mercedes' lock. It went in easily, but the key wouldn't turn. Lindsey fiddled with it, slipping the key in and out several times before she finally got the door unlocked. So much for her friend's fancy car. Even Lindsey's old Toyota opened without a problem.

What a weekend. Now she even missed her car, she mused, sliding into the driver's seat. She checked the rearview mirror and then maneuvered her way into the sparse Sunday-afternoon traffic. In a few short hours, she'd be home again. Then she could begin to put this bizarre weekend behind her.

Not that she'd ever forget it. Not that she wanted to until the killer was in custody, locked away so that he couldn't kill again. That might take a long time without a description of him, identifying details she should have been able to provide. She had watched the whole thing, and she was letting everybody down, especially a young blond woman who should have had her whole life in front of her.

Lindsey glanced at her watch and then pulled over into the left-turn lane. She'd be cutting it close, but she had to drive by the LeBlanc house one more time. It was a long shot, but returning to the scene of the crime just might trigger some memory that would lead to a positive identification of the killer.

A warning nagged at the back of her mind. She'd promised Graham she'd butt out and let him handle things. But this wasn't breaking her promise, she assured the nag. She was just going to drive by for one last look before she left town.

Lindsey eased her foot from the accelerator as she neared the house. She didn't have the address, but she had no trouble locating it this time. She drove by slowly. There were lights in at least one window.

That was odd. The LeBlancs were supposedly out of town, and surely Ruby wouldn't be working at six o'clock on a Sunday evening. Lindsey pulled around the corner and parked. It wouldn't hurt to take a look. She could take a brisk walk by the house and still make it to the airport in time.

She dropped her keys into her pocket and scooted out of the car, stepping over the roots of an ancient oak. The house was about half a block away, enough distance to give her time to study it as she approached.

There were lights on the first floor, in one of the rooms facing the street. The second floor was bathed in total darkness, and so was the turret that topped the house like a crown. Lindsey stopped at the edge of the property and bent over as if tying a loose shoelace. She lingered as long as she could, but there was nothing to see but the impressive architecture of a St. Charles mansion.

She walked slowly past the house, trying not to be too obvious in her spying. There was a car parked in the drive, old and sporting a front end that had weathered a few New Orleans fender benders. It might belong to Miss Ruby, but it hadn't been there yesterday.

A car door slammed somewhere behind her, and her heart crashed against her ribs. She turned and watched a family of four climb from a van and enter a house down the street. She took a deep breath, forcing air into her lungs. The murder had left her jumping at shadows.

By the time her gaze had returned to the LeBlanc house, a male figure was walking out the front door, his silhouette framed in the soft glow of streetlights. Lindsey slipped behind one of the oaks that lined the avenue. The man couldn't see her here. Unfortunately, she couldn't see much, either.

Angry voices carried across the manicured lawn, and Lindsey strained to hear them above the traffic noises. Eavesdropping was not her style, but the volume wasn't making it much of a challenge.

"You lied to me again. I told you about that. I can't trust you anymore!"

The voice was Miss Ruby's. Lindsey scooted around the tree trunk until she had a partial view of the action. Growing darkness masked their features, but there was still enough light to make out their shapes and movements. The young man with the housekeeper looked to be in his mid-twenties, overweight, and with scraggly hair that hung to his shoulders. So much for honest Ruby's vow about never inviting anyone to the house. Or maybe she hadn't invited him.

"I told you I'm sorry. I took the key one time. That was all. I just wanted to show the place to someone."

"Don't lie to me." Her voice became a whine. "You were with that girl you've been hanging out with. She's nothing but scum. She and all her friends. I told you to stay away from them, but you just won't listen, will you?"

"They're not scum. They're my friends. But you won't have to worry about Roxy anymore."

"Like I believe that, any more than I believe the rest of your lies. You move into your own place and take up with riffraff. Just like Jerome. You forget your raising and take up with worthless scum. You're breaking my heart, and you don't even care.''

Lindsey stretched to her full height and peered over an overhanging branch. Miss Ruby followed the boy down the walk, her shrill voice whistling through the twilight air.

''Friends, humph! They're just using you. That's all. You better wake up before they get you in a lot of trouble. And I might not be able to help you this time. Mr. LeBlanc doesn't like getting involved with the law, and I promised him you'd keep clean.''

''I am clean, Mama. I told you. I didn't take nothing. Just the lousy old key, and you got it back, didn't you?''

Mama. So Miss Ruby had a son, one who had taken a key. She'd have to tell Graham about this. He couldn't be mad at her for coming here once she gave him some helpful information. Not that it mattered if he was mad or not. She was a private citizen with a perfect right to stop on a public street.

''Sure, I got the key back. But I don't want you lying to me. I don't want you ending up like Jerome.'' Now she was all but pleading.

''No, Mama. I won't. I promise.''

''And I hope you mean it. I sure hope you mean it. Now why don't you come in and get a bite of supper? I've been cooking all day, getting ready for Miss Katie. She'll be coming in tomorrow, and soon as she does, she'll be filling the house with company. That woman thinks about nothing but having a good time. Not like the late Mrs. LeBlanc. God rest her soul. Now that was a lady.''

''You save your cooking for Miss Katie, Mama. I'm not hungry.''

"Of course you are. I made pecan pie. You know that's your favorite."

Shoulders down, the boy turned and headed back up the stairs, following meekly behind his overbearing mom.

Lindsey started back toward her car, but a strong hand grabbed her shoulder and swung her around.

"Did you miss your plane?"

"Graham, you frightened me! I didn't expect to see you here."

"I could say the same for you. There's a little difference, though. I'm a detective. I'm supposed to be here. And if I remember correctly, we made a bargain." His fingers dug into her flesh.

She pulled away. "I've kept my part of the bargain, although it was a stupid agreement to begin with. I was just driving by, and I wanted to take one last look. Just to see if it would help me remember anything."

"You only have to remember one thing, Lindsey. Stay out of this."

Same old Graham. He had been understanding at the police station, but that had been when she was doing things his way. Now she had acted of her own accord, without his permission, and he was jumping right down her throat again.

"I'm an adult, Graham, and I'm perfectly capable of making decisions about where I go."

"Excuse me, I guess I just expected you to keep your word," he growled through clenched teeth.

"Sure, I just need to go home and leave the big, bad criminals to the tough guys. This may come as a surprise to you, but I'd like to do just that. Unfortunately, I don't have that option. I'm the one who witnessed the murder."

Graham pushed up a sleeve to look at his watch. "So

your option was to miss your plane deliberately so you could hang out in front of the LeBlanc house like some two-bit private eye. Real smart.''

She glanced at her watch. Damn. Twenty minutes until takeoff. She'd never make the flight. And it was the last one tonight. Okay, she'd made a mistake—but she didn't have to admit it to Graham, not when he was in the know-it-all mood he was right now.

''As a matter of fact, stopping by here was pretty smart,'' she quipped, tossing her head back and glaring at him. ''I found out that Miss Ruby has a son.''

''She has two sons, to be exact,'' he told her. ''Garon and Jerome Oleander. Ages twenty-two and twenty-four.''

''How do you know that?''

''It's all a matter of public record, if you know which records to look at.''

''Well, I bet you didn't find this in any public record. One of the sons has been in trouble. I don't know exactly what, but apparently Mr. LeBlanc had to come to the rescue.''

''Garon Oleander. Busted for possession of marijuana. Two years ago. Paid his fine and got a suspended jail sentence.''

Graham's smug manner was growing as irritating as the mosquito that was buzzing around Lindsey's face. She slapped at the pesky insect and wished she could do the same to the good detective. His present manner was making it a lot easier to forget their past. At least the good parts.

''Well, you might be interested to know, Mr. Detective, that Gargoyle, or whatever his name is, stole a key from Miss Ruby, and I'm sure it was the key to the

LeBlanc house. And somehow I doubt if that's public record.''

"The name is Garon. And what makes you think he stole a key?''

"I've been standing right here listening to them arguing. And Mama Ruby doesn't like his friends, either. They're all scum. Her assessment, not mine.''

"Do you think Garon could be the soldier with the dagger?''

"No,'' she admitted reluctantly. "In fact, his build is totally different from what I remember.''

"Okay, Lindsey. I appreciate your concern with identifying a suspect, but you've done your part. More than your part. I tried asking you nicely to stay out of this. Now I'm telling you. Go back to Nashville, and leave the investigation to the experts.''

Lindsey's blood pressure shot skyward. Graham Dufour hadn't changed one iota. But she was no longer in love with the handsome rebel from her impressionable youth. She didn't have to play the game his way.

"I'm afraid I won't be able to follow your orders, Graham. Unless, of course, you have a warrant for *my* arrest.''

"I can get one, if I have to.''

"Then you might have to do just that.''

Anger smoldered in Graham's eyes. "My car is parked over there, Lindsey,'' he snapped, motioning toward the blue sedan parked a few yards down the avenue. "Get in it.''

"Thank you for the invitation,'' she answered, not bothering to hide her sarcasm. "But I have my own car.''

"Look, Lindsey. I know I come on strong sometimes.'' His voice softened, but didn't lose its irritating edge. "But I only had three hours of sleep last night, I haven't eaten since breakfast, and…'' He looked at the grass under his feet and took a deep breath. ''And I'm worried about you.''

Damn him. There it was again, that concern that came from out of the blue and cracked her resolve. ''There's nothing to worry about. I can take care of myself.''

''I know. But humor me.'' He gestured toward his car. ''Now, get in.''

''My car is parked—'' He silenced her protests with a firm grip on her hand.

''Give me this, Lindsey. It won't take long, but we have to talk, get a few things straight, especially since you're not leaving town like I thought.''

''Okay,'' she agreed. She'd hear him out, but she wasn't making any promises. Finding the killer depended on her ability to identify him. She wasn't ready to give up yet. ''And just where do you plan to take me?'' she questioned, climbing into the front seat of the blue Ford.

''My place.''

LINDSEY STARED into a flickering fire and tried to make some sense of the emotions warring inside her. She was sitting in Graham's apartment, the last place on earth she'd ever have thought she'd be, while he cooked dinner for the two of them. She leaned back against the couch cushions and took another sip of the chilled wine he had poured for her.

Graham Dufour, hotshot star of the Brother Martin High School football team, cocky and rebellious, determined to show everybody in school that he was tougher than all of them. Graham Dufour, warm and sensitive, quick to anger, quicker to passion.

She had met him at one of Brigit's parties. He'd swaggered into the room like he owned the place, his jeans riding low like some country singer's, his shirt stretched over muscles that a grown man would envy. He'd asked her to dance, and she'd all but fallen into his arms, her schoolgirl heart ripe for the plucking.

From that night on, he'd been the only boy for her. Being with him had become the most important thing in her life, even more important than pleasing her dad. For the first time, she'd ignored her father's wishes, defied him openly, going so far as to threaten running away if he tried to keep her from seeing Graham.

A log on the fire slipped lower, crackling and spitting flames. Lindsey shook her head to clear unwanted ghosts from her past. Growing pains, the price of transformation from little girl to woman. That was all it had been.

She moved her gaze from the flames to the man in the adjoining kitchen. He was no longer the tempestuous teenager who had once dominated her life. Now he was Graham Dufour, homicide detective. But he was as cocky, and as bossy, as ever.

"Do you still like your steak so rare it moos?" he called, waving a spatula in her direction.

"You got it. And do you still burn yours to charcoal?"

"Yeah, if I have a choice. I usually don't. The NOPD makes sure I never get to stay home long enough to cook them to that stage."

Lindsey twirled the sparkling liquid in the crystal goblet. It was funny the things she remembered about Graham. He liked his steaks well-done, his po'boys not dressed, his milk icy-cold.

And he liked his women docile and compliant. She hadn't filled that bill ten years ago. She definitely didn't fill it now.

"Are you sure you don't need some help in there?"

she called, eager to have something better to do than conjure up old memories.

"No, you just relax. Dinner's almost ready."

She took another sip of the fruity wine. "Then do you mind if I use your phone? I need to find a hotel room for tonight."

Graham appeared at the door, wiping his hands on a cook's apron that sported a feisty crawfish jumping from a boiling pot. "I thought you were staying with Brigit."

"No. She offered, but they have a houseful of guests in for Mardi Gras. I decided I'd get a lot more rest in a hotel. Only problem is, I checked out of the one I was in this morning."

Graham set two mismatched bowls of leafy salad on the small dining table in the far corner of the room. "So you're stuck with no place to stay for the night?"

Prickles of irritation danced up Lindsey's spine. Graham's tone sounded more amused than concerned. Surely he didn't think she was fishing for an invitation. She'd sleep on the streets before she'd share his place.

"I'm sure I can find a room, somewhere. Mardi Gras's not for another nine days. The hotels can't possibly be booked already."

"Think not? Partying starts early in the Big Easy. You should know that, after the weekend you just had."

Partying and a lot more, she reminded herself, as images of the bizarre stabbing played again in her mind. Suddenly the sleeping-on-the-streets idea lost all its appeal.

"Steak's ready. Why don't we eat first, then worry about a hotel? No use letting the food get cold. Thirty minutes more or less isn't going to make a lot of difference in finding a room. Besides, if worse comes to worst, I can always arrest you for loitering on the street corners and let you spend the night in the comfortable confines of Central Lockup."

"Thanks a lot."

Lindsey joined Graham at the round table, which was barely big enough for the two of them. He cut into his thick filet with relish. She nibbled at her salad.

"Do you need to make a call to anyone else—you know, a roommate, boyfriend, whatever—to let them know you won't be home tonight? If you do, you're welcome to use my phone before you go."

Lindsey wondered if more than hospitality or idle curiosity had prompted his question. She tried to read his expression, but there was nothing there except signs of immense satisfaction as he started on another bite of his overcooked steak.

"No, I live alone. Not even a goldfish that needs to be fed," she remarked, her mind suddenly swinging into gear. "In fact, I don't have to go back to Nashville until I'm ready. I have weeks of vacation time I haven't used."

Averting her eyes to the pattern on her fork, she avoided the angry stare that had replaced Graham's look of complacency. "I could stay in New Orleans, and you could get me into the LeBlanc house. If I could go into the turret where the murder took place, there's a chance it would all come back to me."

"Forget it. It's out of the question. And that's exactly why we have to talk tonight. You seem to be enjoying playing supersleuth, but the stakes in this game are a lot higher than you're bargaining for. If you need gruesome details of murders in this town, believe me, I can supply them."

"No, I'm not interested in police party games. And I'm not playing. So, do you have a better idea? You told me yourself that there's no suspect, no body, no motive, just one semidependable witness. But if I could remember what the guy looked like, we'd have something to go on.''

"You're going to be on the first plane out in the morning. We have a bargain, remember?''

"And I'm going to keep the bargain. I'll be on the first plane out…''

"Good.'' He took another bite of his steak.

"The very first plane that leaves after I've been in the turret,'' she explained, taking advantage of his full mouth. "The quicker you get the search warrant, the sooner you'll be rid of me.''

Lindsey watched the irritation in Graham's eyes burn into something far more disconcerting. His gaze caught and held hers, and the old stirring returned once more to haunt her. Stay angry, Graham, she pleaded silently. Scream and yell, but don't look at me like that.

"I don't want to get rid of you, Lindsey.''

The fork grew heavy in her trembling fingers, then slipped from her grasp, sliding noisily to the table. Graham reached over and took her hands in his.

Lindsey lowered her gaze to the patterned cloth on the table. She didn't want to tremble at Graham's touch, didn't want to feel the old desire inside her rising up like smoke and stealing her breath away. She didn't want to, but she did.

She shivered as he scooted his chair closer. Taking his right hand from hers, he slipped a finger under her chin, tilting her face upward. Mysterious passions smoldered in the deep depths of his eyes, capturing her, cruelly awakening feelings that should have died years ago.

"I've never wanted to get rid of you,'' he whispered huskily, his finger sliding from her chin, tracing the line of her neck down to her shoulder and then up again.

She wanted to pull away, to lash out at him for playing so ruthlessly with her feelings, for stirring desires she had so carefully buried away. But words wouldn't come, and her body had suddenly grown far too weak to pull away. He leaned toward her, his very nearness washing over her in sensual waves she couldn't escape.

And then his lips were on hers, warm and inviting. She shuddered, but couldn't pull away. The intensity of his craving melted her resolve, rolling away the years like morning mist. It was only her and Graham, lost in each other, the way it always was in her dreams. Love surged inside her, suffusing her body with warmth.

She parted her lips, the hunger inside her demanding she savor the taste of Graham's lips, the feel of his probing tongue. Her mind followed her body, whirling feverishly, passion as hot as fire controlling her senses, burning away her ability to think of anything but Graham and her own maddening desires.

Oh, God, she loved him so.

No. What was she thinking? What was she doing? Struggling for breath, she forced herself to focus. She couldn't forget the past, couldn't exchange one glorious moment of passion for a new lifetime of pain.

A low moan tore at her throat as the sting of memories struck deep in her soul. Slowly, reason returned, replacing the fire in her blood with cool determination. She placed her hands on Graham's chest and pushed him away.

"I'm sorry, Lins." Graham's voice was low. "I didn't plan that. It just happened. It's just that seeing you again…"

She forced a cold authority to her tone, denying the inner hunger that still tormented her body. "What we had is in the past," she assured him, cutting his explanation short. She didn't need to hear it. All she needed was to get her own emotions under control, and to remember the price she had paid ten years ago for believing his kisses meant something.

"Of course." The sharp tone of authority returned to his voice. "I was out of order. It won't happen again." He scooted his chair back from the table. "But I do have a job to do, and right now my first priority is keeping you safe. So you can just forget these foolish ideas about interfering in police business. Under no circumstances will I allow you to become involved in this Mardi Gras murder mess."

"I am involved, Graham." She took a deep breath, determined to stand her ground. "I didn't ask for it. It just happened. But now that I am, I can't just walk away."

"You can, and you will," he demanded, all traces of his recent passion lost in the determination that pulled his mouth into firm lines.

"No." She swallowed and forced the words past the cotton that dried her mouth. Nothing had changed between her and Graham. Not the passion that burned beneath the surface of every touch, every word. And not the differences that had torn them apart and left her heart too battered and bruised for her to even attempt another chance at love. But she was all grown up now, and responsible for her own decisions. "You gave the orders and ultimatums ten years ago, Graham. But you can't give them now. I'm not a young, lovestruck girl anymore."

His gaze grew cold as ice, and he clenched his hands into fists. "You're right. I can't make you return to Nashville. But I'm warning you, Lins. Murder is serious business. These guys play for keeps, and if you get in over your head, even Daddy's millions can't save you.''

Lindsey intuitively girded her strength about her for the fight that had always followed his outbursts. But there would be no fight tonight. She could no longer be influenced by what Graham said or thought.

Toying with her salad, she eased a forkful to her mouth.

''You're right. A description of the killer *would* make solving this case a lot easier,'' he continued. ''But you need to know what you're up against.''

''No wonder there are so many unsolved crimes in New Orleans, if this is your modus operandi. Do whatever you can to frighten the witnesses into silence. Besides, even if the killer did look at me, he can't possibly know who I am. I was costumed and masked.''

''He'll know if you keep snooping around the LeBlanc house.''

''Not if I'm Officer Green. Just an efficient female detective, doing my job. You've set everything up.''

''Yeah,'' Graham commented, cutting into the steak with a ferocity that would have sliced leather. ''Leave it to me to pave the way for the *efficient* female cop.''

''I'm in your hands. I'm sure I'll be safe.''

''That makes one of us.''

Lindsey finished her meal in silence, but with a sense of relief that restored her appetite. Going into the turret might not jog her memory, but at least she'd have done everything she could. She'd sleep a lot better at night knowing that.

Now all she wanted to do was find a room, any room, as long as it was far away from Graham Dufour and the painful memories he'd brought back to life. She needed rest. It had been the longest weekend of her life.

THE ROOM was suffocatingly small, and musty smells hung in the air like cheap perfume. Or was it after-shave? Lindsey tossed in the narrow bed and then jerked to a sitting position. It was her heartbeat that pounded in her ears, but it was not her footsteps shuffling along the carpet, not her heavy breathing filling the room with a deadly threat.

It was the middle of the night, but someone was in the room. She could hear them, could feel their presence. But how could she have an intruder? She'd carefully locked the dead bolt and slipped the night latch into place.

She lay deathly still, moving nothing but her eyes. Somehow she had to see through the curtain of darkness. The shuffling sounds grew closer, and she tightened into a knot, scarcely daring to breathe.

A scream gurgled inside her, fighting for release. And then he was there, the towering figure coalescing in the blackness like the shadow of death.

"Who are you?" The scream she'd so desperately needed had locked in her throat, but her whispered question managed to escape.

The only answer was a menacing laugh. Lindsey struggled, but two hands clasped her wrists and pinned her to the bed. He leaned closer, the smell of rotting earth, dank and potent, surrounding her.

"Tell me who you are and what you want," she pleaded.

Then, as if by magic, the figure came into full view. He was in a soldier's uniform with his cap cocked to one side. Hair shiny as onyx fell over his forehead. But the face… Oh, God, no… There was only an empty shell, dark sockets, horrifying blankness.

The scream finally flew from her lips, bloodcurdling, freezing and holding in the room. Lindsey jerked to a sitting position, cold sweat beading on her skin. Nothing held her now. She reached for the lamp and flooded the room with light. It was as dingy as ever, but there was no one here. The door was still closed tightly, the night latch safely in place.

She swung her legs over the side of the bed and grabbed her kimono from the chair, clutching it around her. Fingers trembling, she retrieved her watch from the table by the bed. It was four-thirty. Two hours ago she'd been praying for sleep. Now, one nightmare later, she wasn't sure she'd ever trust sleep's hold again.

She slid into her slippers and started toward the window.

"Are you all right in there?"

A gruff male voice penetrated the door, and once again Lindsey's heart accelerated to racing speed.

A banging accompanied the voice. "Hey, you all right in there? Somebody heard a scream."

She forced her heart to slow down and managed to push words past her own jagged breathing. "I'm fine. It was just a nightmare. I'm sorry if I woke the other guests."

"Are you sure you're okay?"

"Quite sure."

"Well, we're right downstairs if you need us."

"Thank you, but I'm fine. Really I am."

"Okay, if you say so."

Relief was evident in his voice. Lindsey dropped back to the bed. She wouldn't sleep again tonight. She was sure of that. And she didn't want to lie in the dark, reliving the murderous scene over and over again, as she'd done for the last two days.

Tomorrow she'd go with Graham to visit the LeBlanc

home one last time. If nothing jogged her memory then, she'd leave the investigation in Graham's hands.

It was definitely the way he wanted it. And it was the way she needed it. She couldn't keep living with these nightmares.

Fatigue settled over her, and she dragged herself back across the room. Lifting her tapestry carryon, she flung it onto the bed. She'd filled this bag with souvenirs and a couple of books she'd bought for herself. She might as well start one. It would still be a long time before the sun rose and eased the nightmare's hold.

She fingered the clasp and then swung the top open.

Oh, no! It couldn't be! She squeezed her eyes shut as frigid fingers clutched and choked her breath away.

Eyes still closed, she leaned against the bed for support. She was awake. The nightmares couldn't come now. It wasn't possible. The trauma of the past few days was playing tricks on her, driving her mad.

She opened her eyes again, determined to push the macabre images from her mind.

Her stomach lurched sickeningly. Yards of velvet, green velvet, coated in dried and hardened blood, stared back at her from beneath the linings of her case. "No, please, don't let this be happening…" she whispered into the silence.

As if to taunt her, the folds of haunted fabric pushed their way up from their cramped position in the small carryon, billowing out of the case, threatening to steal her fragile hold on reality.

She slapped the top of the case shut as heated tears welled and then escaped from her eyes, rolling down her trembling face. The horror was fully alive again, just as it had been two nights ago. Then the velvet ball gown had been on the victim. Now it was here, in Lindsey's hotel room.

Visions of the beautiful Southern belle swam before her eyes. And of the faceless killer.

The killer. She had no idea who or where he was, but he knew about her. Somehow, he had found her. And he had left his calling card, in the form of a bloody souvenir.

Forcing her breath through burning lungs, Lindsey reached for the telephone and dialed Graham's number.

## Chapter Five

Morning sunshine filtered through the faded curtains of the hotel window, casting a sinister glow over the dingy furnishings. Lindsey rubbed at her half-closed eyes and then jerked awake as the tapestry suitcase came into view. A chill of foreboding quickened her heartbeat, but she forced herself under control.

Finally adjusting to the dim light, she ran her fingers across the bedside table and located her watch. Six-thirty. She must have dropped off to sleep for a little while. This time, the nightmare had not returned.

Stretching her legs, she crawled from between the sheets and crept to the window. Wide-awake now, she pushed the curtain aside and peered into the parking lot. An array of cars, vans and pickup trucks, most far older than Grace Ann's Mercedes, surrounded the painted brick building like dented sentinels. A red van on the far side of the lot revved its engine and pulled into the quiet street.

Lindsey drew the curtains to and headed for the shower, carefully avoiding sight of the tapestry luggage and the dreaded surprise from last night. The surprise she had still not shared with Graham.

His last words ran through her mind like a stuck record. "If anything unusual happens, call me at once." She stepped under the tepid spray.

She had tried to call him—several times, in fact, at home and at the number that rang in his office—but there had been no answer. Of course, she could have just called the police station, but she had wanted to give the information to Graham.

Besides, the immediacy had already been lost. The dress had apparently been planted in her luggage yesterday afternoon, while the Mercedes was parked near the LeBlanc house. Finding it had sent her into a fitful panic, but she wasn't in any immediate danger.

The dress was obviously meant as a warning. If the killer had wanted to strike again, this time at the witness, he would have delivered a bullet, not a bloody ball gown.

And there was still the outside chance—way outside— that the person hiding the dress in her car had not known who the car belonged to. The Mercedes had been parked all afternoon on a quiet side street. A perfect dumping spot for incriminating evidence.

She picked up the phone and dialed the first three digits of Graham's number. She hesitated, then dropped the receiver back in its cradle. Guilt gnawed at her conscience, but she pushed it aside.

The dress was in her possession. A dress without a body.

But there was a body somewhere. That was the problem. The body of a young woman who hadn't had a fighting chance at life. And Lindsey was the only one who could lead the police to her killer. At least she could if her memory would only return.

Graham had agreed to let her go with him to the LeBlanc house, but he had done so reluctantly. One hint that the killer might know who she was would change his mind forever.

And a bloodstained dress last worn by the victim was a hell of a lot more than a hint. As soon as Graham heard about its unconventional delivery, she could kiss away any chance of ever getting into that house again.

She'd tried to play by his rules. It wasn't her fault he didn't answer his phone. But since he didn't know yet, what possible difference could another hour or two make? She would tell him everything, gladly place the bloody ball gown in his hands, as soon as they returned from the LeBlanc house and a thorough investigation of the turret.

The shrill ring of the telephone sent her nerves jangling again. Grabbing a towel, she dashed across the slippery tile floor to the bedroom.

"Hello."

"Lindsey, is something wrong? You sound breathless."

"I was in the shower."

"Good. I didn't wake you, then. Did you sleep all right last night?"

"Like a baby," she lied. "Do you have things set up for us to visit the LeBlancs?"

"I'm working on it. If all goes well, the warrant should be in my hands by ten."

"That long?" Guilt reared its ugly head. She was holding evidence. She wanted desperately to keep it a secret until she got inside the house, but something inside her pushed toward total honesty.

"I'll pick you up about nine," Graham offered. "That way, we'll have time to grab a quick bite first."

"Sounds fine."

"Okay, I'll see you then."

"Wait, Graham. Don't hang up yet." She was losing the battle with her conscience. "Something's changed."

"Don't tell me you finally came to your senses. I was hoping you would. It makes absolutely no sense for you to go with me to the LeBlancs'. It's police business, and no place for amateurs."

Agitation knotted Lindsey's stomach and weakened her resolve to come clean. His words didn't surprise her. She'd already known exactly how he felt. He hadn't tried to keep it a secret.

"No, Graham. I was only going to suggest we meet at Camellia Grill. I've been hungry for their Mexican omelets and chocolate freezes for ten years."

"Okay." His disappointment was evident. "Camellia Grill it is. By the way, I checked the flight schedules this morning. You can get a direct to Nashville as late as two-thirty. I'm sure we'll be through in plenty of time for you to make that."

There it was again, that undeniable eagerness to push her out of his life, the sooner the better. He clearly had no time or inclination for an old lover turned star witness.

"Don't worry, Graham. I'm as eager to get out of here as you are to see me go."

"What do you plan to do until we meet for breakfast?"

Load a bloody piece of evidence in the car, check the parking lot for snoopers—or was it stalkers?

"I don't know. Probably read a little. Maybe I'll give Brigit a call, or Danielle. She's in a down mood these days."

"Good idea. But, Lins, don't…"

"Don't what?"

"Don't talk about what you saw the other night. Like I told you, it's better if we keep everything between the two of us for a while longer."

"Whether I talk about it or not, it happened."

"I know. But just let it ride. It'll be better that way."

"Whatever you say. I'll see you at breakfast."

Lindsey hung up the phone and stole another glance out the window. A tall man in a gray overcoat was climbing into a car on the street, and a woman was hoisting two youngsters into a minivan, the wind whipping her skirt against her long legs. Evidently the cold front the weatherman had predicted yesterday had arrived.

Satisfied that life was going on as usual, Lindsey wiggled into panty hose and then chose a straight brown skirt from the hanger. Thankfully, her clothing had been packed in the hanging bag and duffel. Only a few souvenirs and a ratty chenille robe had been left in the tapestry bag. They could stay there, buried below the yards of green velvet. She wasn't about to touch any of them.

Five minutes later, Lindsey was fully dressed, her coral silk blouse tucked neatly into her skirt, her hair brushed into place, a touch of lipstick smoothed over her lips. She paced the room, knowing her nervous energy wasn't about to let her sit around and twiddle her thumbs until it was time to meet Graham.

But she wouldn't check out of the hotel. Somehow she couldn't force herself to load the tapestry bag back into the car. Her rational mind might believe that the green velvet dress was a harmless inanimate object, but her heart knew different. She shivered and hugged her arms around her.

It was as if the ghost of the dead girl had arrived with the dress. Its cold and shimmering image played with Lindsey's psyche. It demanded things of her, pushed her to do its will.

Perhaps that was the real reason she hadn't been able to tell Graham about the dress. A dead girl was calling out to her to see that her killer was found and punished. Lindsey hadn't been called on to do much in her life. Now that she had, she wasn't going to fail.

She'd been pampered and spoiled for most of her life, the only daughter of a self-made millionaire who loved nothing more than showering his little girl with everything money could buy.

Why not? She'd been all he had left after the beautiful fashion model he'd married died in a fiery car crash. She'd been rushing home from an assignment, determined to make her daughter's second-birthday celebration. Lindsey couldn't remember anything about her mother. Her dad had trouble remembering anything else. Anything, that was, except how to make and spend money and how to give orders.

But his little girl was all grown up now, and taking orders from no one. She could take care of herself. And, if her memory would cooperate, she could also identify a heartless killer.

The man in the soldier suit had been young and handsome. That much she was sure of. A man about the age of Garon Oleander. Only he'd been much thinner and…straighter. And no scraggly hair had hung beneath the soldier's cap.

A cap.

Lindsey grabbed a pencil and a piece of the freebie stationery from the table and began to sketch an image. She'd forgotten the hat, but the man had been wearing one. It had tipped low in the front, and a lock of dark hair had peeked out, falling over his right eye.

A uniform, a cap, dark hair, broad shoulders. Breathtakingly handsome. That was the way her eye had framed him. Picture perfect. The form taking shape on the paper looked nothing like that. She dropped the pencil in disgust. Drawing was not one of her strong points, and her mind had returned to its disgusting void, leaving the killer faceless.

Tapping her fingers on the thick telephone book, Lindsey closed her eyes again and tried to concentrate. A positive identification from a witness who'd seen the murder from a distance wouldn't seal the case, but it would give Graham something concrete to go on. Identified suspect, corpse, weapon, motive. That was what he'd said he needed.

And opportunity. Someone in the right place at the right time. Like someone who'd stolen a key. Garon Oleander. Thick neck, pudgy face, scraggly hair that crawled down his neck and into his shirt collar.

No, stolen key or not, he wasn't the man. She'd make book on that. Even from a distance, he wouldn't be as dashingly handsome as her soldier had been. Not even in *his* dreams.

Lindsey flipped open the phone book and thumbed through to the *O*s. Garon Oleander. Not the murderer. But maybe he was the accomplice to one of his scum friends. She skimmed through the pages.

There were three Oleanders in the book. One had a Dr. in front of his name. The next was Richard, on Riviera Street. She dialed and let the phone ring eight times before giving up. The next was R.A. Again there was no answer.

"Buy an answering machine," Lindsey ordered into the mouthpiece.

R.A. That was the best guess. Ruby something-or-other. With a nervous glance at the tapestry bag, Lindsey grabbed her handbag and the phone book and pushed into the hall, pulling the door to behind her and checking to make sure it had locked.

AFTER A STOP at a McDonald's drive-through for coffee, and forty minutes of driving through Monday-morning traffic, Lindsey finally pulled off of Gentilly Boulevard and onto Music Street.

The narrow street was lined with trees of various sizes and with older homes, settled, with character.

She slowed and studied the numbers. It was another block to the home of R. A. Oleander. She returned a wave from an older lady sweeping the street in front of a house bedecked with shimmering strands of purple, green and gold foil. Signs of the season, Lindsey noted, and in New Orleans, Mardi Gras was *the* season.

Thirty-two twenty-four, the middle of the block. Lindsey stopped in front of a double shotgun house, smaller than most of the others, but with fresh paint and a manicured lawn bordered with budding azaleas.

There were two windows in the front, but the blinds were closed tight. A woman with any sense at all would get out of here on the double, Lindsey warned herself. As Graham had said, murderers played for keeps. And she'd already received a warning, in the shape of a slightly used ball gown.

But an officer of the law couldn't be intimidated. Lindsey climbed from the car and smoothed her slim skirt, adopting her most professional Officer Green manner. Threading her fingers through the strap of her shoulder bag, she marched up the walk.

"Ain't nobody home there, honey."

Lindsey jerked around to face the owner of the crackly voice. A thin man with wire glasses and a walking cane looked up from his position at the foot of the front steps. He eyed her appreciatively, letting his eyes run the gamut from her high-heeled pumps to her dark hair. He had to be nearing eighty, but his eyes and imagination were apparently still working fine.

"Miss Ruby's been gone for hours."

"Too bad. I was hoping I could catch her before she left for work. I had some good news for her," Lindsey lied, wondering if starting up a conversation with the nosy gentleman would glean her any wisdom.

"Hard to catch her in the morning. She works slave hours for them LeBlancs. 'Course, they pay her a fine penny. Too much. She wastes it all on those lazy boys of hers. One too ornery to work. One don't know enough."

"They do seem to give her trouble, but they're very important to her. She talks about them all of the time." Might as well go along with him for a minute.

"Humph." The man stopped his train of thought to spit a tobacco-colored wad into the grass. "She'd be better off not even talking to them. The younger one's going to turn out as bad as his brother, if you ask me. And Jerome's worthless. He's handsome enough, though, when he's sober and cleaned up. He gets the girls. That he does."

The old guy nodded his head in appreciation of his worthless neighbor's prowess with women. "He had a leggy little thing yesterday, a-hangin' on him like he was the only port in a storm."

Lindsey walked back down the concrete steps to stand beside the man. He was on a roll, and she needed him to keep talking.

"Problem is, soon as Jerome shows up back in town, Miss Ruby gets nothing but trouble from Garon. Now he's up and moved out. Got himself an apartment somewhere near his brother's. And his poor old mama'll end up havin' to pay for it."

"Well, you never..."

"You hear what I tell you?" he continued, ignoring her attempt to speak. "Probably have to bail him out of jail again, too."

"So Jerome is back in town. I wasn't aware of that." Or that he'd ever been out of town, she noted to herself, hoping her comment would keep the neighbor sharing his tales.

"Yeah, he's back. Nothing but trouble. Now, you take Miss Lee's sons. She lives over there in that white house." He pointed across the street, toward a two-story clapboard with decorative iron bars on the front windows. "If I had children, I'd have kids like hers. One's a doctor. One's a teacher. Now those kind of kids do you proud."

"Surely Garon and Jerome aren't all that bad, are they?" she asked, determined to steer the conversation back where she wanted it.

"The doctor, now he don't come around much. Got one of those highfalutin wives. Thinks she's too good for..."

Lindsey stepped away, eyeing her own car. The neighbor was off on his own agenda, and she didn't have much time to spare, not if she was going to meet Graham by nine.

She took one step back to her car, but a man on a motorcycle pulled up, nosing her Mercedes' bumper before coming to a complete stop.

"You looking for someone?" the driver barked, jumping from the bike and taking swift steps in her direction.

"Ruby, but I missed her. I guess you did, too." She managed a sweet voice and a friendly smile. The man in front of her was unimpressed. The snarl on his face intensified.

"What do you need her for?"

"I wanted to ask her a few questions."

He stepped closer, his breath reeking of last night's garlic and booze. He was muscular and tall, and a large white bandage covered the right side of his face. His nose poked out, black-and-blue and swollen two sizes.

"A few questions." He pushed back long strands of sun-bleached hair that had fallen over his forehead and then put his hands in his pockets. "You wouldn't happen to be that little policewoman I heard about, now would you? The one that came snooping around the LeBlancs' the other day?"

The tangled web of deceit. Well, she hadn't woven this one. The whole Officer Green idea had been Graham's. If it worked to her benefit in finding the killer, so be it. If it worked against her... She fought back a shudder and answered. "I might be."

"Why don't you leave my mother alone? Like she told you, she doesn't know anything."

"Do *you* know anything?" she asked, keeping her voice as steady as she could manage.

"I might. Come on in." He gestured toward the front door.

She hesitated for a moment and then followed him back up the steps, while the man next door continued his monologue, totally oblivious of his departing audience.

"Crazy old man. Ought to be locked up."

"He seems harmless enough."

"He's nuts. Gets on my nerves. Always babbling away like some fool."

He opened the front door and stood aside while she entered in front of him. His touch of manners surprised her.

"Tell me, Jerome, when was the last time you were in the LeBlanc house?"

"How did you know my name?" he asked, whirling around to face her.

"It's my job." And a lucky guess, she added to herself. "You didn't answer my question."

He dropped into an upholstered chair and motioned her to a matching sofa. "Aren't you forgetting something?"

"Like what?"

"Like advising me of my rights. If you don't you can't use anything I say in court."

She swallowed a curse. She was playing detective, and she didn't know the rules as well as the suspects. But was he a suspect? She studied his face. The swelling had blurred his features, but he had a strong chin, and he was attractive in some rugged, unkempt way.

Dark hairs had popped out all over his chin, begging for a shave. He probably needed a bath, too, she decided, judging from the stains on the front of his wrinkled shirt. He looked as if he'd slept in his clothes.

"Don't worry," he snapped, not waiting for her to answer. "I don't have anything to hide. You couldn't pay me to go into that stinking museum they call a home. Money, money, everywhere, and not a drop to share. Unless you beg, of course, like a good employee."

"Your mother seems to like working for them," she pointed out, baiting him.

"Yeah, well, she's gotten used to bowing and scraping. I haven't."

Contempt added a sardonic bite to his words. Lindsey couldn't tell if it was for the LeBlancs or his mother, but one thing was certain. There was no love lost between Jerome and the LeBlancs.

"You'll have to excuse me for a minute, lady. I need a beer. You want one?" Jerome asked, heading for the kitchen. "No, I guess you wouldn't," he went on, "not this time of the morning. But there might be a soft drink in there somewhere.''

''No, nothing for me.''

Thankful for a few moments to get her thoughts together, Lindsey studied the cozy living room. She'd never really expected to get in the house. In fact, she wasn't sure what she'd expected when she looked up the Oleander address. Perhaps she'd only wanted to kill some time while she waited for Graham. Or maybe to catch a glimpse of a handsome, dark-haired man.

The phone rang, and Jerome grabbed it on the kitchen extension.

''Yeah. No way. I'm telling you, it ain't going to happen. Stay in control, man. I'll take care of everything.''

She strained to hear every word, but it was a waste of effort. He wasn't going to say anything incriminating, even if he knew something. Not with Officer Green in the next room.

She tiptoed to the hall that separated the two sides of the house. There was a bedroom to the front, and a room to the rear with a closed door. She opted for that direction.

Easing open the door, she stood motionless, letting her eyes adjust to the darkness. There wasn't much to see. A single bed with a green cord spread, a wooden dresser, and a bedside table with a cypress-knee lamp and a color photograph in a heart-shaped frame.

The photo was of a girl with flowing blond hair. Lindsey stood dead still as fingers of ice traced a pattern along her heart. Afraid to look closer, but knowing she had to, she reached for the photograph.

Icy fingers tightened around Lindsey's heart. The girl staring back at her with the constant smile was the same one Lindsey had seen in the turret. There wasn't a doubt in her mind. The frame shook in her fingers and slid to the wooden floor. She bent over to retrieve it.

"Looking for dust bunnies?" Jerome stopped in the door, his eyes and voice making threats his tense muscles could easily keep.

She jerked back to a standing position, using the toe of her foot to push the edge of the frame under the bedspread and out of view. "No, I was looking for a bathroom. I wandered in here by mistake, and the back fell off my earring."

Her breath quickened as the lies flowed from her lips. It was amazing. A week ago, she couldn't have told a lie to save her life. Now there had been so many she couldn't keep up with them.

"Here, let me help you look for it." He walked over and lifted the edge of the spread.

"No, it's okay. Really. I have plenty of extras."

"I insist." He bent down and retrieved the picture frame from the floor.

"Sorry, no earring back, nothing but a picture." His voice was mocking, and the knowing look he shot her way made it clear he had not been fooled. "So you stopped to nose around? A sneaky look without a warrant. And it appears you found something of interest."

"Who's the girl, Jerome?"

He studied it as if seeing it for the first time. "I'm afraid I couldn't tell you. She's a…looker," he remarked, evidently searching for a word not too offensive to a policewoman. "This was Garon's room before he got a place of his own. I guess you'll have to ask him about her."

"Then do you mind if I ask you how your face got banged up?"

"I took a spill on the Harley." He scowled and placed

the picture back in her hands and moved closer, towering above her menacingly. "Sorry, pretty officer lady, but I'm afraid the party's over."

"What do you mean?"

All of a sudden, Graham's warnings to stay out of this were front and center and screaming doom. She forced herself to stand perfectly still. She couldn't back down, couldn't let Jerome sense her fear.

With slow but purposeful movements, she ran her fingers across the clasp of her handbag and loosened it, slipping her hand inside. She held her hand still, right on the spot where her gun would likely rest, if she really were an officer, as Jerome believed.

"I mean our time together is up, though I can't say I haven't enjoyed it." His gaze never left her hands.

She wrapped her fingers around a lipstick and glared at him. "You're right. I'll be leaving now, but I'm sure we'll talk again," she said, her voice strangely firm.

Pulling courage she didn't know she had from somewhere inside her, she pushed past him and toward the front door.

"Yeah, another time, pretty officer. Count on it," he added menacingly as she let the front door slam behind her.

GRAHAM SWERVED into the last parking spot and headed into Camellia Grill. He was twenty minutes late, but surely Lindsey had waited for him. He'd been working since long before sunup, but the first big break had come only minutes ago.

He pushed through the double glass doors and looked over the old-fashioned drug counters that linked the place to its earlier glory days. The days when the waiters behind the counter entertained the customers with jokes, songs, whatever it took to keep the tips big when times were hard.

Even at 9:20, the place was still crowded. He skimmed the seats and found Lindsey, sipping a chocolate freeze and making notes on a scrap of paper. His heart took a dip. The same plunge it took every time he saw her.

He eased onto the circular bar stool beside her.

"Sorry I'm late."

"No problem."

She smiled her usual devastating smile, and Graham felt the heat in certain parts of his body rise to the level of steam.

"I haven't been here long, myself," she added. "Traffic crawled along St. Charles."

"Yeah. I thought about that after I talked to you this morning. I called back to suggest you take the streetcar from your hotel, but you didn't answer."

"No, I went out for a while."

"What'll it be?" the waiter asked, stopping in front of them and twirling his pencil like a baton. "Oh, it's you, Mr. Dufour. How's it going?"

"Going great, Arno. Better all the time." Graham lifted his hand to exchange a high five with him.

"Yeah, looks that way." Arno gave Lindsey a nod of approval and Graham a knowing wink. "Sure does look that way."

A faint blush colored Lindsey's cheeks. Graham knew the waiter's implication had not escaped her, but she was here strictly on business. Arno might not know that, but Graham did.

And if she hadn't been, he wasn't interested. He'd paid his heartbreak dues. It would take a fool to renew a relationship that would lead to more of the same. He wasn't a fool, but his heart and body and mind had definitely been making motions like one ever since Lindsey had walked back into his life.

They gave their orders, and Graham started on his fourth cup of coffee of the morning. Lindsey picked up her pencil again and started writing. Graham read her words out loud.

"Handsome, good posture, soldier uniform, cap at an angle, dark hair. Sounds like you're casting the hero in a new movie."

"It does. But in this case it's the villain in a mystery."

"Have you remembered anything new?"

"Actually I have. The man wore a soldier's cap, tilted at a rakish angle, and a lock of dark hair fell over his right eye."

Determination etched new lines in the soft features of her face, and dark circles surrounded her eyes. The strain of the past few days was taking its toll.

"I think you're worrying about this too much, Lindsey."

"I'm fine."

"I want you to stay that way." He slid his fingers over hers. He hadn't planned to touch her, not like this. But he couldn't seem to help himself.

She looked into his eyes. Damn. This wasn't working. He had to keep their relationship strictly business.

"Do you remember what you said, Graham, about what you needed to solve a murder mystery?"

"No, not offhand." He didn't remember much of anything right now. Not with Lindsey staring at him with those dark, misty eyes.

"You said you needed a corpse, a suspect, a weapon, a motive, and opportunity to commit."

"You have a good memory."

"We know Ruby had access to the house, but she can't be a suspect."

"Not if you saw a man do the stabbing."

"Right. Her son Garon stole a key to the house, so we can assume he also had the opportunity to commit the crime."

"Right again. Only you've already said you're certain Garon can't be the murderer. He's carrying too much flab."

"But he could be an accomplice, and so could Ruby. Wouldn't that put both of them under suspicion, at least give us just cause to bring them in for questioning?"

"Give *us* just cause?" He felt the muscles in his jaw and neck tighten. "There is no *us* in this case. You are a witness. That's all. I knew I shouldn't have agreed to let you go with me to the LeBlanc house today."

Lindsey stiffened shotgun straight. She was silent, no doubt biting her tongue and waiting for inspiration to hit and supply her with a remark sharp enough to cut him to shreds. Her obsession with this case was clearly out of hand.

"Just simmer down," he warned as the waiter approached with steaming plates of chili-topped omelets. "I said you could go with me, and I plan to keep my word. You can look, not talk, and definitely not ask questions."

"Then you did get the search warrant?"

"No, turns out I don't need one." He raised a forkful of food to his lips and savored the taste while Lindsey stared at him, impatiently waiting for an explanation. "Mrs. LeBlanc has returned from Europe, and she is eager for my visit."

"Then you must have told her about the murder?"

"No," he answered slowly, enjoying keeping her

guessing about his revelation. "I didn't tell her anything, but she requested my presence anyway. It seems murder isn't the only crime that took place during the LeBlancs' absence."

He placed another forkful in his mouth. "Eat it while it's hot, Lindsey. It's delicious."

"Come on, Graham. Give. What else happened at the LeBlancs'?"

"Well, according to the lady of the manor, there are a few jewels missing from the family safe."

"A few jewels?"

"An expensive few. Half a million dollars' worth, more or less. Probably more."

Lindsey reached to the back of the chair and grabbed the strap of her handbag, ready to bolt to her feet. "I can't believe it. Why are we sitting here eating, if there's new evidence?"

"Because I'm hungry." He took another bite and chewed slowly. "And because Mrs. LeBlanc requested we not come for at least a half hour. She just woke up, and she wants time to get ready for company."

"Police officers investigating a crime are not exactly company."

"Evidently Mrs. LeBlanc thinks we are. She insisted on time to shower and dress before we arrived. It seemed a reasonable request."

"Not to me."

Graham sipped the last of his coffee. "Then finish your breakfast, so we can get out of here. *One* of us has an investigation to handle."

## Chapter Six

Lindsey sat beside Graham on the plush LeBlanc sofa and studied her surroundings. It was the same spot where Ruby had parked them two days ago, but the sedate Southern mansion had suddenly sprung to life. The heavy drapes and underlying lace panels were pulled back and held in place by ornate bronze magnolias, and glorious streams of sunlight reflected off antique furnishings that had been polished to a see-yourself sheen.

Anticipation—or was it apprehension—crackled in the air, and Lindsey tried hard to concentrate on maintaining her Officer Green persona. Graham had ordered her to keep quiet, and indeed she had, although she was certain he hadn't meant it quite as literally as she had taken it.

He wouldn't approve of her keeping secrets from him, especially essential details like a bloody ball gown appearing in her suitcase and the discovery of a photograph of the beautiful lady who had been stabbed while wearing it.

No doubt about it. She would have a lot to tell him as soon as they finished at the LeBlancs'. Pieces of the puzzle were suddenly dropping into her life like Louisiana lagniappe. Too bad none of them seemed to fit. And now there were more pieces—jewels worth half a million, disappearing into thin air.

She settled back, determined to steady her nerves. The puzzle wasn't hers to solve. All she had to do was pose as Officer Green and make a visit to the turret. Then her part of this investigation would be over, and she could return to her quiet and orderly life. A life without the constant threat of faceless murderers waiting behind every closed door.

A life without Graham Dufour.

The weight of ten years of fooling herself settled to the pit of her stomach. She had fought so hard to convince herself she was better off without him, and her attempts had appeared to be working. A week ago, she had thought he was all but forgotten.

"Remember, Lindsey, leave the talking to me." His voice, low but insistent, broke into her reverie and startled her back to the here and now.

"I heard you the first time you said that, and the second and third," she answered, avoiding meeting his gaze.

"It's not your hearing I'm worried about."

"Who does Mrs. LeBlanc think took the jewels?" she whispered.

"That's what we're here to find out."

"Are you going to tell her about the murder?"

"It all depends."

"On what?"

"Shh… I think I hear them coming."

Lindsey settled back in her chair as Mrs. LeBlanc swept into the room, an emerald silk tunic swaying about matching slacks. Her fiery red hair cascaded in ringlets past her shoulders and down her back. *Vivacious.* The word so aptly described her, it was all but tattooed across her forehead.

Lindsey watched her performance in total surprise. This was not at all the stuffy aging socialite she had expected to rule over the impressive manor. Mrs. Le-Blanc was no more than forty and far more flamboyant than stuffy.

"I'm so glad you've come," she announced in a girlish voice oozing with charm. "It's so terrible. I just can't believe it."

Hands flew as she talked, brightly manicured nails punctuating her distress. Lindsey took in the show and racked her memory. She hadn't attended half the high-society functions her dad was involved in, but she'd accompanied him enough to have met most of the rich and powerful at one time or another.

Not Mrs. LeBlanc, though. Lindsey would definitely have remembered. She was not the kind of person who went unnoticed, especially not in a world where understatement was the mainstay.

Lindsey nodded as Graham flashed his badge and introduced the two of them. He waited only until Mrs. LeBlanc had taken a seat before diving into the nitty-gritty.

"Exactly when did you discover the jewels were missing?"

"When I called you. I mean, that was the first thing I did, call you. Well, after I called Richard, of course. He insisted I inform the police at once." Her long eyelashes fluttered in Graham's direction.

"So you didn't discover they were missing until this morning?"

"Right. It was about eight-thirty. I hadn't been awake long, but I wanted to unpack the jewels I had taken to Europe and put them in the safe before I got busy and forgot them."

"When did you get back into town?"

"Last night. Quite late, and I was totally exhausted. You know how tiring those flights across the Atlantic can be."

"No. I'm a home boy myself." Graham drawled the words innocently. Not his usual style. No doubt he'd learned to use his boyish charm as a detective's guise to put rich Southern women at ease and keep them revealing information. "I know you're upset," he continued, "but try to be as accurate as possible. When was the last time you actually saw the jewels in the safe?"

"Three weeks ago, January 21. It was a Saturday night, or the wee hours of Sunday morning, to be exact. I remember the date precisely because we had just returned from a Mardi Gras ball, and we were flying to London the next day."

"Okay, let's see if I have this straight. You came home late on the night of January 21 and checked your safe. Is that what you normally do?"

"No, of course not. I usually slip out of my clothes and drop into bed, just like I did last night. But, like I said, that night I was getting ready to leave the country. Richard insisted I go with him. He knows I don't like to miss a minute of the carnival festivities, but he hates it so when he has to be away from me. The poor dear. You know how men are."

The last remark was directed at Lindsey, and she nodded her agreement, though she was sure Mrs. LeBlanc had a lot more experience in the men department than she did. She was putting on quite a show, but Lindsey could tell from the irritated way Graham's eyebrows rose that he was not buying the performance.

Same old Graham. Nothing irritated him more than the rich talking about their jet-setting and society bashes.

"So, Mrs. LeBlanc, you came in on that night, and you were leaving the next day. Why, exactly, did you check the safe? Had you had problems before?"

"Heavens, no. Never. And please, call me Katie. Everyone does. I opened the safe to return the diamond necklace and tiara I had worn to the ball. I wanted to make sure they were safely locked away before we left."

"And this particular necklace and tiara are worth half a million?"

"No, no, not nearly so much as that. The appraisal on those two pieces came in under two hundred thousand. But there were other pieces in the safe, as well. Everything was taken."

Lindsey studied Katie's expression. She threw around talk of million-dollar pieces of jewelry like the butcher giving the price of steak, but something in her voice didn't quite ring true. Perhaps it was the accent that escaped from time to time, a hint of blue collar in a world of black tie. Lindsey's guess was that the striking redhead had married into her first taste of riches.

"Half a million. That's a lot of baubles. Most people I know wouldn't keep that kind of investment lying around in a little home safe."

Katie bristled with indignation. Graham's line of questioning was obviously not sitting well with her. She expected sympathy and efficiency, not the suggestion that she had been careless.

"I can assure you this is not a *little* safe, Detective. There are banks in town that would envy the LeBlanc vault."

"A vault? Sounds impressive. Why don't you show it to me?" Graham asked. "We can talk while I look it over. Be careful what you touch, though. The fingerprint crew will be here any minute now."

"Oh, dear. Fingerprints, thieves. It gives me the creeps. Really it does. To think some total stranger broke into my house and just helped himself to my things."

"Well, at least *someone* did it. There's always the chance it wasn't a stranger. It might not have even been a *him*."

A cloud of disbelief darkened Mrs. LeBlanc's fiery eyes. She shook her head, not willing to even consider Graham's suggestion that it was an inside job.

"No. I'm sure it was a stranger. Ruby was in charge, and Richard says she is completely trustworthy."

"I take it she's worked for you for quite a while."

"Well, not for me, exactly. Richard and I only married five years ago, but she's been with the LeBlanc family for years. Besides, she doesn't have a key to the safe. It's not likely she could even locate it. It's quite well hidden." Graceful as a ruling house cat, Katie rose with a toss of her head. "Follow me," she said as she stepped toward the winding staircase.

The carpeted steps led to a hall that stretched out before them like a landing strip, long and narrow and bordered by electric sconces. Lindsey followed far behind, grabbing the opportunity to peek in every open door they passed. And the selection of doors was endless. Room after room met her gaze, each filled with expensive antique furnishings, marble fireplaces, bronze-and-crystal chandeliers, and enough dark corners and half-hidden crevices to hide an army of thieves.

Or one lone soldier, she mused, her heart constricting at the thought. A handsome soldier with a dagger, and a beautiful Southern belle by his side. The murder, the jewel theft, the stolen key. Somehow it was all connected. The trick now was in finding the link and putting the responsible parties behind bars.

She peeked into a room on the left side of the hall and then stopped. Unlike the elegantly furnished rooms she had come to expect, this one was nearly empty. She stepped inside. Boxes were piled in one corner, and old newspapers were stacked haphazardly in another. A wooden desk stood in the middle of the room, but it was far too cluttered to provide a work space.

A ghostly chill snaked through Lindsey's body, and she pulled her sweater over her chest. It didn't help. Looking up, she spotted the source of the cold air that barreled down like a wintry blast. A pull-down staircase to her left spiraled upward, leading into a dark, ghostly hole above her head. No wonder the room was used for storage.

"Are you with us, Green?" Graham called back, the agitation in his tone making it clear that this was an order to keep up with them, and not a friendly question.

"Right behind you." She hastened her pace and caught up with them just as they opened the door to a massive room, paneled in dark wood and filled with overstuffed chairs and reading lamps. Katie LeBlanc marched inside and led the way to a wall of mahogany bookcases laden with hardcovers. Everything from leather-bound copies of Shakespeare's sonnets to Grisham's latest stared back at her, all filed neatly in alphabetical order.

The silence of the room was broken by Lindsey's sigh of appreciation. "What a wonderful room, and so many books. I could hide away in here for days and never once be bored."

"Unfortunately, Richard could, too," Katie answered, dropping to her knees as she spoke and retrieving a copy of *War and Peace* from the bottom shelf. "But not me. It's far too stale and dark. I prefer people to books— young ones, full of life."

Lindsey inched closer and knelt at Katie's side as she slid her hand to the back of the space *War and Peace* had occupied. Sliding her finger around, she located a button-size knob and twirled it to the left.

Then, right before Lindsey's eyes, a four-foot section of wall, books intact, swung open.

"Pretty impressive," Graham admitted, stepping out of the wall's path.

Actually, it was amazing, Lindsey decided. She had heard there were houses in the Garden District with secret passages and hidden rooms, but she'd never imagined anything on this scale. Behind the wall was a heavy door, at least six feet tall, and wide enough for two oversize men to walk through side by side. The top was curved like a cathedral, or a tomb.

Katie reached over and slipped a small bronze key into the palm of Graham's hand. "Why don't you do the honors, Detective?" she offered. "Just slip the key into the LeBlanc crest, right in the lion's mouth."

Graham turned the key over in his hand and then poked it into the middle of the insignia. To the untrained eye, the crest looked as solid as the rest of the door, but when Graham wiggled and pushed, the key slid inside and turned, letting the door swing open.

Cold, dank air slapped them in the face, and Lindsey noticed Graham's right hand slide instinctively to the pistol at his waist. "Is there a light switch?"

"No, there's no electricity in there. But there's a battery-operated floodlight that illuminates the whole area. It's just inside, to the left of the door. Just go on in. You can't miss it."

"Why don't you get it, Mrs. LeBlanc, and turn it on? You must have done this many times before."

"Of course, but you told me not to touch anything."

"Didn't you already touch the light this morning?"

"Yes, but…"

"Turn it on." This time his words were an order.

"You see?" Katie stepped inside the damp vault and flicked on the beam of light. "It's empty, absolutely empty."

Lindsey stepped backward as an icy tremor snaked its way up her spine. Secret vaults, ghostly entries, faceless murderers. Her pulse raced, and she longed to run from the room, from the house, from this whole crazy mess.

She closed her eyes and forced herself forward, closer to Graham and closer to the vault door. He reached back and took her hand.

"Stay right with us, Lins. You're doing fine," he whispered in her ear. He gave her hand an extra squeeze before letting go.

Her pulse slowed to near normal, and she followed them inside the uninviting tomb.

"This is pretty elaborate for a home safe," Graham acknowledged, taking the light from Katie and directing it over and around stacks of small metal safes, all opened and empty.

"The vault was originally part of a system of secret passages," Katie explained. "Richard says he has no idea what they were used for originally, but his father had them closed off. He cemented this part in to make a safe. It's as safe as any bank." She ran her hand over one of the empty safes. "At least it was."

"Who else knows about this secret entry?" Graham asked, stepping to the back of the vault and running his hand along the concrete wall.

"Just Richard and I now. At least that's what Richard thinks. It was a family secret, and his only brother and both his father and grandfather are dead."

"So you and Richard are the only ones with a key to the vault?" Graham questioned.

"That's correct. Richard gave me a key on our first anniversary, at the same time he gave me the tiara. He said I could keep my jewels here and they would be safe. The original Mrs. LeBlanc had. It's insurance approved."

"No doubt. But surely there's another key somewhere. What would happen if you misplaced yours while Richard is out of town?"

"You don't misplace the key to a half-million-dollar treasure, Detective. But you're right. There is one more key. It's in my safety-deposit box at Whitney Bank."

Lindsey stepped back, easing herself from the circle of light and back into the library. The dampness of the air, and an unfamiliar acrid smell, were clogging her lungs. Besides, she doubted seriously there was much more to be discovered in the empty vault.

"Is there any other way leading…"

Graham's voice drifted from hearing range as Lindsey slipped out the door and back down the hall. She tiptoed across the carpet, determined not to alert Ruby that she was on her own in the house. If she could find the turret, she could have privacy and silence while she searched it, and her mind, for hidden clues.

The only problem was, she had no idea how to get there. The turret sat alone on the third floor, but the wide staircase they had climbed earlier stopped on the second floor.

There had been the other staircase, of course, the tiny metal one that disappeared into the black hole. But that couldn't be the entry. The pull-down steps were narrow and treacherous, like the steps to an attic.

She moved quickly, retracing her earlier path, but this time opening each door. The stairs to the turret had to be somewhere. But where? She was at the front staircase now, and she hadn't a clue as to how to get to the third floor.

She stopped and listened. Everything was quiet, except for the sounds of Ruby rattling around below, probably in the kitchen. Katie and Graham had not reappeared.

As far as she could tell, the metal steps were the only possible way to the turret. It didn't seem likely, but she was dealing with architecture from another century. Maybe the turret had served as an attic then, or maybe access to it was simply meant to be hidden away. If the builder had wanted secret passageways, he might also have wanted hidden stairwells.

Lindsey tiptoed back down the hall and stopped at the storage room. The door was still ajar. She stepped inside, and the same cold air, the same sense of foreboding, attacked, this time with renewed vigor. It was almost as if someone, or something, were warning her to stay away. But that was ridiculous.

She took a deep breath and stepped on the bottom rung of the ladder. Tilting her head back, she studied the cold darkness above her. There was no light, no sound. She was ascending into emptiness.

She climbed to the next rung, whispering reassurances to herself. "Get a grip, Lindsey, old girl. You're imagining things. It's the middle of the day, and you're in the house with a would-be socialite, an overbearing housekeeper, and Detective Graham Dufour, champion of right and might. Nothing evil would dare happen under his nose."

Finally, she reached the top, and her head pushed through the opening. It was still dark, but a narrow strip of dim light beckoned from a few feet away. She ran her hand over the floor. It was bare wood, but solid. Using her knee as a wedge, she pulled herself up to the attic floorboards.

Lindsey took a step and stretched her arms and hands out in front of her, feeling her way. She was in a narrow passageway. Although it was wide enough to maneuver through easily, she had to stoop to keep from hitting her head on the ceiling. A rectangular pattern of illumination was about four feet in front of her. She inched closer until, palms out, she could trace the actual door that spilled light from the top, bottom and one side of the facing.

Her hands were clammy now, and trembling, but she managed to locate a rounded knob. She hesitated, her breath heavy and jagged, her body fighting a nameless fear. But she had come this far. It would be foolish not to have a look. Holding her breath, she twisted the knob and then pushed. The door caught at first, but then gave, all but dropping her on the floor as it swung open.

Relief coursed through her body, and laughter bubbled up inside her as she enjoyed the release of her foolish fright. She was standing in the turret, and morning light poured through the open windows, illuminating an elegant room of jewel-toned colors and muted patterns, far more modern than the rooms she had seen in the rest of the house.

A low-slung sofa stood against one wall, and the tables placed at each end were made of thick panes of beveled glass atop curving legs of green metal. A massive desk and leather chair stood in a corner, and a marble statue of a shapely nymph finished out the furnishings of the rounded room.

Even the cold had an explanation. The windows were flung wide open, and an icy February wind was bringing the chill inside. Lindsey shivered and stepped over to close the inside shutters, carefully avoiding the spot in front of the window where she had seen the soldier pull the dagger and murder Garon's blond friend. The one whose picture Garon Oleander still kept by his bed. The one whose green velvet dress was now in Lindsey's hotel room.

This was the house. This was the room. Lindsey pushed aside the fears that racked her mind. She had to concentrate. A lean soldier in uniform could easily maneuver the climb she just made to get here, but a girl in a bouffant skirt that billowed out forever? No way.

Lindsey stepped back from the window. For that matter, why in the world were these windows open? And who cleaned this room? Someone did. It was spotless. But she sure couldn't imagine Miss Ruby squirming her way up here.

Nonetheless, a costumed couple had been here, in this very room, only a few feet from where Lindsey was standing right now. She stared at the spot in front of the window. If she could just block every other thought, every other image, from her mind, she might be able to see them once more, just the way she had seen them that night. And this time, just maybe, she could also remember the man's face.

The sights and sounds of the parade came back to her, the teeming throngs of excited spectators, all begging for the colorful throws. She could see the blurred faces again, swimming in front of her, could visualize the hands waving wildly.

And she could see the victim, the striking outline of her face, upturned, staring into the eyes of her lover. She could see her lips parting, for a kiss. Or maybe not for a kiss. Maybe she was laughing, or telling the soldier something.

Lindsey stood as if in a trance while the thoughts tumbled hauntingly in her mind. The soldier, straight and tall. There were no pudges in the uniform, just the firm muscle of youth. That was the image—strong, firm, in control.

The hat had sat at a cocky angle, and a dark lock of hair had fallen over the right eye. Irritation pulled at Lindsey. She knew all this, had gone over it in her mind a thousand times. There had to be something more. If she could just visualize his profile the way she could the girl's, she could at least give the police artist an accurate description.

Nothing. Long nose, pointed jaw, mustache, clean-shaven? Nothing. She could remember nothing that would help, not one thing to help identify a suspect.

The police didn't have to rely on eyewitnesses. She'd seen enough movies to know that. Fingerprints and blood samples could be just as effective in getting a conviction. They'd find the killer. It would just take a lot more time with no suspect and no corpse.

But there had been plenty of blood. Lindsey stared at the Persian rug that covered most of the floor. It had to have been soaked. Stepping to the center, she dropped to her knees for a closer look.

The rug was old and well-worn—no older than the rest of the carpets in this house, but definitely the oldest thing in this room. She ran her fingers across the thick pile. If this rug had been here that night, someone had done an excellent job of cleaning it.

Lindsey smoothed the pile with her bare hand, keeping her eye peeled for any discoloration. Her fingers found the spot first, a rough spot, stiffer than the rest. And the color was lighter—not much, but it was noticeable, a

rough circular pattern of stiff pile and an almost indis-
cernible stain.

Her mind swung into overdrive. Whoever had cleaned
this rug had either committed the murder or was covering
up for the guilty person. The suspect might be a lot closer
than they thought.

A gust of cold air filled the room again, and Lindsey
glanced at the window. One of the folding shutters must
have blown open again.

She was wrong. They were closed tightly, and the wind
was coming from behind her. She raised up on her knees
and twirled around, her heart punching into her chest with
breathtaking force. The door she'd thought went to the
closet stood open, and a tall man was leaning against it,
a wicked smile dancing on his lips.

"Looking for something, Officer?"

## Chapter Seven

Lindsey glanced up from her awkward position, her knees grinding into the expensive Oriental rug. The man in the corner stared back, a smirk on his face that highlighted the threat in his dark eyes.

She swallowed the panic that rose to her throat. "Who are you?" she stammered, trying to force authority into her voice. "And how did you get here?"

"Ah, I thought you would know such simple things. After all, that's what you get paid for, isn't it, Officer Green? And from what I hear, you've certainly spent enough time snooping around here lately."

Damn. Everybody seemed more informed than she was, or misinformed. At any rate, her Officer Green character was certainly a popular one.

A sardonic smile twisted the man's lips as he let his gaze roam the length of her and then linger on her breasts. The muscles in her stomach clenched sickeningly.

"But *I* didn't expect to have the pleasure of your company." He reached back and shoved the door to with his foot—the heavy wooden door that led to the outside.

She longed to kick herself with the same ferocity he'd used on the door. Of course the turret had its own outside entry. She should have thought of that, since there was no inside entry, except the one reserved for pack rats and amateur sleuths.

She returned his stare. His body was lean and mean, the type that left coeds drooling and middle-aged matrons longing for their youth. He acknowledged her stare with a toss of his head that shook a lock of jet black hair over his forehead.

"Did you break into my room, or did my aunt furnish you with a key?"

"Your aunt?" she asked, easing back to a standing position while she tugged at her skirt, determined to keep her knees and upper thighs completely covered.

He shook his head and chuckled, apparently enjoying his little game of one-upmanship. "My, my... You don't know much, do you? My aunt, Katie, the mistress of this pretentious monstrosity. Surely you've met her by now."

"Katie LeBlanc? Of course I've met her."

Lindsey turned away from the arrogant man who apparently lived here and studied the room with new insight. Tingles of terror slithered along her spine. In this very spot, a woman had been murdered by a young man as dark and as handsome as the one standing beside her. She forced her feet to inch toward the door.

"In fact, your aunt knows I'm here. She's supposed to meet me any minute," she said, bluffing. "Probably on her way up right now."

"Not likely," he answered, stepping between her and the door. "My aunt hates the narrow steps and the steep climb from the balcony. Total privacy. That's the nicest thing about this hideaway. Besides the price, of course."

He tucked his thumbs into the front pockets of his jeans and lounged against the door, blocking any chance of a hasty exit. "Where's your partner?"

"He's around."

"I'm surprised he let you out of his sight. A sexy woman like you shouldn't be visiting a man's apartment all alone. Anything might happen to you. Or are you the kind who likes taking risks?"

"No," she answered, recoiling at the suggestive tone in his voice. She wasn't the risky type. *Stupid* was a much better description of her actions.

"So what's the big, bad crime you're investigating? Did Uncle Dick cheat the IRS out of a few million? If he did, just ask him. He has plenty lying around, and heaven knows he doesn't need it."

Lindsey breathed deeply, forcing her jangled nerves into a semi calm. "I thought everyone needed money."

"For what? He'll never see sixty again, and he's already bought a new wife. Got his money's worth, too, from what I can tell."

Lindsey's pulse slowed a little, her curiosity overpowering her fear, at least temporarily. She might be standing in this room with a killer, but he didn't seem inclined to repeat his performance. At least not at this minute. She tried to concentrate. His nose was classic, and his jaw jutted out just a little. The sun had bronzed his skin, but hadn't taken its toll in wrinkles yet.

Still, nothing struck that chord of déjà vu. She still couldn't remember the man's face at all. Too bad she hadn't been close enough that night to see the eyes. The ones staring at her now were coldly calculating and hard as nails. She had to keep the man talking, and hope Graham missed her soon.

"I take it you approve of your uncle's new wife."

"Seems nice enough. And she's a hell of a lot more generous with the LeBlanc money than the rest of the family."

"Generous enough to support you?"

"You might say that. I prefer to think of it as sharing the family wealth. Besides, my aunt likes having me around. My uncle's friends tend to be a tad stuffy."

"And I'm sure no one says that about you."

"I haven't had any complaints."

"Too bad Katie wasn't here Friday night. She said she loves Mardi Gras. She could have watched the Minerva parade with you."

Fury flashed in his eyes and the muscles in his jaw tightened briefly before he brought them under control. Lindsey fought the dark foreboding that weakened her knees. The man was sophisticated and sauve, but there was something else. Not something she could put in a police report, just a chill that tingled along the nerves, dark and ominous.

She was playing a dangerous game, but logic told her she was safe, for now. What man in his right mind would kill a policewoman with another officer in the house? Besides, even if he was the killer, he wouldn't suspect a woman he thought was Officer Green of being the masked witness.

"It was a great night for a parade," she said, baiting him.

"I wouldn't know about the parade. I was out Friday night. All night. With a friend," he answered, leaning in her direction.

"Too bad. I heard it was great. Of course, there were a lot of elegant parties going on that night, too. A friend of mine went to a masquerade ball. It made quite an impression on her."

"Why do I think we're playing a little game, Officer? It's not necessary, you know. If you have something to ask me, get on with it. No need to stand on formality now. You've already broken into my room.''

Graham was going to kill her as it was, as soon as he discovered she'd not only gone exploring on her own, but had interviewed a prime suspect, as well. Information gathered by a woman impersonating a police officer. The judge would throw it out in a heartbeat. She might even go to jail herself.

''I'm not playing anything. I was merely making polite conversation.''

''Sure you were. Polite conversation, the investigating cop's stock in trade. And it sounds as if I'm about to be honored with another uninvited guest.''

Breathing a sigh of relief, Lindsey focused on the approaching footsteps. She stepped back as the door swung open with a blast of frigid air and a fuming detective.

''What in the devil are you doing up here? Did you listen to anything I told—'' He stopped in midsentence and stared at Katie's nephew. ''And who in the hell are you?''

''Thomas LeBlanc.'' He nodded toward Graham. ''I would invite you to come in, but then, you already have. And that is no way to talk to a lady, and certainly not one as beautiful as Officer Green.''

He was back to his innocent routine, and he was good at it, obviously well practiced at playing the debonair bachelor.

Graham glared, first at Thomas, then at her. He flashed his badge in Thomas's face. ''Thomas LeBlanc, this is a surprise. Your aunt just told me you were out of town. Said you'd been gone for weeks, and she had no idea when you'd resurface.''

''True. I returned on Saturday, but I've been out most

of the weekend. I haven't had a chance to welcome Katie home yet.''

''You just said you were out Friday night, with a friend,'' Lindsey pointed out, her tongue jumping into gear before her brain.

''Exactly, and I was. I returned to New Orleans on Friday, but not to my apartment. Like I told you, I was with a friend—all night,'' he added, a satisfied smile playing at his lips. ''I have her number, if you'd like to chat with her yourself.''

He was lying. Lindsey was sure of it. She'd tell Graham that later—that is, if he ever spoke to her again. Right now, the way he was staring at her, she was just thankful the old adage about looks being able to kill wasn't true. If it were, she'd be nearing extinction.

''Mrs. LeBlanc said this apartment belongs to her,'' Graham commented, his gaze already covering the room. ''She gave us permission to look around up here. If it's all right with you, we'll go ahead and do that now.''

''Certainly. I'm just a guest.''

Apparently one with his own key, Lindsey noted silently.

Thomas reached for a faded jean jacket, the designer type. ''I don't think you'll find anything, but then, since you didn't bother to answer my question, I don't even know what you're looking for.''

''I'm sure your aunt will fill you in on the details.'' Graham walked to the window as he talked. ''The bottom line is, somebody made off with her jewelry, a half-million dollars' worth.''

A low whistle escaped Thomas's lips. ''You're kidding. Stole them from the inner sanctum? Must have been some ingenious crook.''

"Yeah, must have been. Either that, or someone who had an inside track on the hiding place."

"Well, well… Who knows, it might have been old Uncle Dick himself. Perhaps the insurance money was more appealing than a few sparkles on his wife's fingers and impressive cleavage."

"Maybe. Anything's possible. But rest assured, we'll find out who did it."

"I would hope so. I'll tell you what, if you don't need me for anything, I think I'll go talk to my aunt. She could probably use a little comforting. Those jewels were her security, you know, the only thing of value in her name, thanks to a LeBlanc-worded prenuptial agreement. They like to keep everything in the family, you know. The immediate family."

"Talking to Katie is probably a good idea. But, Thomas, why don't you jot down the name and address of your Friday-night friend?" Graham ran the toe of his shoe across a faded area of carpet as he spoke. "And if you have any ideas about cutting out of town before this thing is solved…don't."

"Surely you don't consider me a suspect?"

"Everybody's a suspect."

"Then you'll be busy. But don't worry, I'll be around."

He scribbled the information down on a piece of scratch paper and tossed it on the table without a word. Lindsey watched as he swung the door open and stepped outside. He turned, stopping dead in his tracks, and stared at her, his gaze once again raking across her body.

Her skin crawled beneath his scrutiny. His face still sparked no memories, but the indefinable something about him gave her the willies…the kind that woke you up screaming in the middle of the night.

He asked Graham something about the lock on the door, but she only half listened to the conversation. The spirits of death seemed to suddenly fill the room, and the walls began to close in around her. The images that had haunted her for the past two days were all but alive now, re-creating the scene right here where it had all transpired. She fought the urge to run, to escape this place and its murderous memories.

Instead, she waited quietly until the door slammed behind Thomas, leaving her alone with Graham. Then, dropping to her knees, she pointed out the faint circle of stained carpet.

SUNLIGHT BURNED through the windshield of Graham's unmarked car, and Lindsey squinted in the strong glare. She glanced in the rearview mirror and watched as Graham exchanged information with the arriving fingerprint team. Hopefully they could come up with something more than she and Graham had.

They had spent thirty minutes alone together in the turret, but all they'd discovered was the slightly soiled spot on the carpet.

Graham had been furious with her, his frigid silence proof of his disapproval of her daring to go off on her own. Fine. It would be good preparation for everything else she had to tell him, especially the part about her early-morning visit to the Oleander household. She stared out the window and concentrated on getting her story straight.

Finally Graham climbed in beside her and gunned the engine to a hurried start, swerving left in front of an oncoming streetcar.

"Graham?"

"Yeah." He kept his eyes straight ahead, avoiding even a glance in her direction.

"I found something today. I think it's important."

"Good. I'd hate to think your little escapade was a total waste, *Officer Green.*"

"Wait a minute. Don't blame that on me. The name game was your idea."

"It's not my first mistake."

"Nor mine." No use beating around the bush. She might as well throw everything at him. The mood he was in, there was no reason even to try apologizing. "I went to Ruby Oleander's house this morning."

He shook his head in disbelief. "Why am I not surprised?"

"I had some time to kill before meeting you, so I just drove by the house. Ruby wasn't there, but a neighbor stopped to talk to me."

"Another Thomas LeBlanc type with roving eyes?"

"You noticed."

"Of course I noticed. The man was oozing lust. It was all I could do not to belt him one."

Jealous. Graham was so mad at her he was barely civil, yet he was still jealous. For some reason she couldn't begin to fathom, a satisfied smile curled around her heart.

"It was another Thomas type, but this one was about fifty years older."

"Good."

Graham swerved around a corner, the momentum swinging Lindsey toward him. She straightened up, but didn't pull away. She'd been through so much in the past few days. It was nice just to have the warmth of a body close by, one that wasn't a suspected felon's.

"So hopefully you left without confronting the Oleanders."

"I planned to, but then I ran into her other son, Jerome. I was talking to the neighbor when he drove up on a motorcycle. He invited me inside."

"You didn't go. And you didn't tell him who you are." His voice had become strained, and he took his eyes from the traffic to see her face when she answered. "Just tell me you didn't let him know you're the one who witnessed the murder."

"Of course not."

The muscles in his face relaxed, and a long sigh escaped him.

"He knew I was Officer Green. I mean, he knew I'm supposed to be Officer Green."

"Oh, God. Not another one. I'm beginning to think even you believe that's who you are."

"No, Graham. I know all too well who I am." Her voice broke on the words. Suddenly she'd had enough. Enough of criminals. Enough of danger. Enough of fighting with this man she only wanted to hold, whose strong arms she wanted to fit herself into and never let go. The man she should have gotten over years ago.

A tear started down her cheek, and she wiped it away with the back of her hand.

The car swerved again, this time throwing her up against Graham. His arm curved around her shoulder. Without speaking, he eased to the curb and slowed the car to a stop.

"I'm sorry, Lins. I know you didn't ask for any of this." He took a clean white handkerchief from his pocket and dabbed at her eyes. "I know you're only trying to help, but—"

"I know. You just want me to go back to Nashville."

"I think it would be best."

Graham wiped her eyes again and tried hard to swallow the words that he longed to say, the words that were eating away at him like acid. He didn't want her to go back to Nashville. He didn't want her to go anywhere at all. He only wanted her safe.

He wanted her in his arms, only not like now. Not with tears of regret. He wanted her happy and secure, and loving. Heaven help him, he wanted her in his bed.

"Graham, I know I shouldn't have, but I went in. I have to do what I can."

"After all the times I told—"

"Wait, just hear me out." She shivered against him, and he tightened his arm about her.

"I can't figure out why he invited me in, but he did. We were just standing in the living room talking, getting nowhere. Then the phone rang, and he took it in the kitchen. While he was gone, I looked around."

"You can't go snooping without a search warrant. I told you that."

"No, Graham, *you* can't go snooping. I'm just a private citizen who visited someone's home."

"While impersonating a police officer." God, he needed his head examined to see what had replaced his gray matter. He'd thrown out the Officer Green lie on the spur of the moment, never dreaming it would take on a life of its own.

"I was wrong. I know that now, but nonetheless, I found a picture of the girl."

"The girl?"

"The blonde who was murdered. It was in a heart-shaped frame, beside Garon's bed."

"I thought we'd established that Garon had moved into an apartment. What made you think it was his bed?"

"Because Jerome said it was."

"Mighty helpful of Jerome. Okay, so you saw a picture that you believe was the same girl you saw from the float?''

"I know it was the same girl. Jerome came in when I was looking at it. He said I'd have to ask Garon who she was."

"So, Garon has a picture of the dead girl. Possibly the girlfriend Ruby was asking him about. The one he said he wouldn't be seeing again."

"That would make sense," Lindsey agreed, "especially if Garon is in on this somehow."

"I wonder why Ruby didn't approve of his girlfriend."

"I can't imagine. She was beautiful, like a model. It's so sad to think she got involved with someone who would take her life."

The tremor in her voice swallowed her words. She tilted her head to face him, and Graham sucked in his breath to halt the rush of blood that fired his senses. He moved his hand from her shoulder and placed it on the steering wheel. He had to keep his thoughts clear. Lindsey's safety was on the line, and he couldn't afford any more careless mistakes.

"But Garon wasn't the soldier in the turret," Lindsey insisted. "His profile, his figure, they're all wrong."

"What about Jerome? You must have gotten a good look at him."

"The build was right, but I couldn't tell much about his face. It was bruised and swollen, and there was a bandage over the right side. One of those bulky ones that stretched from temple to chin. He said he'd had an accident on his Harley. Anyway, he was a sun-bleached blonde, and the soldier had dark hair."

"Like our friend Thomas LeBlanc."

"Exactly. His profile didn't ring any bells, either, but everything else fits perfectly. Plus, he apparently lives in that room, compliments of Aunt Katie. Only one problem. He claims to have a valid alibi.''

''Suspects have been known to lie, Lins, especially the guilty ones. And almost everybody's guilty of something.'' Graham tapped his fingers on the wheel. ''The hard part is sifting through the lies to find the truth.''

''Graham, there's something else.''

She wrapped her arms about herself, as if fighting off a chill. He reached for her hand and wound his fingers through hers. Her hands were cold in spite of the warmth of the car.

''There's something else you should know about, Graham. Something in my hotel room that I need to show you.''

Graham stared into her eyes. They were dark as night, but misty, like early-morning dew. ''What is it, Lins?''

Damn. His voice choked on her name. He couldn't bear to see her hurting. He never could. That was the real reason he'd listened to her father ten years ago and just walked away.

''I'd rather show you. It will be easier that way.''

LINDSEY SLIPPED the key into the lock and pushed open the door to her hotel room. The air was even staler than she remembered, and the dust and corner cobwebs were omnipresent in the beam of sunlight that poured through the room's one window.

''You slept in this dump?'' Incredulity colored Graham's voice.

''I didn't have a lot of choice.''

The suitcase glared at her from the shabby armchair, where she had flung it last night. She just wanted to get this over with, to hand it and this whole sordid murder case over to Graham and be on her way.

"The surprise is in the tapestry bag, Graham." She motioned toward the chair, without stepping away from the door. She was as close as she cared to be. "Why don't you open it?"

He eyed her suspiciously, but didn't hesitate. Two long strides, and he was across the room.

"Be careful. There may be fingerprints." God, she was even beginning to sound like a cop!

Graham used his handkerchief to unlatch the case and swing it open. Lindsey sank to the bed as the bloody velvet poked out, turning the brightness of the day dark with its silent threat.

Graham's face turned white, then a fiery red, as a string of curses flew from his lips. Still using the handkerchief, he lifted the shoulder of the dress above his head, letting it fall its full length. The front of the skirt was ripped, hanging from the bodice by frayed threads. A sticky sweetness filled Lindsey's nostrils, choking the life from her lungs.

"When did you find this?" His voice was hoarse with fury.

"Early this morning."

"But you didn't call me?"

"I tried to. You didn't answer." Her heart constricted painfully. She'd been prepared for his anger, but not for the hurt she could hear in his tone, could see in the bewildered shrug of his shoulders.

He dropped the dress back onto the chair, but something slipped from the folds. She followed the curve of bronze as it rolled silently across the worn carpet. Graham bent down and retrieved the shiny gold button from its resting place beneath the table.

He turned it over and studied the pattern. "Looks like some type of military insignia."

Lindsey walked to his side. His muscles were taut, the hard lines of his body stiff and tense.

"Get your things, Lindsey. You're coming with me."

"That's not necessary, Graham. I'm ready to take your advice. I'll be on the next plane to Nashville."

"It's too late for that now. The dress changes everything. Someone knows who you are, and is following your movements. You'll have to come with me."

"Where?"

"To the only place I can make sure you'll be safe. You'll be staying with me, in my apartment."

## Chapter Eight

Lindsey lifted the glass of brandy to her lips and sipped again. The slow burn slid down her throat and continued its attack on the knot in her stomach. Dropping her head against the soft cushions that lined Graham's sofa, she gave in to the heaviness of her eyelids. It was much better this way. She could blot out the glare of the afternoon sun, the grimness that tugged at Graham's lips, the urgent tone of his voice as he spoke into the kitchen phone.

The receiver clinked back into its cradle, and she forced her eyes open. His steps were heavy, and the lines in his brow deepened as he joined her in the compact living area.

"You could be overreacting to all of this, Graham. The dress may not mean anything. Just because it was hidden in the trunk of my car doesn't necessarily mean the killer put it there, or that he knows I'm the witness."

His eyebrows arched questioningly, but his penetrating stare didn't soften. "No? Then why do you think you were chosen to be the lucky recipient? Because you looked so needy driving around in Grace Ann's *extra* Mercedes?"

"Sarcasm isn't necessary." But, strangely enough, it

helped, she decided. Irritation with Graham was a far more productive emotion than fear or denial.

"Everybody seems to think I'm Officer Green. Maybe someone knows who did it, and they wanted me to have a clue. Or maybe they just needed a place to dump the evidence, and my trunk was available."

"It's possible," he admitted. "But not likely. Sneaking around hiding bloody ball gowns in locked cars isn't as easy as you make it sound. Especially right off a busy street corner."

"*If* the car was locked. I'm not sure it was. It's always hard to open. Grace Ann apologized for it, but said she just hadn't had time to take it in for service. But last night, when you took me back to get the car, the key turned easily. I didn't think about it at the time, but later, when I found the dress, I remembered. So, you see, it could have nothing to do with thinking I'm a witness."

"So there's not a thing to worry about. Is that what you think?" Frustration pulled at the corners of his mouth. "You obviously haven't listened to anything I've been saying. You still think this is some mystery game. How to find a murderer. Be the first kid on your block to gather the clues and show up the police."

"That's not true. But now you're not listening to me. If my scenario is correct, then the dress isn't a threat. It also means that someone out there besides me knows who the killer is, and for some reason, they're afraid to say. But if we can convince them…"

"I hope you're right. But I'm not betting the bank on it." He scooted closer and took her hand in his, his thumb nervously fondling the tops of her fingers. "I won't let anything happen to you, Lins."

His strong voice grew husky, and he turned toward her, capturing her eyes with his. His gaze held her, dark as night, but fiery with the passion she'd tried so hard to forget. A searing warning exploded inside her, demanding she pull away. She couldn't. Her mind had lost the power to make rational decisions, hurling her into the danger zone.

She leaned into Graham as his face lowered to hers. Once more she closed her eyes to hide from a truth she didn't dare face. His lips brushed hers, gently at first, as if she might disappear at his touch. She didn't. How could she, when she longed so desperately for more than he had ever been able to give?

His mouth grew rougher, demanding, claiming her last vestige of control with a bittersweet pain. The blood inside her surged into a whirlwind, rushing through her body, demanding a release from everything she had endured the past few days. Everything that had eaten away at her heart for the past ten years.

She pressed against him, her pride forgotten. His body was hard and straight. He pulled her closer, his fingers digging into her skin. A groan, deep and soulful, rumbled from deep inside him. With a forceful jerk, he pushed her away.

Only then did she hear the pounding at the door.

"Dufour, you in there?"

"Yeah. Hold on a second, Rooster."

"Were you expecting someone?" Lindsey asked, her breath punctuated by ragged gasps. She slid her hand down the front of her blouse, smoothing away the telltale wrinkles.

"Yeah. A detective friend of mine, with his usual bad timing." He kissed her again, thoroughly, breathtakingly.

"Just keep that thought until I return," he whispered, easing up from the couch and heading toward the door. "I have to run down to headquarters. There's a million things to put in motion now that we finally have something to sink our teeth into. The theft, the girl's picture, fingerprints.''

''C'mon, man. It's cold out here!'' the voice from outside the closed door yelled impatiently, to the accompaniment of stamping feet. ''Get your pants back on and open the door.''

''Yeah, yeah…''

''This is my protection?'' Lindsey asked to Graham's back as he turned the latch.

''Don't worry. His humor's a little off-color, but you'll like him. Everybody does. And he's one of our best cops,'' Graham assured her, swinging the door open.

''Come in, Rooster, and pretend you have some manners. I told you this is a lady, not the kind of woman you're used to.''

Manners or not, he was big enough to be a formidable bodyguard, Lindsey decided, as he stooped to duck under the door facing. His face and hair were bright red, and a mouthful of bright white teeth showed when he smiled.

Graham stepped backward and caught her hand.

''This is Jeff Rooster, Lins. Ugly as sin, but he's halfway decent. Only man on the force who can match me on the accuracy test. And he makes a great cup of cappuccino.''

Rooster beamed at Graham's introduction and took her hand. ''Ah, Miss Lindsey. My old buddy told me you were a special lady, but he forgot to mention you were a knockout. It is indeed a pleasure to meet you.''

''And you.'' She shook his hand and then pulled her own away. ''But I don't need a baby-sitter.''

''Good, then I'll get right to the cappuccino and we can catch the Rockets game. Unless, of course, you want to neck or something.'' His easy smile and laughing eyes were contagious.

Lindsey managed to ignore them. ''Graham, I am perfectly capable of taking care of myself.''

''I know. Like you have been for the last three days.'' He grabbed a beat-up leather bomber jacket from the pile of clothes and newspapers at the foot of the couch. ''And, Rooster,'' he instructed, oblivious of her protests, ''if she tries to sneak out of here without you…shoot her!''

GRAHAM RUBBED the stubble on his chin and shuffled through the papers on his desk, moving the burglary report to the top of the stack.

A string of curses slipped from his lips, and he banged his fist on the desk, sending a pencil into orbit. A routine break-in—that was how it had been reported.

Routine enough to guide the murderer to Lindsey. Fortunately, somebody on the force had had enough insight to realize the impact it might have on the LeBlanc case. They had highlighted it and stuck it on his desk.

The burglary had apparently occurred during the afternoon, while the owner of the house was out. They hadn't taken much. Some cash, a TV, a CD player. But the house had been generally ransacked, including the file cabinet that held the records for the Krewe of Minerva.

Most of the krewes kept secret membership records, files on who rode on which float, past costumes. It was traditional. Of course, in most cases there were few real secrets. In fact, the owner hadn't been upset at all about the records when Graham questioned her. It was the ransacked house that had made her furious.

Graham raised his feet to the top of the desk and pushed back in his swivel chair. Reaching for the phone, he dialed his number and waited as it rang. He was paranoid, he knew. He'd called the house a half-dozen times since he'd left.

"Hello." The answering voice was male and gruff.

"How's it going?"

"God, Graham, it's one o'clock in the morning. How do you think it's going? Lindsey's trying to get some sleep."

"Everything's fine, then."

"Of course it's fine. What's going to happen, with me on the job?"

"Nothing, you're the best. Is Lindsey still asleep?"

"Yep. As peaceful as a new puppy with a full belly. Any word yet on the various fingerprint samples?"

"Nothing definite. That's why I'm still hanging around. Like we thought, the lock on the LeBlanc safe was picked by an expert. I'm going back out to the LeBlancs' in the morning, and over to talk to Garon about that photograph."

"What about the costume-rental spots? Any leads there?"

"No. We got started too late on that. Those places close early. But there'll be a team on it first thing in the morning. They'll hit them all—Uptown first, then Metairie and the Westbank."

"So, why don't you call it a night? Sooner or later you've got to sleep."

"Yeah. I'll be home soon."

"Good. In the meantime, don't worry about us, pal. Nothing's going to happen to your woman with me on duty."

"Right. Later. And thanks."

*My woman.* Graham mouthed the words into the empty room as he dropped the phone back into position. He had thought she was his woman once. He had been wrong.

So why was he still so drawn to her? Why was being with her blowing away his resistance as if it were a cardboard house in a hurricane? He'd been fighting the return of that damnable attraction ever since Saturday morning, when he first walked into her hospital room.

Well, he wasn't doing a very good job of fighting anymore, and neither was she. That had been evident tonight, when she melted in his arms, when she returned his kiss, pressing her body against his, as hot and as willing as she had been that one night ten years ago.

He slammed his feet back to the floor. Damn. He was losing it, going against the very edict he insisted his men live by. Don't get mixed up with anyone on your case. If you're already involved, let someone else take over for you. Emotion causes mistakes in judgment. It puts people in danger.

It gets people killed.

He pulled his coat on and headed for the door. This edict would have to be broken. He wasn't pulling himself off the case. Not when Lindsey was in danger. He'd give his life protecting her. Why not? He'd given his heart for her years ago.

The outer office was bustling with the night noises of city crime when he headed for the front door.

"Hey, Dufour. I figured you'd gone home to get some sleep hours ago. I was about to call you with the fingerprint report."

"What'd you get?"

"Nothing at the site of the break-in. Must have used gloves. We searched everything, sure they'd have made a slip, but so far nothing. Nothing around the safe, either, except Mrs. LeBlanc's prints, of course."

"What about the suitcase?"

"Prints everywhere. Couldn't have left more clues if they'd been trying."

"Have you identified them?"

"The Oleander boy. Garon. The one that was busted a couple of years ago. Got off when LeBlanc intervened for him."

"Yeah, go on."

"His prints were all over everything. The car trunk, the suitcase, and on one of the souvenir paperweights in the bottom of the suitcase. Looks like you may have your man."

"Don't bet on it."

"No, I won't. I've learned not to take anything for granted in this job."

Graham grabbed the pen and notebook from his pocket and scribbled a few notes to himself. "Thanks, and keep a lid on this, will you?" he called as he threw a handful of notes into a manila folder. "I don't want a word leaking out to the press."

"I never talk. You know that. So where do you go from here? Is there enough evidence to haul Oleander in?"

"Not for what I need. But there's enough for police questioning, and for a search warrant to check out his house. And I'm putting a tail on him tonight. I want to know every move he makes."

"It'd be a nice feather in your cap to wrap this one up quickly. Jewelry heist and murder in a St. Charles Avenue mansion. At the house of Richard LeBlanc, no less."

"Yeah, well, the fat lady hasn't sung yet. There's nothing to tie the dress to the jewels. And I can't solve a murder case that doesn't exist. There's still no corpse and no missing-persons report."

"Sorry, old boy. But I did what I could. I'm calling it

a night. The old lady may start looking for a replacement if I don't get home to warm her bed soon.''

''Judy's too good for you, anyway.''

''Yeah. Go home yourself, Graham. Get some sleep. There'll be plenty of crime for you to fight in the morning.''

''I'll do that.'' He turned to go, a million ideas somersaulting through his mind. ''And thanks again for the hard work. One lead is a hundred percent improvement over nothing.''

A half hour later, Graham pushed out into the night, with one thought hammering away in his mind. Somewhere in the city, a vicious killer was looking for his next victim, and somehow he had to find him before he succeeded. Lindsey's life depended on it.

IT WAS DAMP, and bitterly cold. Lindsey pulled her sweater tighter and hastened her steps. She should never have come out alone. But the faceless man was here somewhere, in the crowd that was watching the parade. There were hands flying in front of her eyes, shimmering beads pounding her in the face and on her head, but she pushed forward through the crowd.

She had to find him. She swung around. He was here. She felt him. But he was leaving the parade.

She followed him into the narrow alley. He turned, and she quickly crouched behind a green Dumpster. The odors were pungent and nauseating. She eased backward, her body pressing against a cold brick wall.

No! No! The scream caught in her throat as two large hands came over her mouth and nose, squeezing the life from her lungs. She fought, pushing, clawing, scratching, until she could look into the eyes of the killer.

Oh, God, no! Not again! There was no face, nothing

but terrifying darkness. Her body grew limp, and finally the scream came, filling the night with her terror.

"Lins, Lins... Wake up!"

The man's hands wrapped around her shoulders, but he was losing his strength. His hands were gentle now. She struggled to open her eyes.

"Wake up, baby. You're having a nightmare."

The eyes above her swam in a sea of darkness, then coalesced into a face. Graham's face. Lindsey's body trembled, but her mind began its grateful reentry into reality.

He dropped to the bed beside her and rolled her into his arms. He wiped loose strands of hair from her forehead and rocked her gently to him. "Are you all right?"

"I think so. It was just a dream, like the others. But they're so real." She pulled the blanket around her, but it couldn't stop the chills that shook her body.

"Do you want the light on?"

"No, not if you'll stay with me, for just a little while."

"I'll be here as long as you need me. Do you want to talk about it?"

The dream didn't vanish from her mind. Even if it had, she could have explained it in detail. It had come in one form or another every night since the fateful Minerva parade. She stumbled for words to bring her fears into focus.

"It's so real. The soldier...with the dagger. He's there when I dream, but he isn't. There's no face."

The icy tremors increased, and she cuddled against the warmth of Graham's body.

"I know, baby. The last few days have been a living nightmare, but I won't let anything happen to you."

"But it's not just fear. I can't explain it. I don't understand it myself. It's like I owe it to the murdered woman to find her killer.''

"Don't be ridiculous, Lins. That's what the police are for. You owed us a report of what you saw. You gave us that. Your responsibility is over.''

"No, it's more than that. It's something I have to do. It's like she's calling to me. Like her spirit will never let me rest until I identify the killer.''

"You have to let it go, baby. You've done all you can do.'' He placed his finger on her lips to silence her. "You have to get some rest.''

She couldn't let it go. The dream had been too real. Her emotions were too strong, too choked. "I'm sorry, Graham. I can't change the way I feel. Not about this.''

His fingers raked through her hair, twirling around a curl and pulling her toward him. "I wouldn't change a thing about you, Lins. I'd never tamper with perfection.''

His voice broke on the words, and she stared into his eyes. Love showed in their dark depths, so tangible she could almost reach out and touch it. The tenseness, the undertow of fear, slowly ebbed from her body. She cuddled against Graham, clinging to his strength.

He held her against him, rocking her in his arms like a baby. His lips touched her hair and brushed across the lobe of her ear. The feathery tingle of his breath spread across her skin, melting the chill of the night she had come to know so intimately.

Lindsey tilted her head, her lips craving the gentleness of Graham's kiss. He let his mouth roam tenderly across her cheeks, to the tip of her nose, finally finding the passion of her waiting mouth.

His hand traced a path down her neck, sweeping across the flesh at the base of her neck and plunging to the curve of her breast above her nightgown.

His touch was heating her body, confusing her thoughts, clouding her memories. Her body arched toward him as his fingers played along the lace, dipping to sear the flesh of her breasts.

"You're so beautiful, Lins. You took my breath away the first time I saw you. You still do." His voice was husky with desire.

The past, the present, the future. The boundary lines were blurred now, mingling in the moment. Lindsey felt the hardness of Graham's chest beneath her fingers, the heat of his breath as his lips left her mouth to push away the thin silk of her nightie. She buried her mouth in the salty sweetness of his flesh, her teeth skimming the wiry hairs, the peaks of his nipples.

"Oh, Lins, Lins…" He slipped his hand under her chin and tilted it upward, once more seeking her lips with his. And then there was no room for reasoning, no reason for doubts. She parted her lips, eager to lose herself in his kiss.

The years fell away, and she was young and reckless again. And with the man she loved. His lips roved from hers, across her chin, down her neck, slow and deliberate. But she didn't want finesse, not now. Her emotions were raw and on edge from dealing with life and death, from too many things she couldn't understand.

She was on fire, a raging blaze, and she craved release. Her hands and fingers kneaded the flesh of his back and down his buttocks, pulling him so close his passion burned between her thighs.

"Take me now, Graham. I want to feel all of you, inside me, deep inside me."

"I can't, Lindsey. Not like this." His body cursed his honor. He wanted her, all right. More than he'd ever wanted anyone in his life. "I won't take advantage of your fears. When we make love, I don't want any regrets.''

Her arms wrapped around him, strong and sure.

''There won't be any regrets, Graham. Not about that. There never have been.''

His hands shook as he pulled her to him, the bittersweet ache inside him driving with devastating force. He'd dreamed of this moment so often, woken up sweating and hot as a fever with the need for her.

He lifted her to the top of him, pushing her up so that he could see the smooth outline of her firm breasts, the gentle curves of her hips that narrowed into the mysterious dark triangle. He looked into her eyes, shiny and moist, mirroring the need that was eating him alive.

He held his breath. He couldn't rush. After waiting ten years, he had to cherish every touch.

But his body wouldn't cooperate. Her movements, her hands on his body, her desire… Desire for him. Graham Dufour, poor detective, who'd loved her too fiercely to ever really let her go.

A soft moan escaped his lips, and he eased her shapely body into place, sliding her down until he plunged deep inside her. Only then did he close his eyes, the passion pushing him out of control as the rhythm of her body swept him away, until there was nothing but her tiny moans, soft, bubbling with joy, merging with his.

She cuddled against him, passion spent, her body moist from their lovemaking. His own body ached from the desire that had left it riddled and worn. Only once before had it been like this. Ten years ago. The one night he'd made love to Lindsey Latham.

The next day, she had walked out of his life.

THE TALL MAN scrunched behind the steering wheel and stared into the dark night. Perspiration poured like rain *down his face. It was the headaches, or maybe the liquor. They were both a part of his life now.*

*He rubbed his fingers across the scratch on his arm. He wasn't sure how he'd gotten it. Probably during his attempts to get rid of Roxy's body. Beautiful Roxy. Sexy, teasing…*

*He wiped the sleeve of his shirt across his brow. How had things gotten so far out of control? A simple robbery, taking from people who had far more than their share. That was all this was supposed to be.*

*Damn Roxy for double-crossing him. This was all her fault. He hadn't meant to hurt anyone. He certainly hadn't expected to have to kill her. He pulled the flask from his jacket pocket and lifted it to his lips, gulping down the last few drops.*

*Now things were out of his hands.*

*He listened to the front door slam in the distance. He couldn't see much in the predawn darkness, but he didn't have to. Like it or not, he knew what he had to do. Someone else was about to die.*

# Chapter Nine

The loud jangling of the telephone was a cruel alarm clock. Lindsey jerked to full wakefulness while Graham stretched sleepily beside her. Reaching across him, she managed to catch it before it completed the second ring. She had the receiver to her mouth before she reconsidered. No need for anyone to know she was here.

She shook Graham awake and pressed the phone into his hand. Groaning and muttering, he stuck it to his ear. "Dufour here. What's up?" he asked, his voice groggy with sleep.

Lindsey pulled her feet from under the covers and threw her legs over the side of the bed. She was awake— might as well start the coffee. Halfway to the kitchen, she stopped in her tracks. The strain in Graham's voice warned her that something was dreadfully wrong.

"How did it happen?"

Padding back across the thin carpet, she stopped in the door and listened to his side of the conversation.

"Is she going to live?"

The concern etched in every line of his face told her the answer was not what he wanted to hear. She waited, afraid to hear more, knowing she had to. At last, Graham placed the receiver back in its cradle. Determinedly she formed the question she dreaded to have answered.

"What's happened, Graham?"

His lips remained silent, but his eyes telegraphed part of the answer.

"It's the soldier, isn't it? He's killed someone else."

He held out his arms, and she slipped inside them.

"It's your friend Danielle. She was hit by a car."

Despair clutched at Lindsey's heart, wringing away her fragile hold on control. Would this madness never end? "She'll be all right, won't she?"

There was no reason to wait for an answer. It was written in the strain that pulled at Graham's face. It was painted in the black depths of his eyes.

"I'm sorry, Lins." His hands tightened around her. "She's dead. She died instantly."

The strength evaporated from Lindsey's body, and she collapsed on the bed, a quaking inside her all but robbing her of the ability to speak. "How did it happen?" she whispered.

"It was a hit-and-run."

"I don't understand. It's barely sunup now. It's a mistake, Graham. It has to be." Too much had happened in the past few days. Her mind refused to accept another shock.

"There's no mistake, Lins. She was walking her dog." Graham dropped to the bed beside her. His hand curled around hers.

"Apparently she's an early riser." Graham's voice was low and troubled. "Her neighbors told the police she walks Fluff every morning at 5:00 a.m., rain or shine."

"And the person who hit her didn't even stop." She tried to choke back tears, but they pushed from her eyes. "The rotten, no-good... He must have been drunk."

"I don't know. It doesn't sound like an accident. One of the neighbors saw it from his window. He said the car rounded the corner at high speed and then jumped the curb, coming up on the sidewalk and onto the lawn to hit her."

Lindsey buried her head in her hands. It wouldn't stop. The pain, the murderous surprises, just kept coming. "Where was her husband?" she demanded, a sudden bitterness clutching and clawing at her insides.

"In bed. Sound asleep. The neighbor who saw the hit-and-run woke him."

"Then he paid someone to do it. He did. I know he did. He was a rat. Everyone but Danielle knew it." Ragged sobs shook her body.

Graham held her to him. She knew he meant to comfort her, but the tense strain in his muscles only made her more afraid. "Did the neighbor get the license number?"

"No. Not according to the police report. He told them there wasn't enough light to see clearly. Even his description of the car is sketchy. Dark, compact, low to the ground. That's it. It could fit half the cars in the New Orleans area."

"But it has to be her husband's doing. He's the only one with a possible motive."

"We'll check him out, but…"

"Go ahead, Graham. I want to know everything," she urged, bracing herself for the worst.

"There was a break-in yesterday, Lins. I didn't tell you, because I didn't want to frighten you."

"What are you saying? I talked to Grace Ann last night. I wanted to be sure she didn't need her car back. She would have mentioned it if Danielle's house had been burglarized."

"Not her house. The one where the Minerva records were kept. Someone took the files that told who was on float seven the night of the parade."

Graham watched the color drain from Lindsey's face as he filled her in on the details. Anger—or was it desperation—knotted in his stomach and burned in his chest. Seeing her suffer this kind of anguish was far worse than experiencing his own. Last night, for a few hours, they'd been in heaven. Now they were racing into hell.

"I hate to leave you like this, Lins, but I've got to get down to headquarters. Rooster's on his way over. I won't leave until he's here. He'll be assigned to you full-time until this mystery soldier is caught."

"And my other friends, the ones who were on the float with me? The ones I've put in danger?"

"You haven't put anyone in danger. You're not the killer. But they'll be protected, just like you will."

She pulled away and reluctantly Graham let her go. As much as he would have liked to stay by her side, he couldn't. If anyone else was hurt or, worse, killed, as a result of his failure to catch the murderer, their blood would be on his hands. It was the unspoken law of the force. If it's your case, it's your responsibility.

And he *would* find the killer. But now he had another enemy. Time, and it was running out. Silent curses rushed through his brain.

"I want Rooster with you every second, Lins. Don't even go out for the paper unless he's with you. *Every second.* Do you understand?"

"Every second," she agreed. "Get your shower, Graham. I'll make some coffee."

He watched as she turned and walked away. Tears moistened her eyes, but her strength was visible in her squared shoulders, the determined tilt of her chin. Graham was certain he had never loved her more.

LINDSEY SETTLED BACK in Rooster's car. The memorial service for Danielle had left her emotionally spent. She hadn't know her as well as she'd known the other Daredevils, but she'd liked her. Danielle had been the quiet, studious one, the one more interested in books than in parties. That was why it hadn't surprised anyone when she spent her last two years of high school studying in Europe.

Blinking back tears, Lindsey stared out the window as they drove. Endless rows of ladders lined St. Charles Avenue like wooden soldiers, each topped with a small seat and safety bar that would hold a child or two in comfort and safety, far above the excited crowd that would gather below them at tonight's parade.

*Comfort and safety.* Words that had suddenly lost all meaning for Lindsey. She lived in fear now, for herself and for her friends. The only thing that made it any easier was Graham. His strength was the one unwavering factor she had to hold on to.

Relationships. Were they never what they seemed? Ten years ago, she had been so much in love with Graham Dufour, she had thought their relationship could withstand anything. Then she had decided to go to college in Nashville, against his wishes, and he had tossed away everything she thought was permanent.

She'd called and she'd written, numerous times, sure he'd understand her need to have some time alone to find herself, sure he'd forgive and forget once he calmed down and realized it wasn't her love for *him* that was in question.

Big mistake. He'd never even bothered to say goodbye. He'd walked straight into the arms of another girl, leaving her to hear about his new love and marriage from her friends.

Now the trauma was starting all over again. Seeing him had brought it all back. But it was more than that. It wasn't only memories from the past that were pulling them together. There was a new bond now, different, but just as overpowering.

He was strong, and hard as nails when he had to be. But he was also warm and loving, passionate and exciting.

She couldn't keep herself from falling in love with Graham all over again. She probably already had, if the other night was any indication. But she had to keep things in perspective.

Graham had been just as loving and as passionate ten years ago, and yet he had walked away without a backward glance. There was no reason to think he wouldn't do it again when this was over.

New tears filled her eyes, and she squeezed them shut. The nightmare *would* be over soon. It had to be. She wouldn't stand by and let her friends die in her place. If the police couldn't stop it, she would. Even if it meant her own life. After all, she was the one the killer wanted.

"Looks like everyone's gearing up for the big day. Fat Tuesday's only a week away."

Rooster's words cut into her thoughts. It was the first time he'd spoken since they'd left the service. Graham was right. He was a good man.

"What do you do for Mardi Gras, Rooster?"

"Work. I complain like the rest of the guys about the long hours, but the truth is, I love it. Always have, since I was a kid sitting right on top of one of those ladders.

I'm a native New Orleanian, you know. Carnival gets in your blood.''

He pointed out the window. ''Must be in Mrs. Le-Blanc's blood, for sure. Looks like she's getting ready for her big ball, in spite of Graham's warning.''

Lindsey studied the action in the LeBlancs' yard and driveway. She'd been so lost in her own thoughts, she hadn't even realized they'd driven this far.

''They must throw some kind of party,'' he continued. ''Looks like they're hanging lights from the tops of every tree. And there's three delivery vans in the drive.'' He slowed down to get a better look.

''I'd like to be a fly on the wall at that party. Imagine what you could find out,'' Lindsey added, possibilities swirling through her mind.

She leaned back and concentrated on intriguing prospects while Rooster maneuvered through traffic, turning off on a narrow side street that cut short the drive to Graham's apartment. The houses were smaller here, interspersed with family businesses. She looked, but barely saw the procession of neatly trimmed lawns, sprawling houses, a dress shop, an antique shop, a costume shop.

Costumes. That was it. Her mind flew into overdrive. ''Wait, Rooster! Stop here.''

''No way. The boss will have my hide. When he left us at the church, he said straight back to the apartment.'' He slammed on his brakes as the light in front of them switched from yellow to red.

Lindsey loosened her seat belt. ''You can go in with me. I just want to run into Dumas' Costumes and Dance. See, it's right there. I'll only be a minute.''

''The answer is no.'' He stared straight ahead, refusing to look into her pleading eyes.

Impulsively she popped the handle down and jumped

from the car, breaking into a run as her feet hit the pavement. She didn't look back. She didn't have to. She knew Rooster would park the car and be right behind her.

Head down, she ducked inside the shop and into a noisy crowd of people.

"You better take a number, honey. They're not waiting on anyone today unless you have a number."

Lindsey nodded toward the pudgy redhead who was giving out advice and pulled a number from the dispenser.

"Might not even get waited on with a number," the man beside her volunteered. "We've been in here thirty minutes, and the line's barely moved."

"I guess everyone wants to dress for Mardi Gras," Lindsey offered, moving over to pick up a brochure from the table. That would give her something to stick her nose into while she got her thoughts and a plan of action together.

A green velvet dress for a Southern belle, and a Civil War soldier's uniform. They had to have been rented from somewhere, and this place was right around the corner from the LeBlancs'. Everything she and Graham needed to identify the killer and the victim might be right here in the records. She was surprised Graham hadn't already thought of that possibility, but he hadn't said a word about it.

Sticking her head above the brochure, she glanced toward the door. Just as she'd expected, Rooster had joined her. He was leaning against the wall and glaring in her direction. It was the same look Graham had given her repeatedly during the past few days. A cop technique, she decided, to intimidate the witness. She turned back and started talking to the redhead in front of her.

Forty minutes dragged by before she got her turn at the counter.

"Sorry to keep you waiting, but it's been like this for a week. It'll be worse before it's over, though. By Saturday, there won't be a thing left." The clerk barely slowed for breath. "Are you looking for something for the big day itself, or something formal for a party?"

"Actually, I'm here for information. Could I talk with the manager? It'll only take a minute."

"I'm the manager. What kind of information are you looking for?" The easy smile disappeared from her face.

"Could you tell me if you rented a green velvet Southern belle dress last week?"

"No. Now, if that's all you want, I'll have to ask you to move over, so we can wait on the customers."

"No, you didn't rent one, or no, you can't tell me?"

"Are you a policewoman?"

"I'm Off—" The lie almost slid from her lips. "No, I'm just looking for a friend of mine. I thought I might get her address from you. I know she rented a gown here last week."

"Sorry, honey. If you're not a cop, I can't tell you anything. We don't reveal that kind of info on our customers unless you have a badge." Her voice softened a little. "You might try asking the NOPD, though. We've told them everything we know."

Lindsey stepped aside. She should have known Graham would have already thought of this. Once again she had stuck her nose in where it wasn't needed. Now Graham and Rooster would both be furious with her for not cooperating.

She glanced back at her innocent-looking bodyguard. He was still standing by the door, staring at the couple who had just walked in. Oh, no. Just what she needed.

Katie LeBlanc and her nephew. And Katie was looking right at her.

"Officer Green, what a surprise! I wondered if I'd get to see you again." Katie swept past the waiting peons and hurried to Lindsey's side. The heavy scent of her perfume permeated the small building.

"I asked that nice Detective Dufour about you," she crooned, "but he said you were off the case. I wanted to invite you to the party, too. He's coming, of course, but we always need an extra pretty girl, don't we, Thomas?"

"Absolutely. You must join us, Miss Green."

Thomas emphasized the *Miss*. And he was doing it again, staring at her with his see-right-through-your-clothes look.

She shifted uncomfortably. She didn't want to go back inside the LeBlanc house, didn't want to think about what had happened there, or who might be responsible. But Danielle had been killed, and the rest of her friends were in danger. The clues to identifying the killer were buried somewhere in Lindsey's mind. Somehow she had to re-cover them.

Her mouth was suddenly dry as cotton, but she forced a lightness to her tone. "I'd love to come."

"Good. I'm here to pick up my costume now," Katie announced, excitement adding a youthful bounce to her manner. "I can't tell you what it is. It's always a surprise until midnight, when we unmask."

"And what about you, Miss Green? What will you come as?" Thomas asked, a mocking smile curling his lips.

"You'll have to wait until midnight to find out."

"No, I'll know you. You have a charm that no mere costume can hide."

"We'll see, Mr. LeBlanc. We'll see."

She turned and took a new number. This time she'd be a legitimate customer.

GRAHAM PACED the floor of his cluttered cubicle of an office, stopping to viciously kick a straight chair out of his path. Dead ends. Every time he thought he had a lead, it led to nothing but another lousy dead end.

A murder without a corpse. A photo of the victim that had disappeared before he could get his hands on it. A drop of blood taken from a washed-out stain in a piece of carpet that didn't match anybody's. One suspect with an airtight alibi, another who didn't match the eyewitness's description.

And seven more females whose lives were in danger because one of them had witnessed the crime. The killer would strike again. It was only a matter of time. Years of experience made Graham as sure of that as he was about death and taxes.

But he wasn't sure what was going on at the LeBlanc house. Katie had reported some strange happenings during the past few days. Nothing she could prove, but she suspected her things were being rifled when she was out of the house. She was adamant it couldn't be Ruby. Graham was inclined to agree with her, though he wasn't sure why. Katie was also adamant it couldn't be Thomas.

There their agreement ended.

Of course, it could be anybody. Katie LeBlanc had ignored police warnings and insisted on having her stupid society ball. The house was already crawling with strangers—florists, caterers, even electricians. The ways the rich could waste money would always be beyond him.

It didn't matter. The bottom line was, he had a killer on the loose who obviously planned to do whatever it took to destroy his only witness. And that witness was the woman Graham loved.

He raked his fingers through his hair, pushing it back from his forehead. Frustration was driving him nuts. For ten years he'd dreamed of what it would be like to hold Lindsey in his arms, to have her back in his life.

Now she was back, stubborn as ever, and just as irresistible. But he was having to resist her, even though she was right there in his bed while he slept on the living room sofa.

It was the only way. He'd given in to his own needs one night, and he'd live with that memory forever. But he damn well wouldn't do it again. Not until this hell of a case was solved and he knew she was safe.

He knew what emotion could do to a detective. It threw you off guard, took away your professional edge. It let you make costly mistakes.

He wouldn't let it interfere here. There'd be plenty of time when this was over to tell Lindsey how he felt. For now, he wasn't about to take advantage of the woman he was sworn to protect, and he wouldn't risk her life or the lives of the other women by losing sight of his first responsibility.

He grabbed his coat and headed out the door. In the meantime, cold showers weren't all that bad, once you got used to them.

LINDSEY STARED into the half mirror, the best that Graham had to offer in his compact apartment. Her long hair was pulled high atop her head, and loose tendrils framed her brown eyes and high cheekbones. Dark shadows gave her eyes a haunted look, but they wouldn't show beneath the mask she'd purchased for tonight's party at the LeBlancs'.

Graham walked up behind her and circled her waist. The loose coat of his river gambler costume swung handsomely about his hips.

"You look quite dashing," she acknowledged, sure it was the understatement of the year.

"And you look even more beautiful than usual," he whispered in her ear, his breath tingly and warm on her skin. "Scarlett O'Hara herself would be green with envy if she could see you tonight."

Graham had been angry over her insistence that she attend the ball. But something more dangerous than mere anger crackled in the air around them. Something mysterious and magnetic, an undefined element as thick as the fog that hovered over the Mississippi on wintry mornings.

Tonight, a silent truce had been called. The calm before the hurricane came swirling out of the Gulf, Lindsey decided. It couldn't last. No matter how she tried to follow Graham's orders, she never quite succeeded. Her stake in this case was far too high.

"I wish you'd change your mind about tonight, Lins."

Light from his eyes reflected in the mirror. They were dark as midnight, and just as deceiving. The other night, she had been sure they reflected love. Tonight, she saw nothing there but an ominous warning.

"But you do understand why I have to go to the ball."

"I understand that you're putting your life in danger. I've done everything possible to keep your identity a secret, yet you've done everything short of having it printed in the *Times Picayune* to reveal it. I know you're not afraid, but—"

"You're wrong, Graham. I am afraid." Her words struggled past the lump in her throat. "But not only for myself. Who knows which of my friends will be next?"

He twirled her around to face him, his hands gliding across the shimmering red fabric of her ball dress. "I told you, Lins, I have someone watching everyone who was on the float that night. I don't know how long the chief will let me keep up the twenty-four-hour guard, but for now, it's in place."

"What do you mean, you don't know how long? Why would he deprive them of protection when there's a killer on the loose?"

"Money. Politics. The nature of the beast. The police department chases down criminals. They seldom use their resources for individual protection."

"You mean they would just let them be murdered to keep from spending a few dollars on protection?"

"Don't worry, Lins. They haven't pulled the protection yet. If they do, your friends are among the lucky few. They have plenty of money to hire their own bodyguards. Most citizens don't."

"Lucky? Lucky to have a stalker on your tail, a heartless thug with no qualms about taking your life? I don't think they would agree with you, Graham. And neither do I."

"You know that's not what I meant." He dropped his hands from her sides and wrapped them around hers. "Do you remember our rules for tonight?"

"Of course I remember. We've gone through them a dozen times this afternoon." At least a dozen, she mused. It was the only way he'd consent to her going. And she had willingly agreed to them all. She hadn't lied to him earlier. She was afraid, far more afraid than she wanted to admit.

"You have to do what I've asked, Lindsey. There is a good chance the killer will be there tonight."

"Why would he come back? He surely knows there

will be costumed police mingling among the guests. It seems to me he would stay far away.''

"Because everything points to this being an inside job. Only an insider would know about the hidden safe. And a close friend or relative's absence would draw suspicion.''

"But you keep insisting Garon is the chief suspect. He's the housekeeper's son. He'd have no reason to be at the party. Besides, you have someone watching him.''

"We *had* someone watching him. They were following him last night on the outside edge of the French Quarter, right off the river. They lost him in the traffic. When they couldn't find him, they alerted headquarters and went back to his apartment to wait. There's still no sign of him.''

"He's not the murderer, Graham. That's the only thing I'm sure of.''

Graham loosed his right hand from hers. Drawing it to her face, he tucked a loose curl into place. Delicately he drew a line down her cheek with his finger.

"That's all the more reason for you to be careful tonight. His fingerprints were on the suitcase and on the car trunk. He may not have killed the woman in the turret, but he's in on this somehow.''

"So you think he's the mastermind behind all this?''

"It's possible. That, or an accomplice who takes orders well. Either way, you don't want to be alone with him. Or anyone else.''

"No. I'll do like you said, Graham. I'll stay in the main ballroom, mingle with large crowds, try to keep you or one of the other officers in my sight. And maybe, just maybe, I'll see someone who will trigger my memory, the same way the broken shutter triggered it last Saturday.''

Graham left her side and crossed the room to the CD player. He flipped on a song by a local artist, slow and soulful. "Just one more request before we leave, Lins. May I have a dance with the belle of the ball?"

He switched off the overhead light as he crossed the room, leaving nothing but silvery beams of moonlight to play on the strong lines of his face. Lindsey slipped into his arms. It was a night for facing ghosts. Later, at the ball, they would be murderous and frightening. Right now, in Graham's arms, they were loving and devastatingly haunting.

She leaned into him and rested her cheek against his broad shoulder. The ache inside her swelled, gripping her heart and wringing it raw. Graham Dufour. The boy she'd loved ten years ago. The man she'd love forever.

The music ended too soon, and Graham led her to the door. "Are you ready for the ball?" he asked, reaching for her satin cape and pulling it about her shoulders. Something burning in the dark depths of his eyes sent tingles of apprehension skittering up her spine.

"As ready as I'll ever be. And I will be careful, Graham," she assured him. "I'll follow your rules precisely. I'll be perfectly safe."

"I hope so." He touched the tip of her nose with his finger and then planted the lightest of kisses on her lips. Flicking off the inside light, he pushed open the front door. "God, I hope..."

The rest of his words were lost in the wind and the darkness of the night.

## Chapter Ten

If flaunting riches were an athletic event, Katie LeBlanc would walk away with the Olympic gold medal for the night's performance. Lindsey had grown up in a world where money was king, but no private party she had ever attended compared with this.

The ballroom itself was lit by giant crystal chandeliers, circular balls of tiny lights that twinkled like starlight. Silver streamers and glittery balloons hung in clusters from the high ceilings, reflecting the iridescent magic that permeated the room.

A gurgling champagne fountain surrounded by silver platters of exotic cheeses and imported fruits dominated one corner of the room. Rex, the king of carnival, impressively carved from a huge block of ice, graced the opposite corner.

Lindsey fondled her half-empty glass of champagne as another waiter glided by. She didn't dare give up her glass. Katie obviously deemed it a mortal sin for a guest to walk around empty-handed.

She glanced at her watch. It was after eleven. Fortunately, the evening had passed in relative calm. Lindsey had floated through a world of elegantly costumed ladies, their necks, ears, arms and fingers adorned with enough diamonds and other costly jewels to pay off the national debt.

But with all that, they did not outshine the men. Velvet britches, lacy shirts, even powdered wigs, were everywhere. She glanced across the crowded room and quickly spotted Graham. He was in a circle of laughing men and women, playing the part of debonair society chap with a practiced air that surprised her.

No Mississippi River gambler had ever looked more handsome. Lindsey was not the only one to think so. A curvaceous Marie Antoinette was hanging on his arm and staring lustily into his eyes.

A stir across the way caught Lindsey's attention, and she stepped back to watch as Katie LeBlanc waltzed back into the room. There was no mistaking the hostess. She wore a silvery half mask over her eyes, but her pouty lips were painted their usual shade of deep red, and the low-cut dip of her fitted bodice revealed a lot more than a hint of her cleavage.

"Don't you love it?" Katie asked, stopping at Lindsey's elbow. "All these marvelous men from fantasyland."

"They're gorgeous, all right. It's a great party." Lindsey hoped she hadn't been recognized. A three-quarter feathered face mask revealed nothing but her mouth and chin. She'd even worked on changing her voice and walk for the evening. So far, she'd been amazingly successful.

"And the nicest part of all is the suspense," Katie crooned. "You have no idea whom you're dancing with, or whom you kiss in the moonlight. So who can blame you later for your sins?"

She twirled about without waiting for an answer. "Oooh, look at that one. The riverboat gambler. I don't know who he is, but I'd love to play a game of chance with him. Ta-ta now, whoever you are. And have fun while you can. The mystery ends at midnight."

Lindsey breathed a sigh of relief. Evidently her disguise had worked even with Katie. That made her feel a lot safer. That, and Graham's command to stay in the main ballroom. Even though the party itself spread through the house and into several tents set up on the manicured grounds, there were far too many people in here for anything to happen to her.

She backed against the wall, studying the figures of the males in the room. She recognized a few as acquaintances of her father, but, fortunately, she hadn't run into any real friends. It would have been much harder to hide her identity from people who had known her well when she lived in New Orleans and traveled regularly in these circles.

"Ah do declare, ma'am, you're looking luscious and tempting tonight."

Startled, she jumped impulsively as a strong hand clutched her elbow.

"I'm sorry. I didn't mean to frighten you. But you're much too pretty to be all alone."

"No, I'm not alone. I'm waiting for someone," she lied. Something about the man's voice made her nervous. She scrutinized his appearance as best she could. His face was fully masked, but he wore the dress outfit of a Rebel soldier, one that fit his muscular body all too well. A shock of dark hair peeked from beneath his hat, which was cocked at a jaunty angle.

Her breath constricted.

"You look alone. So why not honor a poor veteran with a dance? I swear, I served right alongside General Jackson in the Battle of the Bulge."

She took a step sideways, finding a better position for

studying his profile. He was tall, muscular, and dark-haired. But that was as far as it went. The magical recognition she'd hoped he might trigger didn't come.

"The Battle of the Bulge was fought in Bastogne in 1944," she answered, hiding her face behind her fan like a true Southern belle.

"And it is still being fought in America today." A smile played on his taunting lips. "But not by you. You are absolutely gorgeous." He wrapped an arm around her as the band broke into a spirited number. "Now about that dance?"

Lindsey acquiesced. It was less conspicuous than refusing. She followed the stranger's lead and jumped right into an offbeat Mardi Gras tune that had even the oldest partygoers moving their feet.

He twirled her, spinning her wickedly and then catching her in his arms as she struggled for equilibrium. Katie was right. Men of mystery were titillating. Unfortunately, they were also dangerous.

If Graham was right, someone in this room was capable of snuffing out a life for no reason except his own monetary gain. Maybe worse. For all she knew, he was a madman who actually got his kicks destroying innocent victims, like the beautiful blonde and poor Danielle.

The dance ended, and Lindsey escaped her secret admirer. Her thoughts had turned sour, and even the music couldn't lighten her mood. She needed air. Quickly she searched the room for Graham. He could walk with her to the wide porch.

Head down, she managed to slip through the crowds, avoiding eye contact that might lead to unwanted conversations. It was almost like the Minerva parade again. Multitudes of faces and pushing crowds. Air filled with a too-sweet mixture of perfumes and soaps, after-shaves and the musk of excited bodies.

She pushed forward as the walls of the ballroom began to close in around her. Finally, she reached the double glass doors that led to the side veranda. Bracing her body against the door facing, she gulped the cold air. It helped. The queasiness in her stomach began to settle, and her hands lost their clamminess.

She reached into the pocket of her gown and slipped her fingers around the tiny whistle Graham had given her. She was to use it in case of immediate danger. One blow on the whistle, and Graham would be able to find her from any place on the premises.

She breathed easier. She wouldn't need the whistle. Not tonight. She was merely a party guest who had gotten overheated. Squaring her shoulders and tossing her head determinedly, she rejoined the party.

It was almost midnight now, and the masquerade would soon be over. When the masks came off, she would have her chance. Graham had told her to scan the crowd early, pick out the men with body types similar to the killer's, men who appeared to be in the right age range.

She'd done that. And the amorous Rebel soldier was tops on her list. Now all she had to do was wait until the masks came off. Right after twelve, Graham would meet her here by the champagne fountain. He'd escort her through the rest of the party area. They would move quickly, not stopping to talk unless she squeezed his hand, the signal that she suspected someone or needed more time to study his unmasked profile.

Perspiration clung to her hands. Midnight, the witching hour, was only minutes away now. She had to be successful. Her very life might depend on it. Hers and all her friends'.

"Miss."

"No, thank you. I've had more than enough champagne." She smiled and waved the waiter away.

"No, I'm supposed to give you this. The man said it was urgent."

Lindsey took the folded slip of paper he pressed in her hand. The note was scribbled in red.

> There's been a change in plans. Meet me in the turret at once. Use the outside entry and hurry.
>
> > Graham

"Was the man—" She looked up. She was talking into empty space. The waiter had disappeared in the milling crowds.

But the note had to be authentic. No one else had given even the slightest hint they had recognized her. Her fingers tightened about the paper, and her pulse began to race crazily. Something important had to have happened for Graham to change the plans like this.

Lifting her skirts, she hurried through the knot of people at her left. The band ended a song and broke into the "Mardi Gras Mambo." People were streaming through the doors, hurrying to the ballroom from every corner of the house.

Evidently the midnight unveiling would be carried off with Katie's usual flair for the magnificent. She was heading toward Lindsey now, a lavishly decorated umbrella twirling madly in her hands while a line of people danced behind her.

The famed New Orleans second line. Dancing behind the leader, white napkins and handkerchiefs waving from uplifted hands, the masked partiers followed Katie as if she were a New Age Pied Piper.

Graham's timing couldn't have been worse. It was all but impossible to buck the traffic. Finally, her breath coming in quick, jagged gasps, Lindsey pushed through the front door.

Thousands of tiny lights flickered from the treetops like fireflies as she dashed around the corner. It was darker here, but still light enough to find and race up the stairs that led to the second-floor balcony.

Once on the balcony, she wasted no time in rounding the corner to the back of the house. The turret was directly above her now, and its light spilled through the curved windows, illuminating the last leg of her climb. She had to go slower here. The steps were narrow strips of iron that caught and held the heels of her shoes.

Finally she reached the entrance to the turret. She hesitated, for just a second, her heart pounding against her chest. But Graham had sent for her. There was no reason to be afraid. She took a deep breath and knocked softly on the wooden door.

There was no response.

Putting her ear to the closed door, she listened for a voice, a sound of any kind. All was quiet. She stepped back uneasily and squeezed her finger around the whistle. Had she been too trusting? Could the note have been a cruel hoax, not from Graham at all?

There was no way to be certain, but she couldn't turn back now. For all she knew, Graham was inside, hurt or…worse.

She wrapped her fingers around the whistle and pushed the door, bracing herself for the worst. But everything looked exactly as she'd seen it days ago. She stepped inside. Music from the ballroom drifted up into the brightly lit room.

"Graham."

A gust of wind caught the door and slammed it shut. Lindsey moved restlessly through the room, her apprehension multiplying with each passing second. She sniffed, puzzled by the strange fetid odor that wafted on the still air.

"Graham." She called his name again, softly at first, then louder. There was no reply. Obviously he wasn't here, and she wasn't waiting around.

She backed toward the door, but a trail of sparkling glitter caught her eye. It was the same glitter that dotted her hair and her dress. It had fallen from the balloon bouquets in the ballroom, bathing the guests in shimmering hues of purple, green and gold.

Her eyes followed the glimmering path right up to the door that led to the attic nook, the one she had foolishly crawled through on her first trip to the turret.

Cautiously she stepped along the sparkling trail. Someone had left the party and come to this room. They had either crawled through the dark passage to get here or had left that way. It had to be Graham. But what could he have found out that was important enough to change their plans at the last minute?

Once more she reached for the whistle, but her fingers were trembling so that she could barely clasp it in her hand. Fighting for control, she clutched it gingerly and slid it between her lips, ready to sound the alarm if it was needed. She took one last jagged breath, turned the knob, and pulled the door open.

Oh, God, no! Not this. Not this.

The blood rushed to her head, and her legs gave way beneath her. She tried to force air through the whistle, but cold horror had frozen her ability to act on her brain's commands.

The whistle bounced to the floor as a lifeless body tumbled through the door, its cold arms wrapping around Lindsey, its long hair flying across her face and into her mouth.

The silent scream finally escaped her lips as the floor rose to meet her and darkness blotted out the light.

## Chapter Eleven

"Oh, dear. Her eyes are fluttering, Detective. And she's moving her leg. Is she all right?"

Lindsey squinted and struggled to bring things into focus. "Katie," she murmured as the blurring lines in front of her coalesced into a face. "Where's Graham?"

She jerked to a sitting position, the image of the naked body wrapped around her own still pummeling her mind, filling her senses with new dread. Something moved across her leg. She forced her eyes to look, and then gave in to a thankful moan. The lifeless shape around her leg now was only a blanket.

"I'm right here," Graham answered, moving into view.

She groaned and dropped back to the sofa. Somehow she had gotten from the floor to the sofa, but a blinding headache was knifing through her brain. She reached for the back of her head and the painful lump that seemed to be growing larger even as she touched it.

"Are you okay?" Graham knelt beside her and wrapped her right hand inside both of his.

"I don't know. What happened?"

"You must have passed out when you found the body.

You hit your head on the corner of the coffee table, but the doctor says it's not serious.''

"The body…"

"Yeah, it's still here."

"I came when you sent for me, but I couldn't find you."

His brow wrinkled, and his mouth stretched into a worried frown. He placed two fingers over her lips. "Shh… Don't say anything now." He squeezed her hand comfortingly and then rose to his feet.

"I'm sorry about ruining your party, Katie."

"Ruin it? Don't be ridiculous. You've made it the highlight of the season," Katie said comfortingly, kneeling to take the spot beside her that Graham had vacated. "Everybody heard your scream. I'm sure they're downstairs now, panting for details."

Lindsey forced herself to a sitting position. Her stomach lurched as she caught sight of the gruesome collage of limp arms and legs and yards of blond hair still draped across the floor and part of the coffee table. The last thing she remembered was trying to move out of the way of the falling body. Evidently she'd slipped in the process, falling into the table.

"Just lay back and rest, dear," Katie offered, placing her hand on top of Lindsey's. "Fortunately, we had lots of doctors at the party. Dr. Kabel is on the phone now with the hospital. But don't you worry. He'll be right back."

Lindsey finally won the skirmish with her stomach and managed to speak. "Don't you think it's a little late to call the hospital? The lady's been dead for almost a week."

"No, dahling, not for that poor girl, for you. Dr. Kabel is very thorough. He insists you go in for a night of observation, even though he's sure you have no more than a mild concussion. They'll take wonderful care of you.''

Graham paced the room, striving to take in everything at once, but it was hard to think when he was so worried about Lindsey. The doctor had assured him she was not seriously injured, but her face was still a pasty white.

Of course, he probably didn't look much better himself. When he'd walked in that door and found Lindsey stretched out on the floor, lifeless and limp… Hell, he'd felt as if his own life had just gone up in smoke. He clenched his hands into fists. Somebody was damn sure going to pay for this.

He pivoted to face the door as it opened and then slammed shut.

''Looks like there's another party in my room. Now why am I never invited to these little soirees?'' Thomas asked, pushing through the door and stopping to lounge against the frame.

Graham muttered a few choice words under his breath. This was beginning to look like Grand Central Station, the way people were popping in and out. How the hell did they keep getting by his man? He'd told him plainly not to let anyone up the steps who wasn't here on official business.

''My, my… What happened to you, Miss Green? You look as if you just saw a ghost. And the blonde there doesn't seem to be having much fun, either.''

''Lindsey's going to be all right, but someone killed that poor blond lady, Thomas,'' Katie explained, hurrying to his side. ''But who would stash a week-old body in your room?''

''Someone with a rather warped sense of humor, obviously.'' Thomas wrapped a comforting arm about his aunt's shoulders. "A week-old body, Aunt Katie. How interesting. And how would *you* know the body's a week old?"

"Because Officer Green said so."

"Really, a week. Amazing. She just walks in, finds a body, and can tell you how long the person's been dead."

"A week, more or less, Thomas." Graham broke into the conversation. He wasn't sure what Thomas was getting at or what he knew, but the week thing could blow Lindsey's cover right out of the window. It was already hanging by a thread after her recent performance. What kind of cop got so upset over finding a dead body that she tripped and busted her own head?

"It's a rough estimate," Graham continued. "We're police officers, remember? We're trained to know that sort of thing."

"Oh, yes. I keep forgetting. Not about you, Detective. A take-charge man like yourself could hardly be anything else. But Miss Green seems so...normal."

"*Officer* Green," Graham reminded him sharply, ignoring the insult. "You didn't answer your aunt's question, Thomas. How did the body get into your room?"

Lindsey tilted her pounding head and waited for his answer. She needn't have. Thomas only shrugged and turned away. She shook her head to clear it. The room was still a bit fuzzy, but at least now there was only one of everybody.

"Don't try to talk yet," Graham said. His voice was calm, but the warning glare he directed her way told her this was not the time for her to start asking questions.

The police radio started up again, filling the room with squawking voices. "They're on the way to get the body now. Do you want me to take Green home?"

That voice she recognized.

"Tell Rooster I'm fine." She forced herself to a sitting position, hoping Graham would believe her lie. She wasn't ready to go home, and she definitely wasn't going back to the hospital.

Not because she was fine. She wasn't, and she was beginning to believe she never would be again. Still, if she wanted to know what was really going on, and not some watered-down version Graham thought she could handle, she would have to see and hear it for herself.

"Are you sure you're all right? That bump on your head is growing by the minute." The concern in Graham's voice wrapped around her like a cuddly blanket.

"I will be, as soon as my equilibrium kicks in," she assured him, struggling to get her lips to curve into a slight smile.

"I'll get an ice pack," the housekeeper offered.

That was the first time Lindsey had spotted Ruby. She was standing in the corner, quietly watching everything. And good old Thomas had moved over to stand right behind her, still dressed in the Rebel soldier's costume, minus the mask. Somehow she wasn't at all surprised the debonair soldier who had twirled her around the floor with such finesse was Thomas LeBlanc.

At the first sign of trouble, look for Thomas. Lindsey was finding it harder and harder to buy his airtight alibi. Ruby left through the outside door, and Thomas wasted no time in sharing his sentiments.

"Poor woman. She had to recognize the body, but she isn't saying a word."

"What makes you think Ruby knows who she is?" Lindsey perked up, eager to hear Thomas's speculations.

"That's Garon's girlfriend, or at least she was. Everybody knows it. He's been dating her for weeks now, though no one could figure out quite why." He shook his head thoughtfully. "What a shame. It's going to look bad for Garon. But he didn't do it."

"What makes you so sure Garon's innocent?" Graham asked, stopping his pacing and note taking to look Thomas square in the eye.

"He's slow. You know, not overly bright. A mama's boy, to boot. But he's not a killer."

"You seem to know a lot about him."

"He hangs around here sometimes."

Katie broke in. "Ruby brings him some days to help with the heavy cleaning. I pay him, but he earns it. He's a hard worker, as long as you tell him exactly what to do. But I have to agree with Thomas. Garon's gentle and well mannered, almost childlike. He would never do anything like this." She stumbled over the words as her gaze traveled back to the body.

"He had some problems, of course, like everybody else," Thomas volunteered, "especially trying to keep a looker like the blonde there satisfied, but I've never seen him mad enough to go that far." He stepped back as Graham moved to the window, the spot where Lindsey had seen the murder take place.

"Mrs. LeBlanc, I'm afraid I'll have to ask you and Thomas to leave the room now," Graham explained. "They'll be here to pick up the body for the autopsy in a minute. Some other police officers will be coming in, too. You just go back to the party and try to go on as if nothing happened."

"You're sure we're safe, Detective? I mean, you're certain the girl's been dead for a few days? I wouldn't want to think the killer was still here, on the grounds somewhere."

"I don't know where the killer is, Mrs. LeBlanc, but I do know the girl has been dead for a while. Dead and in cold storage someplace for most of that time, waiting to make her grand entrance at your party.''

''A sicko,'' Thomas complained. ''I just wish I knew how they got into the turret. I won't be sleeping up here for a while. I can guarantee you that. Not until that smell of decay is gone completely.'' He turned up his nose and headed for the door.

Graham opened the door to usher him and Katie out. ''Remember what I said. Don't leave town. Make sure I can find you if the need arises.''

''Surely you don't suspect Thomas.'' Surprised indignation was written all over Katie's pretty face.

''I don't suspect anybody, Mrs. LeBlanc, not yet. I'm just investigating a case. The evidence will dictate who's arrested, and a judge and jury will decide the rest.''

''Well, I can assure you Thomas has nothing to do with any of this. Now, if you need us for anything else, we'll be downstairs with my guests.''

Graham tried to push the door closed behind them, but Ruby appeared with a tall glass of cold water and an ice pack. He moved aside and let her in.

Head down, she walked straight to Lindsey, carefully avoiding any glimpse of the body still draped across the Oriental rug. Lindsey reached for the water. Ruby held it back, not saying a word, but capturing Lindsey with her gaze.

''Is there something you want to tell me, Miss Ruby?'' Lindsey asked.

She hesitated, her eyes boring into Lindsey's, silently pleading for something. Lindsey had no idea what.

''No. Nothing,'' she finally answered, her voice a shaky whisper. With trembling hands, she placed the water in Lindsey's grasp and hurried out of the turret.

Poor Ruby. Poor nameless blond girl. Poor Danielle.

How many people would be hurt by this before it was all over? Lindsey took a deep breath and plopped the ice pack on her head as the room filled with a new supply of men. All she could do now was sit quietly and wait.

The action was heating up around her, and she wanted to hear everything that was said. She was in this case up to her neck, and one thing she had learned: Ignorance was not bliss.

"Say, I'd rather carry out the girl on the couch. The live one," one of the young guys joked, nodding in Lindsey's direction.

"Just tend to business," Graham directed, "and handle this body like it was the last cold beer on a hot summer day. I need all the evidence the autopsy can give me."

"You got it."

Lindsey watched as two of the newly arrived police began to snap photos of the crime scene. Graham continued his restless pacing. "Damn psycho," he muttered to no one in particular. "Kills his woman and then saves the body for a party favor."

A frigid tremor slithered up Lindsey's spine. The devious psycho Graham was describing also wanted her dead. He wanted it so badly he was willing to kill all eight women from float number seven, if that was what it took. He'd already killed one.

The murderer knew the witness had been riding on that float. But he didn't know which one of the riders had been watching when he plunged the dagger into his lover's heart. That meant one of Lindsey's scenarios about the dress being hidden in her car was true.

The dress was meant as a warning or a gratis clue. Or maybe the Mercedes really had just been in the right place at the wrong time. A dumping spot for unwanted evidence.

No. That wasn't likely. Too many people were keeping up with her whereabouts these days. Katie, Thomas, Jerome, Ruby. Everyone seemed to know when she visited the LeBlanc mansion. Stashing the dress in her car was probably a planned move. But why? That was the burning question.

She pushed the thoughts aside. She could deal with them later. Right now the investigation was in full swing, and she didn't want to miss a thing.

A serial killer was out there somewhere. Graham would find him. She was sure of it. But she couldn't wait forever. Either Graham and his fellow officers from the NOPD nabbed the killer soon, or she took matters in her own hands.

It was the only way.

SUNLIGHT was peeking around the edges of the closed blinds when Lindsey opened her eyes on Monday morning. She checked out the alarm clock by the bed. Six a.m. She stretched beneath the covers, reluctant to climb from the cozy warmth.

Graham had insisted she take the bed. And since the first night, he'd left her to toss about on the double mattress all alone. Lindsey wasn't sorry. It had been the right decision for both of them.

Not because the night they'd spent together hadn't been everything she'd dreamed it would be. It had been all that and much more. But a passionate fling in the midst of a life-and-death crisis was not what she wanted.

If she and Graham were to have a chance to re-create what they had once shared, it would take time. They would need to get to know each other all over again, to find out if they could learn to trust again. That couldn't happen as long as staying alive and finding a killer dominated their very existence.

She hugged the pillow against her. She was in one room, Graham in another, yet they were so close she could hear his breathing in the middle of the night. It was the right thing to do. She was sure of it. So why was it driving her crazy?

"Are you awake yet, sleepyhead?" Graham asked, pushing the door open a crack and peeking in.

"I am, and you can come in if you're bearing coffee."

He stepped inside, two cups in hand, the steam from the fresh-perked brew curling about his face. "I thought I heard a little movement in here."

Her heart constricted. Even in the morning, his hair still damp from the shower, his face red from the razor, he was devastatingly male. He possessed the same boyish charm she remembered, and the tough hardness of a man she was only beginning to know.

She combed her fingers through her disheveled hair and propped up two pillows, making a spot for Graham to join her on the bed. "What are you doing still lazing around? You're usually up and out before the sun."

"I decided to stick around awhile and make coffee for you. I'm tired of Rooster having all the fun."

She studied the somber lines on his face. "Why is it I don't believe you?"

He reached over and took her hand, playing with her fingers. "You've been around cops too long."

"So what is it, Graham? Is there something new on the case?"

"Yeah. Finding the body Saturday night shed a lot of new light. Unfortunately, it's all pointing in one direction."

"Garon?"

"That's how it looks. The girl's name is Roxanne Brunet, and she *was* dating Garon. He admits it, and so does everyone else who knew either one of them. He seems genuinely devastated by her death. Of course, that doesn't prove anything. How many men kill their wives or lovers and then kill themselves because they can't bear to live without them?"

He took a big gulp of his coffee. "It's a crazy world out there. I see it all the time, but it never ceases to amaze me what people will do."

"What else did they find out about the victim?"

"She has a record, mostly minor things, going all the way back to age twelve. Shoplifting, taking things from a neighbor's house, that kind of thing. But word on the street has it, she was into big-time stuff."

"Big time? Like what?"

"Head of a burglary ring. Jewelry was her forte. She was even the subject of an undercover operation last year, but they couldn't get the goods on her. They arrested a few people, but no one was willing to squeal on the fence. They weren't about to lose the connection who gets them the big bucks for their stolen goods."

"When did you find out all of this?"

"Yesterday. Some of it the day before." Graham slid closer, circling her shoulders with his arm. "I think Garon's our man, Lins. All the evidence points to it, except your eyewitness report."

"So you think I'm wrong." She turned to face him. "But why would I remember that wrong, when I was right on target with everything else?"

"I don't know. I ran it by the psychologist that works with us on difficult cases. He has an idea or two, but he wants to talk to you about them."

"If that's what you want, I'll talk to the psychologist."

She scooted over to her side of the bed and dropped her feet to the floor. "But talking is not going to change what I saw. The killer was tall, straight, handsomely built. He had to stoop to kiss the woman. His hair was cut short in back, but a shock of coal black hair stuck out from under his cap. Garon doesn't fit that description."

"No, not hardly. He's five-ten. The victim was five-eight. He's squatty, if anything, not lean. And his hair is shaggy in front and back."

Lindsey grabbed her robe and slung her arms through the sleeves, pulling it around her. With a forceful jerk, she yanked the blinds open, letting sunlight flood the room.

"So what do you think happened?" she persisted. "If Garon and Roxanne were dating, and she was helping him rob the LeBlancs of their jewels, why did he kill her?"

"We're working on that. Garon had a key to the house. We know that much. Even Ruby admitted he took it from her purse one night. She would have probably never found out, but he lost it in his car and didn't find it until the next day."

"Was that the night of the Minerva parade?"

"No, he'd returned it to her before that, but he could have had a key to the house made. He and Roxanne could have planned the jewel theft for the night you witnessed the murder. With all the cars around for the parade, no one would have noticed his parked among the others. Once inside, it would have been easy enough for Garon to lead her to the secret door that opens onto the safe."

"How would Garon know about the safe?"

"He started going there with his mom when he was a youngster, before he was old enough to go to school. Richard and his wife had encouraged it. He entertained

Richard's father, who had become senile and a general bother to the family. They were like two kids, playing chase and hide-and-seek all over the house.''

"How would Katie know that? She wasn't around then.''

"Ruby told me. She didn't want to, but Garon had already admitted that he had gone there frequently as a child. There was nothing his mom could do but tell us the truth about that.''

Lindsey ran her finger down the cord that operated the blinds. "And what boy would forget something like secret passages and walls opening up?''

Graham walked up behind her and circled her waist with his arms. "We believe Garon is our man. There'll be a warrant issued today for his arrest.''

Lindsey leaned back, letting her shoulders and head relax against Graham's strong chest. If Garon was the killer, life could go on. If not, the wrong man would be behind bars, and a deadly killer would have free rein to strike again.

Graham buried his lips in her hair. "This will all be over soon, Lins. When it is, we can move on to other things. Like how I feel about you. How I've always felt.''

Graham seemed so sure of his feelings. But even now, with desire swelling inside Lindsey, the nagging doubts persisted. She had changed, matured, found herself, in ten years. Perhaps Graham had, too. But ten years of disillusionment, of distrust and heartache, were a formidable barrier. Only one thing was certain. She had never stopped loving him. She never would.

But first, the nightmare of the past few days had to be laid to rest. "Okay, Graham, when do I see the psychologist?''

"This afternoon, at three. Rooster will take you, if

that's all right. There are still lots of loose ends to tie up on the case. Hopefully, we won't hit any more snags.''

"This afternoon at three. I'll be ready."

LINDSEY SMOOTHED the straight lines of her gray wool skirt over her crossed legs and studied the muted pattern of the wallpaper behind the good doctor.

"It's not an uncommon phenomenon," he continued in a matter-of-fact tone laced with conviction. "This may be what happened in your case, Miss Latham."

"So you think that some memory from the past planted itself in the live event I was witnessing?"

"I'm only saying it's possible. You admit you were a little woozy at the time, from champagne and the rocking of the float. It could be that you saw the same characteristics in the man in the window as you remember in some…let's say, some past romantic interest."

Tall, dark, classically handsome. Damn. It was Graham. He was all those things, and since the day she had met him, he had never been far from her mind. The doctor had a good point.

"If I displaced the man in the window with an image, why didn't I do the same with the woman? Why didn't I see myself with…"

"With the man from your past?"

"Right. Why would I confuse just half the scene?"

"I didn't say you confused what you saw, just what you remember seeing. If I understood you correctly, you told me you can't recall distinct facial features about the man, but that you could the woman." The doctor took a notebook from his desk and quickly skimmed a page before continuing.

"I drove by the house in question last night. I wasn't at eye level like you were on the float, but from the street,

I could have easily seen a person in the window well enough to recognize them again. Especially if I had taken time to study them, the way you did.''

''So you think that's why I don't remember the features of the man, because I blocked it from my memory? You think I just replaced that image with one more to my liking?''

''No. I'm only saying it's possible, that it's not unheard-of. You told me you were moved by the sight of two beautiful lovers. Maybe one of the lovers really wasn't so beautiful. In your mind's eye, you may have replaced his unseemly image with one more in keeping with your own memories and dreams of romantic love.''

Only one image had ever been in her dreams of love. Graham Dufour. She'd been thinking of him that night. She couldn't deny that. She was right here in the city where her love for Graham had all begun. And where it had ended.

Only it had never ended. She knew that now. Maybe her unconscious had known it the night of the murder. She got up from her chair and paced the room. The doctor's theory had seemed crazy at first, but was it really? At least it would explain why she couldn't remember the details of the killer's face.

Of course, the fact that she'd been more intent on looking at the Southern belle and her beautiful costume could also explain it, and that made a lot more sense. Once she'd begun to focus on the man, and the dagger in his hand, she really couldn't believe her eyes. At that point, shock and horror had robbed her of all ability to make descriptive distinctions.

''I'm not sure, Doctor. I guess it could have happened like you say. It just seems rather farfetched.''

''The subconscious does strange things to our vision

and our memory, Miss Latham. The powers of the mind should never be underestimated.'' He got up from his chair and walked over to where Lindsey was staring blankly at a painting, the waters of the billowing ocean in the seascape swirling like her thoughts.

''I hope I've shed some light on this for you. I wish I had more time to talk about it with you, but it's almost time for my next appointment.''

''You've helped. I'm not sure I buy your theory in this case, but I appreciate your efforts.'' She extended her hand.

''Think about what I've said, Miss Latham. And if you want to talk again, call. We'll set something up.''

Lindsey thanked him once more and walked out of his office, a thousand questions playing leapfrog in her mind. She wanted to believe him. And all the evidence the police had gathered pointed straight at Garon. Fingerprints, the stolen key, opportunity, motive. All circumstantial, but reason enough for an arrest, Graham had assured her.

She pushed through the double door of the downtown office building and exited into the brisk February air. Rooster waved at her from the waiting parked car, a satisfied smile suggesting he was the cat who had eaten the canary.

She hurried her pace. She'd lived with the police long enough to know exactly what his expression meant. He'd heard from Graham. They'd arrested their man.

But please, God, let it be the right one, she prayed as she opened the car door and slid inside.

''Time for the celebration to begin.'' Graham pointed the champagne bottle toward the wall and ceremoniously popped the cork. ''The long arm of NOPD strikes again. Thanks to Officer Green, honorary policewoman.'' He leaned over, letting his mouth brush Lindsey's cheek and settle on her inviting lips.

He forced himself to pull away. Tonight had to be perfect. He couldn't spoil it by rushing things, no matter how his eager body was reacting to her kiss. If things worked out the way he hoped they would, tonight would be just the beginning.

He filled the only two matching glasses he had and placed one in her hand. "What a day, Lins. First the lady at Dumas' Costumes gives me a positive identification on Garon as the man who picked up the two costumes. Then Garon himself walks in. He knows the warrant is out for his arrest, and he wants to save us the trouble of looking for him."

Lindsey lifted her glass in a toast. "To Graham Dufour, homicide detective extraordinaire."

"And to Lindsey Latham, the bravest and prettiest crime witness I've ever worked with."

Their glasses clinked musically, and Graham leaned closer. Lindsey's lips were moist with sparkling champagne, and her eyes were smoky with something that looked a lot like desire. The same desire that was driving him crazy.

He'd controlled it. He'd had no choice. The first priority had been keeping her alive. Romantic involvement and investigations were a fatal mix. But now the killer was in jail. He set his glass on the table. There were much better things to taste.

He ran his fingers through her silky hair, twirling them about her lush curls and easing her closer. He wanted to feel the soft curves of her breast against his chest, to mold her shapely hips into the hard lines of his own craving.

She smiled up at him and then pulled away.

"Is something the matter?"

Her eyes were still staring into his, but there was something there besides desire. Questions. Or was it doubt?

"Let's go into the living room, Graham. There are some things we need to talk about."

## Chapter Twelve

Lindsey's insides quaked as she walked to the living room and sat down on the couch. The moment of truth had arrived. Each look, each touch, each kiss, had hurled them deeper into a whirlwind of past heartaches and present desires.

Confrontation was inevitable. It had been since the other night, when she'd melted so completely in Graham's arms. The night she'd given in to the passion that had simmered deep in her soul for the past ten years. She didn't regret it.

But there could be no repeat performances. She wouldn't go through another decade of heartbreak. Not even for Graham. If he wanted the kind of intimacy she longed for, she had to believe they could avoid the pitfalls of the past. For her, it had to be all or nothing.

Graham dropped next to her and slipped his arm around her shoulders. "What's the matter, Lins? Is it the arrest? Are you still convinced that Garon is not the man?"

"No. You're the expert. If you say the evidence is substantial, I have to believe you."

He cupped his hand under her chin and tilted her face

upward, his lips only inches from hers. She took a deep breath and pulled away.

"Then what is it?" He danced his fingers down her arm. "I can touch you, but I can't reach you."

"I'm right here, Graham. Where I've always been. I didn't erect the barriers between us. You did, years ago. They're the same ones that sent you running out of my life and into the arms of someone new."

He shrugged his shoulders and slowly shook his head from side to side. "Do we have to rehash all of that?" He leaned back against the cushions, spearing his fingers through his dark hair. "Haven't we been through enough this week without having to dig up old garbage? I just want to be with you."

He turned his face toward hers, and his eyes burned with reminders of the passion that lay just below his cool exterior. "I want to make love to you. And you can't tell me you don't want the same thing. Not after Monday night."

"So what do you suggest, Graham? That we just fall into each other's arms and go at it like some cheap B movie? Happy ever after, or for the next ten minutes, whichever comes first?"

Graham clenched his hands into fists, the muscles in his arms straining under the cotton shirt. "That's not what I meant. You surely know by now how I feel about you."

"How would I? Because you walk into a room and electricity crackles through the air? Because when we make love the fire is so hot I'm consumed with you?"

"I'd say those are damn good indications." Irritation drew his lips into tight lines. "But obviously you don't."

"We had all that before, Graham. In the end, none of it mattered. You rejected me." She turned away, unwilling for him to see the tears burning her eyelids. "I'm the same person I was then."

"I know." He reached for her hand, threading his fingers through hers. "I knew it from the moment I saw you in the hospital room, giving orders to me, the nursing staff, even the doctor. Determined to do things your way. And still able to twist my heart like a toy balloon."

He turned her face toward him, making her meet his gaze. Desire smoldered in his eyes, mesmerizing her, making her want so desperately to trust his love.

"At eighteen, I was obsessed with you." His voice lowered to a husky whisper. "I still am."

Her heart beat painfully. The need for him was all-consuming, but somehow she managed to hold on to her resolve. "Then why did you walk away, Graham? All I wanted was a little time to find myself. To be on my own, away from my dad and his suffocating protectiveness. Why couldn't you understand?"

He dropped her hand and stood up. Walking to the window, he jerked the string on the blinds and stared out into the night. "What was I to understand? That you had a life that didn't include me?" He shoved his fists into his pockets. "You were determined to go away to college rather than go to the university here, like I had to do. That's what I understood."

"You had a scholarship offer to play football."

"Is that what you wanted, for me to come chasing after you?"

"No. I tried not to make demands. But I expected you to get an education. You were too smart not to have ambition."

Graham paced the room, his jaw clenched and his mouth drawn into hard lines. "The poor don't have the same options as the rich. I couldn't take the scholarship.

School had to be a part-time thing for me. Work had to come first. My family needed my support.''

Grief tore at Lindsey's heart. She didn't want to pull painful confessions from Graham. But she had to understand, had to know the real Graham Dufour.

''You had so much, Lindsey. Anything you ever wanted was yours for the asking. I had nothing. You were the beautiful rich girl. I was the poor kid who was lucky enough to worm myself into your circles just because I happened to be a damn good quarterback.'' His voice was hard now, remnants of past anger pushing through the barriers he had built around his feelings.

Lindsey squeezed her eyes shut for one brief moment, but a persistent tear pushed its way through. ''The rich girl. It always came down to that, didn't it, Graham? You could never quite see past what I had, to see who I was.''

''I tried. But what did you expect? We lived in two different worlds. You went to Paris for Christmas. I couldn't even afford to buy you a decent gift.''

''I told you time and again, none of that mattered.''

''It mattered to me. I was a teenager, for Christ's sake. I wanted to be like everybody else. But I was playing out of my league.''

''Has anything changed between us, Graham? I make it on my own now, because I choose to, but one day the family business will be mine. Will the same prejudices still tear at you then like they did before, like some wild creature you can't tame? Will it just be the same story all over again?''

''No.'' He walked over to stand in front of her, his back ramrod straight. ''Not anymore. I'm all grown up. I know who I am. I can be myself in any league, even one with your father. I should have never listened to him back then.''

Old frustrations settled in her chest like lead, stealing her breath away. "My father? How did he get back into this?"

"The day you left for college, your father called me in and offered me five thousand dollars to stay out of your life."

Grief and disillusionment burned at Lindsey's throat and knotted in her stomach. Her father had always believed everything had a price tag. Now it looked like he'd been right. Even with Graham. "So that's why you disappeared so completely. You were bought and paid for." She wiped a tear from her cheek and prayed no more would follow.

"I didn't take a cent of your dad's money. He got what he wanted for nothing." His eyes burned with old contempt and hurt.

"Why, Graham? Why, after all we'd been through together, did you choose that time to listen to him over me?"

Graham dropped to the couch beside her. "Because at the time, he was probably right. But he isn't right any longer." He pushed a wayward curl behind her ear, then let his finger trace a path down her neck and back up again.

Tingles of anticipation followed his touch, but Lindsey couldn't give in to her body's desires. Not yet. "Let me see if I understand this. My dad told you to get out, so you dumped me without saying a word to me about it. You just said, 'Okay, Mr. Latham, if you don't want me to see Lindsey, I'll just go pick up someone else and marry her. No problem. One girl's as good as another'?"

"Now you're being facetious, Lins."

"I'm trying to understand."

Graham picked up his empty glass and took it to the

kitchen counter. He refilled it with a double shot of Scotch. Straight. Tilting his head back, he downed a healthy swig.

"Okay, Lindsey. You're right, as always. That isn't all there was to it. I was seeing red. I asked you not to go to Nashville to college. You went anyway. And then, to top things off, your dad pointed out one too many times that I wasn't good enough to associate with the likes of you."

Graham slammed his right fist into the door facing, the sound rocketing through the small room. "So the hotshot quarterback marched right out and found himself a girl who didn't say no. She all but jumped into my arms. And into the back seat of my old revved-up Chevy. I wanted to hurt you like you'd hurt me."

Pain ripped through Lindsey's heart with the same force it had so many years ago. "That's all it took for you to forget me? A one-night stand?"

"No, but it helped ease the pain. I was eighteen. I wasn't making great decisions."

"You didn't answer my letters. You didn't return my phone calls. I all but begged. You gave me nothing. I even heard about the marriage from someone else." Her voice broke on the words, the familiar pain as cutting as it had been then.

"I wanted to call you. Believe me, I wanted to. But by that time we had a little problem. Sarah became more than a rebound fling the day she appeared on my doorstep and happily informed me she was pregnant. Guess who the lucky father was."

Lindsey felt her heart take the blow of Graham's words. She struggled for breath. "I didn't know there was a baby."

"And I didn't know there wasn't. At least not mine."

Bitterness rang through every word. "The wedding was a hurry-up affair. Sarah lost the baby two weeks after we were married. She moved on a couple of months later, but not before she took great pride in telling me the baby hadn't been mine. It belonged to a married guy she'd been seeing on the sly. Now you know the whole sordid story. Is that what you wanted? To get an up-close look at all my filthy laundry?"

"I'm sorry. No one ever told me."

"No. Probably not. I didn't take out an ad in the paper to announce I'd been had. Besides, by then you were dating some medical student at Vanderbilt. I wasn't about to come crawling back. Not with an ego that had shrunk to pea-size."

His voice grew low and husky, revealing an unexpected vulnerability that caressed Lindsey's heart and melted away her doubts. They'd paid ten years for youthful mistakes. It was time to settle the bill.

Graham turned to stare at her, his eyes smoky depths of regret. "I've made my share of mistakes. I won't deny that, and I can't undo them. But I never stopped loving you. I never will."

She walked over and wrapped her hands around his waist. A warmth suffused her body. For ten years, she'd longed for what might have been. Only it couldn't have been, not then. They had both been too young and far too foolish to know how to handle love like theirs. But now she knew.

"That's all I want, Graham. Your love, forever, the way I love you. No one could ask for more."

A low groan tore from his throat, and he held her even closer. He rocked her in his arms for long minutes, until Lindsey tilted her head back to face him. Her eyes were moist, brimming over with tears of pure happiness. He kissed them away, his lips on her face as gentle as morning mist.

Passion soared inside her, igniting the flame that only Graham could put out. Her feelings had been denied, bottled inside her, for much too long. She parted her lips for Graham's kiss.

Her invitation did not go unheeded. He found her lips again, but this time his kiss quickly lost its gentleness. She struggled for breath, and his mouth roamed lower, to the outline of her breasts, his fingers roving her body in sensuous waves, exploring and finding the secret areas that ached for him.

Roughly, his hands shaking from the same need that ravaged her body, he carried her to the bedroom and laid her atop the smooth spread. "I want you, Lins. I want you so much I ache." His voice trembled, its husky timbre a mixture of passion and pain, tethered to one last thread of control. "But it's your call. If you're still not ready, I'll wait. This time I'll wait as long as it takes."

She wrapped her arms around him, pulling him down beside her. Reason, doubts, heartache, they were nothing now. There was only herself and Graham. And their love. Their endless love.

"The wait is over, Graham. It's finally over."

GRAHAM STOOD in the bedroom door. His heart constricted as it always did upon seeing Lindsey in his bed, her disheveled hair cascading over his pillow, her body curled in sleep. How could anybody be that gorgeous in the morning?

"Happy Mardi Gras!" He threw a couple of strands of purple and green beads across the pink toes that peeked out from beneath the sheet.

Lindsey opened one eye.

He bombarded her with carnival throws.

"What time is it?" she mumbled, her voice throaty from a few hours of sound sleep.

"Carnival time. The big day is finally here." He tugged on the cord of the blinds, washing away the gray darkness with a spray of sunlight. "And what a day. Clear and bright. *Laissez le bons temps rouler.*"

"Let the good times roll." Lindsey repeated the familiar French phrase in English as she swung her shapely legs over the edge of the bed. A low moan slipped from her lips. "I think I already overdid it in the good-times department," she complained good-naturedly.

Graham squatted beside her and gave her a good-morning kiss. As always, she took his breath away, and he had to pull himself back to reality before he lost control. "You didn't overdo it. You just need more practice. We'll have to work on that."

"Let's practice having fun today, Graham. All day." Innocent eagerness lit up her eyes. He wished to hell he could comply with her request. She'd been through so much in the past week. Now that the killer was safely behind bars, she deserved a little fun.

He did, too, and he'd like nothing better than to crawl back into bed beside her. But the case of the Mardi Gras murder and jewel theft was not over. There were still too many questions without answers. At this point, only Roxanne's murder could be linked to Garon. Evidence was still needed to tie him to Danielle's murder and to the jewelry heist. Either evidence or a confession.

Getting the killer off the street made it safe again, but Graham wouldn't be satisfied until this whole thing was settled. The fun would have to wait. "How about half a day?" he offered.

"Don't tell me you have to work. It's Mardi Gras."

"It will still be Mardi Gras this afternoon." He planted a kiss on the tip of her beautiful nose. "We'll do anything you want. Catch a parade, go down to the Vieux Carré, make love in the middle of Bourbon Street. Anything you say."

"The making-love thing sounds nice, but Bourbon Street's not quite the place I had in mind." She danced two fingers up his chest. "And parades are out. I've had enough of those to last a while. But I'd love to go to the Vieux Carré. After the week I've had, letting it all hang out in the French Quarter sounds fabulous."

"Then fabulous it is." He kissed her again and tucked a tempting breast back inside her loose gown. It was hard enough to leave her this morning without any added temptations.

"What will you do this morning? It's your first morning alone. No bodyguards, no reason to be afraid."

"Think of you. And enjoy being alive."

Graham kissed her again, long and hard.

"Are you sure you have to go in this morning?" Lindsey purred, letting a toe run up his trouser leg.

"I'm sure," he answered, slipping the strap of her gown off her shoulder with one hand and undoing his belt with the other. "But it looks like I'll be a little later than planned."

GRAHAM spent the morning unsuccessfully chasing clues. Someone had to know something, but no one was talking. Katie was too busy worrying about today's parade party to concentrate on police questions. Ruby was protecting her son. And big brother Jerome couldn't even be found for questioning.

Shuffling papers with one hand and stuffing the last bite of a slice of king cake into his mouth with the other,

Graham finally located the notes he'd made while questioning Garon. For a second he'd been sure Garon was about to break and tell all, but then Rooster had asked him something about Jerome, and he'd clammed up like a kid caught skipping class.

A wasted morning. Graham drained the strong dregs from his coffee mug and reached for his windbreaker. He had a date to celebrate Mardi Gras, and for the first time in years he was actually looking forward to the madness.

"YIPPEE TI YI YO!"

A cowboy in a leather vest and chaps and little else walked up as Lindsey climbed from Graham's car into the French Quarter revelry. "Nice little filly you got there, partner." He stopped ogling long enough to give Graham a high five.

"The cowboy has good taste—in women, anyway," Graham acknowledged, a devastating smile parting his lips. "But his riding gear looks like it might give a little saddle burn."

"Yeah, I'll bet he's thankful the weather warmed up today. If it had stayed as cold as it was last week, his chaps would be riding goose bumps."

Easy laughter escaped Graham's lips as he reached back into the car and pulled out a long string of beads, strung together in patterns of purple, green and gold. The bright rays of afternoon sun caught them, touching them with a shimmer of sparkle as he draped them about her neck. "Can't go out without these. It's a mortal sin on Fat Tuesday."

"I love them," she exclaimed, fingering the tiny gold bands that separated each bead. "I didn't see any like these, even at the Minerva parade. Where did you get them?"

"A friend brought them to me this morning." He locked the car and wrapped his arm about her. "I'll tell her I put them to good use."

Lindsey doubted very seriously the friend would agree. She was quite sure there would be many a shattered heart when the women of New Orleans found out that Lindsey Latham planned to yank Detective Dufour from the ranks of available bachelors.

"You do look great today," Graham offered, curling his arms about her waist and guiding her toward the busy sidewalk. "I like the way those jeans fit your cute little behind." He stopped and gave it a second look.

"Why, thank you, sir. I'll remember that." The Mardi Gras spirit had finally caught on, adding a skip to her walk. The sights, the sounds, the smells. She wanted to experience it all. After a week and more of living a nightmare, the mere idea of having fun was intoxicating.

"Look at that woman!" Lindsey pointed out a shapely lady across the street. "Her dress is magnificent."

"Pretty classy, all right."

Lindsey slowed her pace to stare. So had everyone else on the block. The woman's hair was bright red and piled high atop her head. The dress had a sequined bodice that dipped indecently low in front and curved into the waist. The skirt billowed out below, yards and yards of organza, so long it all but swept the dirty street.

"Where could she be going dressed like that? There are no balls in the middle of the afternoon."

"*She's* not going anywhere," Graham explained, laughing. "That's a *he*."

"I don't believe it. I mean, look at that figure. I'd trade with her—with him—in a minute."

"Please don't. I'm partial to the body you have right now. But to answer your question about where he's going, there are hundreds of parties scattered about the Quarter today. Besides the really big one on the streets, I mean.''

They rounded the corner from Decatur onto St. Peter. The crowd increased at Jackson Square. Groups of friends stood laughing and talking amid the colorful umbrellas of the sidewalk vendors.

Lindsey slowed to a crawl, trying to see everything at once. A clown skated by on Rollerblade in-line skates, throwing kisses to the ladies. Lindsey threw one back. A man who looked at least ninety danced on the corner with a lively teenager. He didn't miss a step.

''You better pick up the pace. We'll never get to Bourbon Street at this rate,'' Graham told her. The laughter in his voice told her he didn't care.

Without warning, a shudder climbed Lindsey's spine. They were surrounded by strangers, but she had the eerie feeling someone was watching her. She stopped and turned, letting her gaze sweep across the crowded street.

Everybody looked occupied with their own partying. Except for one man. He was standing in the shadows, almost hidden in a brick alcove. A full rubber mask designed to look like a wrinkled old man completely covered his face. But he wasn't old. The straight lines of his back and the muscular bulges beneath his shirtsleeves were proof of that.

Lindsey squeezed Graham's hand, this time pulling him along. It was a day for letting go of fears and inhibitions for everyone, and she would follow suit. She owed it to herself and to Graham.

Forcing a skip to her step and a smile to her lips, she headed for the next sidewalk vendor. A bewitching woman dressed in a low-cut black blouse and black tights sat on a high stool as a smiling young artist did his job.

Dipping his brush in black paint, he created a pattern of gory spiderwebs, weaving them from one almost totally exposed breast to the other.

"Tough job," Graham joked. "Imagine having to do that for a living."

"You mean they do this all the time?"

"No. The rest of the year, they usually stick to portraits or faces, just like they did when you lived here. But anything goes today. It's the day the sane act crazy, and the weirdos become the norm."

"I'd almost forgotten. Remember our senior year, when the whole gang came down together? It was the only time in my four years in New Orleans that I got to spend Mardi Gras Day in the Quarter."

"I remember. Your father swooped you away every year to some ski resort or another. He'd let you go to the pre–Mardi Gras parades, but he wasn't about to let you experience the total iniquity of the big day."

"He was sorry he did that time. I had so much fun, you had to drag me home."

"It's high time you had that much fun again." Graham led her to a street-side bar. "I'll take a beer, a large one. What about you, Lins?"

"I'll have the same."

The man got their drinks, pouring them into plastic cups which already overflowed from the trash cans and lay trampled in the streets. "I'd hate to have to clean this mess," she lamented, stepping over one of the plastic mountains at the curb.

They paused to join a group of people in front of a lone musician who was blowing a jazzy rendition of the "Mardi Gras Mambo." Graham grabbed Lindsey's hand and pulled her into the street.

"What are you doing?"

"Dancing with my lover." He whispered the words in her ear, his warm breath shooting pleasurable goose bumps down her neck. He twirled her around, evaporating her last shreds of inhibition like magic. People were staring, and her beer was jostling from her cup, spraying her shoes and the ground around them. She couldn't have cared less.

The wilder they danced, the faster the musician played, until they were spinning madly like a top set free. At last the music stopped, and Graham gave her a finishing twirl, swinging her into his arms. Heat rushed to her face as the world stopped spinning and she realized what a crowd they had drawn.

And then Graham kissed her. Right on the street in front of everybody. Their audience went wild, clapping and cheering. Graham bowed low, the star of the show, the star of her life. He threw an arm around her and led her away, while the musician started a new song.

"You've added a new step or two to your repertoire since the last time I danced with you," she said teasingly.

"And everything I've got belongs to you."

This was a new Graham, totally different from the one she had lived with the past few days. Today he was free-wheeling and dizzily exciting. Traces of the heart-stopping hotshot quarterback of her past were beginning to break the surface of his work-hardened exterior.

"Are you hungry?" Graham asked.

She stopped, suddenly aware of the odors wafting from the nearby restaurant. The scents of fried oysters and pungent Cajun spices did strange things to her stomach and made her mouth water in anticipation. She suddenly realized how little she had eaten the past few days.

"I'm starving."

The restaurant was relatively uncrowded, considering

the throngs of people who paraded the streets. The hostess led them down a narrow hall to an outside patio, complete with birds in a stunted tree and scavenging pigeons at their feet.

They had made their choices from the limited menu long before the harried waitress arrived. "We'll split an oyster po'boy and each take a cup of the seafood gumbo," Graham explained.

"You want the po'boys dressed?"

"No, not for me," Graham answered. "I want nothing but oysters and mayo, lots of mayo. But dress the other half. Lots of tomatoes."

Lindsey relaxed against the back of the iron garden chair. Funny the things one remembered. Graham remembered how she liked her po'boys. She'd remembered he liked his coffee black, and the way he slumped his shoulders and stuck his hands in his pockets when he was thinking about unpleasant things. Just the way he was doing right now.

"What's the matter, Graham? A few minutes ago you were dancing in the street. Now you look like the morning after."

"I was just thinking about what Katie said about someone prying through her things. I'm sorry, Lins. I promised you an afternoon of fun, and here I go bringing up the case again." He reached across the table and gathered her hands in his. "You need to think about nothing today except having fun. And about me, of course."

Lindsey chose to ignore his advice. He'd brought the subject up. Now it was on her mind, too, so she might as well ask the questions that wouldn't go away.

"I'll officially start a recess from the case when the food arrives," she promised. "Now, who do you think is snooping around the LeBlanc mansion?"

"I wish I knew. It could be anybody. Katie LeBlanc makes it easy, inviting everybody and their brother-in-law over for some party or another every day. She has the worst case of Mardi Gras madness I've ever seen in a grown woman."

"She is a fun-loving sort," Lindsey agreed.

"Fun loving? We're fun loving. She's a party junkie. They should have recovery centers for people like her. I've all but ordered her to stop entertaining on such a grand scale until the murder case is solved and we have some leads on the jewelry theft. I might as well be whistling into the wind."

."The two crimes have to be related."

"Seems reasonable. But proof would be nice. Right now there is still nothing to go on in the jewel theft. We have tracers out all across the country, but nothing has shown up anywhere."

"I think the jewels are hidden somewhere in the LeBlanc house."

"I'd be inclined to agree with you, if we hadn't already searched every square inch of the place with a fine-tooth comb."

Graham drummed a restless tattoo on the checkered tablecloth. "The most obvious scenario would be that Garon stole the key and took the blonde to the house. She broke into the safe, but instead of giving him the jewels, she hid them somewhere and wouldn't tell him where. He lost his temper and stuck the dagger through her heart."

"Meaning she had to hide the jewels somewhere in the house."

"Right. But what puzzles me is where Garon was while Roxanne was hiding the jewels. If he took her there, it seems he would have been in on the whole operation. And now she's dead, and Garon is in jail. So who in hell, if anybody, is snooping around the Le-Blancs'?''

''Suppose it wasn't Garon. Suppose…''

''While you're supposing Garon is innocent, how about supposing how his fingerprints got on the trunk of your car and all over the suitcase that held the bloody ball gown? And how about supposing why Garon stole the key in the first place, and why he was immediately identified in the lineup as the guy who picked up the costumes under a false name.''

''Okay. But he might have been set up. Someone else might have pulled off the crime and found a way to make it look like Garon did it. He doesn't seem capable of masterminding an operation like that.''

''No, but Roxanne was.''

''That still leaves us with no explanation for why someone is rifling through everything in the house, or where the jewels are now.''

The waitress appeared with two steaming cups of gumbo. Lindsey dabbled with her spoon, breaking the surface of the pool of liquid. She drew tiny circles in the thick concoction of brown roux, seafood and fluffy rice, but her mind continued to dwell on unanswered questions.

''Tell me again about Thomas's alibi,'' she asked, not quite ready to keep her promise to let the matter drop.

''He arrived at the airport at 8:10. It would have taken him at least fifty minutes to get to the LeBlancs'. The murder took place at approximately nine o'clock, as near as we can pin it down from reports of when float number seven would have been in front of the LeBlancs'.''

''Fifty minutes after he arrived in New Orleans.''

"Fifty minutes after his plane touched down. It takes a while to deboard and get to your car."

"But, given optimal conditions, it is possible that he could have arrived at the LeBlancs' in time for the murder."

"Given optimal conditions, he could have *arrived.* But I can't imagine his having time to drive there, change into a soldier's costume, stage a robbery and commit a murder. But that's not all of the alibi."

"I know. A houseful of people swear he arrived at a party at *exactly* nine o'clock. He was there with his little brunette until we saw him the next day. She swears to that. So he would have had no opportunity to dispose of the body or clean up the murder scene."

"Right. He arrived and someone said, 'Look who finally made it.' Just at that time, the clock in the entrance hall struck nine o'clock. Thomas laughed and made some comment about how for him it was still early."

"Maybe the clock is slow."

"We checked it. It's right on time."

Graham spooned a mouthful of the spicy soup and then shook in another drop or two of Tabasco.

"But suppose…"

"No more supposing for now, Lins. We made a pact. One afternoon of fun. We deserve it. Tomorrow's problems will come soon enough."

He placed one hand under the table, resting it on her thigh. "An afternoon of fun, and a night of heaven." Leaning over, he brushed his lips across hers. "Now eat up. You're going to need plenty of energy for all I have in mind."

Lindsey worked at complying with Graham's wishes. Surprisingly enough, she was almost successful, thanks to the disarming presence of the sexy detective and the mouth-watering taste of the overstuffed sandwiches.

When the last bite was finished, he glanced at his watch. ''Now that you're fortified, are you ready to hit Bourbon Street?''

''As ready as I'll ever be.''

Graham paid the check, and they headed back to the street.

The crowd was thick even before they reached Bourbon, but nothing like the mass of people who crowded onto the world-famous street. The overhanging balconies were maxed out, lined with double and triple layers of revelers. Many were in bizarre costumes, but some were just there to look.

They inched forward. A girl in a see-through Little Red Riding Hood costume had stopped in the middle of the street, and eager amateur photographers were all but fighting for a close-up shot.

''Hold on to my hand,'' Graham yelled above the noise. ''But if we get separated, go to the next corner and wait for me.''

She clutched his hand tightly. The crowd was pushing into her now, carrying her along with the flow. Someone's drink splashed on her shirt, and she tried to back away. She couldn't. There was no room to move.

The crowd surged forward, and she gasped for breath. They were jammed in like cattle being herded through the narrow street. Only instead of mindless cattle, she was being carried along on a wave of people so intent on partying, they were laughing and drinking their way through the threat of stampede.

People brushed by in a blur. Lindsey turned, and her heart took a sickening plunge. A few steps behind her, the painted mouth of a rubber mask grinned at her above the crowd. It was the same wrinkled representation of an old man she had seen earlier. She held on to Graham's hand and pushed closer to him.

Finally they maneuvered past the action, and once again there was room to breathe, to walk side by side, to choose your own course. She stepped back to catch her breath and to watch the steady flow of incredible sights.

Little Bo Peep came by, with a real sheep trailing along behind her. A masked man in green medical scrubs carried a sign that offered free breast exams. The Phantom of the Opera dragged by them, his shoulders drooping from the weight of a bulky chandelier headpiece that looked as if it might topple at any moment. And a family of clowns marched single file, pulling a baby clown in a decorated wagon.

"Has it changed in ten years?" Graham asked.

"Not the outlandish costumes. Not even the uninhibited freedom. But the size of the crowds has. It was pretty rough back there for a few yards."

"Yeah. The police try to keep everybody moving, but it happens like that sometimes. One person puts on a show, and all of a sudden everyone stops to stare. But, amazing as it seems, Mardi Gras's still one of the safest places to be. The few injuries that are reported are usually minor."

"Look at that," Lindsey shouted, pointing to a man completely covered in tattoos. At least it appeared that way, from what she could see. And since he was wearing nothing but a pair of skimpy briefs, she could see a lot more than she wanted.

"All those needles stuck in your body to paint pictures." Graham groaned. "It hurts just to think about it."

They slowed to a crawl as the crowd came to another standstill. A band inside a local hangout was blasting away, its music carrying into the street for half a block or more. A few couples had stopped to dance, and one scantily clad woman was putting on her own show.

An unexpected shudder snaked up Lindsey's spine as the crowds pushed in around them. She stuck as close to Graham as possible, squeezing his hand for reassurance. The crowd surged suddenly and then came to an abrupt stop.

A man came by pushing a young woman in a wheel-chair. The sign she carried read Throw Beads. I'm From Ohio And This Is My First Mardi Gras. The mountain of carnival throws piled on her chair evidenced the giving nature of the crowd.

Lindsey dropped Graham's hand to give them room to roll through.

A tall man in coveralls followed them through the opening, a dozen or more empty cereal boxes attached to his clothes. The miniature boxes were mangled and torn, and a large metal spoon dangled from a chain around his neck. A cereal killer.

Her hands grew clammy. Even as a joke, the idea was hard for her to take, after the week she'd just been through. She looked over her shoulder. A short guy in a bright green, purple and gold shirt smiled broadly at her, but Graham was nowhere in sight.

She worked her way to the outside edge of the side-walk. It was roomier there—more chance for her to find Graham again. Her gaze scanned the crowd. A tall soldier squeezed past her and stopped, his eyes peering into hers from only inches away. A shock of black hair dipped over his right eye.

Her heart constricted painfully. For a moment, just a moment, she could have sworn it was the killer. Now she really was imagining things. Maybe the psychologist was right. If innocent faces in a Mardi Gras crowd made her shiver in terror, she was losing it.

The next corner, was what Graham had said. Just go to the next corner and wait. Thank goodness he'd had the foresight to make emergency plans. Otherwise she might never have found him in the ever-growing crush of humanity.

Easing around a group of teenagers, Lindsey turned and scanned the crowd again. Her pulse quickened. The same man she had noticed earlier was following a few steps behind her, his fast-moving pace another reminder that the person behind the mask was not old.

She pushed on, determined to find Graham. Her adrenaline was flowing freely now, but there was no way to increase her speed without running over the slow-moving revelers. She ducked inside an open door. Her nervous stomach lurched at the overpowering stench of beer and bodies crushed inside the tiny bar.

A strong hand clutched her elbow. Her breath coming in jagged gulps, she forced herself to turn around. The rubber smile was there, just as she'd known it would be, but the eyes gleaming through the dark holes of the mask were alive and flashing.

"Why are you following me?" She forced the words past the lump that blocked her throat.

"Garon Oleander is innocent." His words were slurred, and he reeked of sweat and whiskey.

"Who are you?"

"It doesn't matter who *I* am. It matters that you are trying to pin a murder rap on an innocent man."

"If you know something…"

A crowd of people pushed in between Lindsey and the man. She grabbed for his arm, but he pulled it away and ducked back into the crowd.

"Wait," she insisted. "You can't go yet."

By the time she could push her way back to the spot by the door, he had disappeared.

Lindsey rubbed her hands across the rough denim of her jeans. Her palms were sweaty, but an icy shudder still lingered in her heart.

She hurried outside. All she wanted now was to find Graham, to feel the comfort of his arms about her, to hear the conviction in his voice when he reassured her that he'd arrested the right man.

He was waiting for her at the corner, frantically stretching his neck to see above the crowd. "What happened to you?" he questioned. "One minute you were right by my side, the next you had disappeared."

"Just the crowd. When I realized we were separated, I headed for the corner, like you said."

"It took you a long time. I was about to hit the panic button. I guess this week has gotten to me more than I thought."

"I'm sorry. I stopped to talk to someone for just a minute."

Graham wrapped an arm about her shoulders and hugged her close. "Are you all right, Lins? You look pale, and you're shaking."

"I'm fine, but I'd like to go home now." Home. Away from this madness, she could tell him about her encounter with the drunk in the rubber mask. "I'd rather spend the rest of Mardi Gras Day with you, just you."

"Sounds like my kind of celebration."

He tipped her head toward his and kissed her hard on the lips. She leaned against his strong chest, letting his love wash over her while she kissed him back. It was Mardi Gras. Who'd notice?

THE NOISE *outside the window was deafening.* "*Damn revelers,*" *he cursed, his voice echoing about the high ceilings and reverberating off the walls. He peeled the rubber mask from his face and hurled it across the room. The restless pacing took over then, sweat pouring from his brow, in spite of the increasing coolness of approaching night.*

*Garon was taking the rap, but things were not going as planned. The lousy cops only had enough evidence to arrest, not to convict. Garon was supposed to be a temporary scapegoat, a ploy to buy time.*

*But things were not looking good. The paper was saying Garon would likely get life, maybe even the chair. He cracked his knuckles. Everything was out of control.*

*If it were up to him, he'd blow this town right now. But he couldn't. And just hanging around here was driving him nuts. The jewels would have to show up soon. If they didn't, who knew what would happen next?*

*He'd already killed one woman from the float. Tonight, to show them Garon was innocent, there'd be another. It wasn't what he wanted, but he couldn't stop it. Not anymore. Everything was out of his control.*

*He shook a handful of aspirin into his hands and downed them in a single gulp. They wouldn't help for long. He knew that now.*

*Out of control. Out of control. Out of control. The words pounded in his head like Roxy's heart had done right before it stopped for the last time.*

## Chapter Thirteen

Ash Wednesday dawned gray and murky. A cloud cover hung low over the city, its somber presence another reminder that carnival was past and winter had a few more blows to deliver before allowing spring to break through.

Lindsey stared out the window of Graham's second-floor apartment and watched a group of well-heeled matrons stroll by, their foreheads dotted with the ashes that symbolized the beginning of Lent. The bawdy riotousness of Mardi Gras, followed by the season of religious traditions. It all walked hand in hand in New Orleans. Another facet of the city's universal appeal.

A horn blared from a passing car, jolting Lindsey back into the present. An answering horn took up the challenge. Everybody had their own agendas as they rushed to start work and school and the thousand-and-one other duties that took people out on a day like this.

For Graham, it had begun much earlier. He had wakened Lindsey only to give her a goodbye kiss and to thank her for staying one more day.

She would have stayed anyway. She already had plans, but it still warmed her heart to know how much he wanted her around. She was having lunch today with Grace Ann, Angela, Brigit and the rest of the Dominican

Daredevils from float number seven. Once again they were all safe to go on with their lives as before. Only this time, one would be missing.

The timorous quaking that always accompanied such thoughts attacked again. Lindsey stuck her head through the swing-out window and gulped in a large quantity of the still air. She had to focus on the positive. Graham was certain he had his man.

Lindsey raised her crockery mug to her lips and drained the last drops of the strong coffee-and-chicory brew. It warmed her spirits and eased the doubts that troubled her heart. Even the coffee in New Orleans was different from anywhere else in the world. Strange that she had been through so much here the past few days and yet she was not ready to return to Nashville.

The truth was plain and simple. As the song said, she knew what it meant to miss New Orleans. It was a city of a thousand ills, but it also offered a million pleasures. Not the least of which was Detective Graham Dufour.

Slipping from her silk kimono, she opened the drawer and pulled out a pair of lacy undies and a matching bra. She laid them on the bed and headed for the shower. She had a busy day coming up. After lunch, she had an appointment with an old friend at Tulane Medical Center, a meeting that might lead to career-changing possibilities.

The water was already running when the jangling phone cut through Lindsey's thoughts. Pulling a towel around her, she raced back to the bedroom.

''Hello.''

''Lindsey.''

The voice on the other end was hesitant, empty. She opened her mouth to respond, but icy dread froze her nerves and paralyzed her muscles.

''Lindsey, are you there?''

"What's wrong, Grace Ann?" The words finally came, but they were the wrong words. She didn't want to know what was wrong. The hollow pain in her friend's voice had already told her far too much.

"It's Brigit. She's been stabbed."

No. It wasn't possible. The danger was all behind them. Lindsey opened her eyes wide, knowing that if she could make herself wake up, the nightmare would have to go away. It didn't work.

"Is she—?" Lindsey stopped. She couldn't bring herself to say the word.

"She's alive. Barely." Grace Ann's voice broke on the words. "A policeman found her, the one who had been pulled from her case. He'd stopped in at daybreak, just to check on her. A crazy hunch, he said. A crazy hunch." Grace Ann was repeating the words as if in a trance, her voice little more than a shaky whisper.

A low curse escaped Lindsey's lips. "How did it happen?"

"When she didn't answer her door, the policeman broke in. He found her sprawled across her bed, choking in a pool of blood. That's all they're saying."

Lindsey's own blood ran cold, with an icy sting that shocked her senses and wrung her heart into a twisted knot. "No. There must be some mistake," she pleaded, knowing the only mistake had been hers. She had brought this curse on her dearest friends.

"There's no mistake. Call Graham, Lindsey. Make him do something. Make him stop the…" Tears muffled the rest of Grace Ann's words, but not the sound of the receiver banging back into the cradle.

But tears didn't come to Lindsey. Nothing came that would offer any release. Instead, she moved like a zombie through the apartment that had only a few hours ago been filled with the sounds of love.

She dialed Graham's number. The phone rang several times before she dropped the receiver back into place. There was no sense in calling, anyway. He would have already heard the heart-wrenching news.

Numbly she slipped into bulky sweats and pushed her hair behind her ears without looking into a mirror. She didn't want to see her empty reflection staring back at her. Grabbing the key to Grace Ann's car, she stepped into her shoes and dragged herself out the door.

THE EMERGENCY SIREN and flashing lights on Graham's car screamed their eerie warning as he dashed in and around cars, stopping only when he absolutely had to. It wasn't the job that pushed him to flirt with danger in his rush to arrive on the scene. It was the clawing guilt deep in his gut.

He had been so cocksure of his own intuitions, his own ability to read evidence and criminals, that he had dismissed all of Lindsey's fears. Garon was not the man— she'd told him that over and over. But he'd been far too arrogant to listen.

He'd even written off her story of the masked man on Bourbon Street proclaiming Garon's innocence. A crackpot, he'd thought, or a friend of Garon's.

His way or no way. She'd said that to him once. Now he'd proven her right. He'd pay with a guilt that would live forever in his heart. Brigit would probably pay with her life.

"Damn!" The curse rolled from his lips as he beat a clenched fist on the steering wheel. "I thought we had our man."

"Yeah. We had our case practically locked away. Now

we're back to square one." Fury clung like leeches to Rooster's voice. "But we'll get him."

"We'll get him, all right, if I have to chase him to the ends of the miserable earth." Graham rounded the corner and screeched to a halt. He cursed again when he saw one of the local TV crews already setting up their cameras.

"How do they do it? We ought to put them in charge of the investigations. They're always the first ones on the scene," Graham grumbled, climbing out from behind the wheel and slamming his car door shut.

A pretty reporter stuck a microphone in his face. "Do you know who attacked the woman?"

"For the record, no comment." He smiled obligingly. She flicked her camera and mike off and started to move away. "Off the record, get your people out of my way. We're here to investigate a murder attempt, not to play a ratings game."

"Then it was attempted murder?"

"When we find a girl with a knife rammed through her, we usually assume it wasn't a friendly game of darts."

She turned and marched away, her high heels clicking on the pavement.

Rooster caught up with him. "Isn't that the car Lindsey's been driving parked in front of the house next door?"

"Oh, no..." A string of low curses flew from Graham's lips, and every muscle in his body coiled into a tight spring. "Looks like Officer Green made it to the scene before we did, too."

"You know, partner, I think you better marry that girl quick, before she takes your job."

"You may just have a point."

Lindsey met him on the porch. He wanted to clobber her for rushing in where she had no business being. He opened his mouth to speak, but one look stopped him cold. Shock and grief had turned her complexion a ghostly white. She looked so young, so vulnerable, standing there. The urge to clobber vanished. Now he only longed to take her in his arms.

He couldn't. He had no way of knowing who was watching. Maybe even the killer, who might have found out by now that one of the riders on float number seven was Lindsey Latham, the ex-girlfriend of Detective Dufour, the girl now posing as Officer Green.

Ex-girlfriend. Past, current and always love of his life. He stepped in front of her and caressed her with his eyes. She would understand. She understood so many things.

"How did you find out?" His voice broke on the simple question, the pain in her eyes striking a new blow to his heart.

"A neighbor called Grace Ann. She called me."

"Are you all right?"

"No, Graham. I'm not all right."

"I'll get another officer to take you home, and I don't want you out of his sight. Do you understand?"

"And the others? What's to happen to my friends?"

"Their protection has been restored. I called for it on my way over here." He touched his hand to hers. "I'm sorry, Lins. I was so sure Garon was the man."

"It's not your fault, Graham. It's mine. I'm the only one who could have stopped this mindless killing. And I didn't."

"Don't say such things. You're just upset. The police let Brigit down. I let her down. Not you. You must never blame yourself." His voice broke on his words. Not only because this attempted killing might have been prevented if he had trusted Lindsey's intuitions, but because of the painful blame she was piling on herself.

"Go ahead, join Rooster and the others," she insisted, her voice amazingly strong. "You have a murder to investigate."

"Okay, I'll be home as soon as I can. We'll talk then." He started through the front door. "We're going to catch him, Lins. I promise you that."

"I know we will, Graham. Tonight, I'll tell you how."

She was in shock. That was the only explanation. Poor baby, she had every reason to be. "Don't move from the porch, Lindsey, not until I release you to the officer."

"No, I'll be right here."

He hated to leave her like this, but he had to get to work. First impressions were often the key that unlocked the secrets. He walked inside the house, and immediately everything except the investigation disappeared from his mind. It was the only way.

LINDSEY STRETCHED to the top of Graham's bedroom closet and pulled her overnight bag from the shelf. Hands shaking, she took panties and bras from the drawer in Graham's dresser and smoothed them into the bag. Then she went to the closet and took down her jeans and a couple of sweaters. Hopefully, she'd only need enough to last a few days.

This was what she should have done in the very beginning. If she had, Danielle would be alive and Brigit wouldn't be fighting for her life. She reached for the cup of hot tea the young policeman had brought her and took a soothing sip.

Graham had called a few minutes ago to check on her and to tell her he was on his way home. She was glad. She needed to see him, needed to feel his strong arms about her. Besides, the sooner she broke the news to him, the sooner he could start the preparations for putting her plan into action.

She tucked a pair of slippers inside the pocket of the overnight bag as Graham's key turned in the front door. Taking a deep breath, she prepared herself for the battle that was about to begin.

Graham would argue. He would rant and rave. He might even issue his famous ultimatum. His way or no way. But her mind was made up. Nothing he could say or do would change it. The killer wanted her, not the others. She planned to make sure he found her.

Graham pushed through the bedroom door. In two long strides, he reached her and took her in his arms, rocking her to him, holding her as if he'd never let her go. "I'm sorry about this, Lins. I would never have dropped the protection if I'd had any idea this might happen." He buried his face in her hair.

"I know that, Graham." She pulled away from him and dropped to the bed.

He sat down beside her, his hand reaching for hers and clutching it tightly. His gaze caught sight of the half-packed suitcase. "You're not going anywhere, Lindsey. Not now. Not after what happened to Brigit." He curled his arms around her. "I know this is hell for you, but I can't let you go back to Nashville. You have to be here, so I can protect you." Anguish roughened his voice and dulled the spark in his eyes.

"I want you to listen to everything I have to say, Graham. And promise you won't interrupt me until I'm through."

"Of course I'll listen."

"And no interruptions. I want a promise."

He pushed a curl back from her forehead, his fingers warm on her skin. "I promise."

She kept her voice calm while she outlined her plan in detail. As she spoke, anger and frustration turned Graham's face a thousand shades of red.

"Absolutely not. I can understand you're upset, but you're talking out of our head."

"You promised to let me finish."

"You *are* finished. I don't want to hear another word of this." He jumped up from the bed and paced the room, his hands knotted into fists, the veins in his neck and face extended as if he might explode at any minute.

Lindsey got up and walked to the kitchen. There was no use in arguing when he was in this kind of mood. Graham stamped in behind her.

"I know you're trying to help, Lins, but your suggestions are out of the question. There is no way I can allow you to do something so dangerous."

She twirled around to face him. "It's not your call, Graham. It's mine. You can rant and rave all you want, but you can't stop me. I'm the one the killer wants. It's time he found me."

"This is totally crazy. Insane. You've let this Officer Green facade go to your head and ferment."

She had expected an argument from him, but he wasn't even trying to see things her way. "It's not crazy," she explained, deliberately keeping her voice low. One raving maniac in the house was enough. "It's the only sensible thing to do."

"Okay, you tell me—how in the world can announcing to the killer that you are the witness be sensible? And to top it off, you expect me to let you move into the turret to make it easier for him to find you?"

"I didn't ask you to let me do anything. I asked you

to protect me while I'm there. When the killer shows up, you nab him. It's as simple as that.''

"Simple? If it were so simple to nab a killer, I'd have done it already." His voice rose again, and his face was returning to the shade of bright red it had been in the bedroom. "And just suppose your little scheme goes awry. Then what? You'll be living bait for a psycho." He slammed his fist into the kitchen counter. "Just forget it, Lins. It's not going to happen. Never. No way!"

"Do you have a better idea?"

"We're working on the case."

"You've been working on it for almost two weeks, and all you have is speculative evidence against a man who may not have had anything to do with this. He's definitely innocent of the latest murder attempt. He was in jail when it happened." She walked to his side and took his hand in hers. "I don't want to argue with you, Graham. I only want you to understand. I *have* to do this."

She stared into his eyes. They were pleading with her, begging her to give in. She turned away.

"I do understand, Lins. But I can't let you do it. And even if I went along with it, you can't just set up a murder trap in a private home."

"You can if the lady of the house gives her permission."

She started to walk away, but he wrapped his hand around her arm, pulling her to him. "You didn't ask her?"

"I did. And she said yes."

"Dammit, Lins. You leave me no choice. I hate to have to do this, but if it's the only way to stop you from this insane game, so be it."

"What are you talking about?"

"I'm calling your father. If I can't talk some sense into you, maybe he can."

"You're what?" She couldn't believe her ears. She'd expected a lot of resistance from Graham, but nothing like this. Especially not from him. "My father is half a world away, Graham. Telling him would only make him sick with worry. But it wouldn't stop me."

"The department will never go along with this, Lindsey." He changed tactics, dropping to a kitchen chair and lowering his voice. Lindsey braced herself for his next round of arguments.

"The department will refuse to provide protection for such a harebrained scheme. The only way they'll consider it is if we get a policewoman to serve as bait."

"Then I guess I'll be on my own, Graham. Katie is going to leak my identity. She's already told Ruby and Thomas. Pretty soon the killer will know, too, if he doesn't already."

"And just what did you tell Katie, besides the fact that you're the witness and you'll be moving into her turret with an engraved invitation for the killer to join you?"

"I told her the truth."

"I doubt that."

"Well, part of the truth."

"Which part?" His eyes bored into hers. But the fire that had sizzled during his recent tirade had cooled to something far more ominous.

"I told her I was not with the homicide division, that I was new on the force. You only let me come with you the first day because I had been riding in the Minerva parade the night before, on float number seven. I was the one who had seen someone murdered in her turret." A shudder shook her body. The realization of what she was doing, what she had to do, washed over her in frightening waves.

Graham dropped to the chair beside her and took her shaking hands in his. "The killer knows there was no Officer Green on float number seven. It's not going to work, Lins. Just let me handle this."

"But there was an Officer Green on the float. She's a friend of Grace Ann's. That's why, when Lindsey Latham couldn't make it, Janice Green was asked to take her place."

"No one's going to buy that story, Lins. It's better to leave things as they are. The protection's been restored to everybody. No one else will be hurt. You have my promise."

Graham walked to the counter and popped a cork on a bottle of red wine. Filling a slender glass to the top, he placed it in her hands. "Why don't you drink this and get some rest? We'll talk in the morning, when the shock has worn off."

Lindsey sucked in her breath, girding her strength about her. She couldn't weaken, couldn't give in to Graham's arguments. Nor to his temper tantrums or even his rational pleadings. It was too late for compromise.

"Katie's already bought the story, Graham. In fact, she wasn't surprised at all. She said Thomas and Ruby had both speculated that something was fishy about me. I wasn't hardened enough to be in the homicide division."

"And they're right. You're not hard at all. You're sweet and innocent. And I plan to keep you that way." He twirled his fingers through her hair. "Let's go to bed, Lins. We're both too tired to think. And way too tired to fight."

"There's nothing to think about." Sadness mingled with fear, tearing at Lindsey's resolve. She hated to do this to the man she loved. She hated to do it to herself. If there were only some other way. But there wasn't.

"Katie's leaving for Rome tomorrow, Graham, and I'm moving into the turret. She said Thomas was going to be staying elsewhere. The official story she's telling everyone is that I'm a rookie on the force and that she's hired me to guard her house while she's out of town."

"It won't work, Lins, but I'm not going to argue the point any further tonight. We'll talk in the morning."

"Fine, Graham, but after we do, you need to set the wheels in motion for a stakeout. Because if you don't there'll be no one to catch the killer when he comes for the bait."

THE SOFA in the circular turret had been opened and transformed into a queen-size bed, piled high with fluffy pillows. Lindsey lay between the satiny sheets and watched the moonlight spill through the open curtains. Outside, parked nearby in the dark, Graham was keeping watch.

"Lindsey, are you still awake?" Graham's voice was barely a whisper.

"I'm awake," she answered just as softly, knowing the microphone taped to her chest picked up the slightest sounds.

"Are you sure you want to go through with this?"

"I'm sure I have to. Do you think—?" She couldn't put words to the fear that was running rampant through her senses.

"I don't expect anything to happen tonight, if that's what you're asking. Unless this is a very foolish killer, he probably realizes he's being set up. And I don't think our guy is foolish."

"Do you think he might not come at all?"

"No, Lins. He'll come. I'd stake my life on it, though I wish like hell I'd be wrong again, the way I was about Garon."

"You just don't think it will be tonight?"

"I think it will be when we least expect it. The culprit's an insider. I'd still bet on that. He'll know everything. When you eat. When you sleep. When you let down your guard for half an instant. He'll know I'm out here somewhere, but he'll still be watching for his chance."

"I'm not afraid, Graham," she lied, almost convincing herself. "Not with you watching over me."

"I could be much closer. I could be in your bed, holding you in my arms. All you have to do is say the word. I'm only seconds away."

His soothing voice, the reassurance of his words, washed over her like a warm ocean spray. "You know that's not possible. Even a stupid murderer is not going to strike when a police officer is in bed with the victim."

"With the *intended* victim. Nothing is going to happen to the woman I love."

"Good night, Graham. I'm going to try to get some sleep."

"Sleep tight, baby. Remember, the slightest sound, and I'll come running."

Lindsey laid her head on the pillow, fearing to close her eyes. While she slept, all alone in the dreaded turret, the faceless man would come to her again. Only tonight the nightmare might be real.

## Chapter Fourteen

Lindsey slipped out the door of the turret. She had made it safely through the night, just as Graham had predicted, but she was unbelievably tired. Sleep had eluded her, but, thankfully, so had the terrifying nightmare.

Opening her umbrella and holding it up to ward off the driving rain, Lindsey carefully made her way down the slippery metal steps. Ruby was working during the day, just as she always did when the LeBlancs left town. Caution had been taken to make everything look as normal as possible. She was even cooking, and she had called on the intercom to say breakfast was ready.

Lindsey was happy to accept the invitation. She needed a temporary escape from the circular trap that would be her home from now until the murderer was caught. Last night, even with Graham's voice whispering reassurances in her ear, fear had hovered over the room, as thick and as suffocating as deadly smoke.

Lindsey ducked in through the side door and walked into the family dining area. The table was already set with silver and china and one rose in a crystal vase. Social amenities could never be overlooked in the LeBlanc household, not even in the midst of a deadly hunt.

Lindsey took a seat and poured herself a cup of coffee

from the silver pot. Seconds later, Ruby appeared with a plate of sausage and scrambled eggs and two buttery biscuits.

"It looks delicious, Ruby. Thanks for inviting me down to eat."

"I always serve breakfast to houseguests," she answered quietly. Her voice was strained, and her eyes were red and swollen. She started to walk out of the room, then stopped. "My son Garon has been released from jail. He would like to talk to you."

"I'm not on this case anymore. Didn't Mrs. LeBlanc tell you?"

Ruby clasped her hands together, nervously tangling them into knots. "Yes, but he says he'll only talk to you. The male policemen frighten him."

"Is he here now?"

"No, but he will be by the time you've finished eating. He's upset. He needs to talk." Head down, Ruby walked from the dining room, leaving Lindsey to her food.

It was twenty minutes later before Ruby returned with fresh coffee and Garon. "Is there anything else I can get you?" she asked, removing Lindsey's half-eaten breakfast from the table.

"No. I guess I don't have much of an appetite these days."

Ruby took Garon's hand and pulled him closer to the table. "My son has a confession to make," she explained, sorrow adding a scratchy edge to her voice. "He didn't tell the police the whole truth when he was in jail. I know *you* can understand that."

Lindsey felt the burn from her accusing words. She hadn't told Ruby the truth about why she had come to the LeBlancs on that first day, and Ruby had not forgiven her. Especially since her youngest son had been arrested for the murder Lindsey had witnessed.

"Tell her, Garon. And this time tell the truth. You can't keep protecting people who use you, even if they are family."

"Your mother's right, Garon," Lindsey pleaded. "Two women are dead, and now another one is fighting desperately for her life. If you know anything that will help us find the killer, you must tell us."

"I don't want anyone to die. That's why I have to tell you." He shuffled his feet and looked to his mother for support.

"Tell us what?" Lindsey urged.

"My brother Jerome knows something about Roxy's murder."

Ruby winced in anguish, but she didn't back away. "Tell her everything, Garon. It's the only way we can help your brother."

"I put that green dress in the trunk of a car," he continued. "But I didn't know it was yours. Really I didn't. I only did what Jerome told me to do."

"Where did you get the dress?" Lindsey kept her voice as calm as possible. Garon was running scared. It wouldn't take much to make him ignore his mother's prodding and retreat back into his wall of silence.

"Roxy told me to go to Dumas's shop and pick up two costumes a friend of hers had ordered. I forgot the name, but I knew it then. Roxy wrote it down and gave it to me. She said I always forgot everything, so she wrote it down."

"What happened after you picked up the costumes?"

"I took them to her house. She was packing her clothes in a suitcase, and she was drinking beer and laughing really loud."

Ruby wrapped her arms around her son's trembling shoulders. "It's okay, son. Just tell Officer Green everything. This will be over soon."

"She said she was leaving town that night, and she wouldn't be back. She wouldn't ever have to put up with stupid people like me again. Stupid people like me. That's what she said."

"Why didn't you tell this to the detectives when they questioned you before?"

"Because Jerome made me promise I wouldn't say anything. He said if I just kept quiet, he could get me out of all of this. If I squealed on him, he said he'd make sure I went to jail forever. He'd do it, too. When Jerome gets mad at you, he doesn't forget. Just like when he got mad at mean old man LeBlanc."

"When was that, Garon?"

"When we were little. Old Mr. LeBlanc told Mama that Jerome couldn't come to this house anymore. And Jerome just doesn't forget. He still talks bad about him."

"Who is mean old Mr. LeBlanc, Garon?"

Ruby answered the question for her son. "It's a long story. I used to bring the boys here with me when they were young. Richard LeBlanc, the current Richard's grandfather, was old and totally senile. He and Garon played games together."

"Jerome didn't play fair," Garon volunteered, "so old Mr. LeBlanc wouldn't let him play with us."

"After a while, the older Mr. LeBlanc got so upset if I brought Jerome with me that I would have to take him home. Jerome was hurt. He wanted to come to the big house and be with his mother and younger brother. He never got over being left behind."

He didn't forgive, so fifteen years later, he stole the LeBlanc family jewels. It was a bizarre story, but for some reason, Lindsey believed Ruby and Garon. Maybe because she just wanted things to be over. If Jerome was the killer in the soldier suit, then the end was in sight.

"Where is Jerome now, Ruby?"

"I don't know. I haven't seen him since Mardi Gras Day. No one has."

Lindsey walked to the window and looked out. A streak of lightning cut through the deep gray of the skies, its jagged light darting and striking its target the way the deadly dagger had a week ago.

A lifetime ago.

"Will I be in trouble for lying to the police?" Garon asked, his voice as innocent as a child's.

"I don't know, Garon. But you told us now, and that helps. It helps a lot." Lindsey walked over to Ruby. "You know I have to tell Detective Dufour all of this, don't you?"

"I know. But telling it to you was easier on Garon. He's a good boy. He just gets mixed up with the wrong people. And he loves his brother." She wiped her hand across her eyes, catching an escaping tear. "We both do."

Lindsey placed her arm around Ruby's shoulders, the woman's sadness pulling at her heart. Ruby loved her sons, both of them. What woman could blame her for that?

It was still raining when Lindsey climbed the slippery steps to the turret. The room would be silent and lonely, but she would be able to talk to Graham. For now, that would have to be enough.

THE REST OF THE DAY passed quietly and in a world of lonesome silence. Lindsey rattled around in the turret, thankful each time Graham or Rooster interrupted her to check on her status. She had house privileges, but there was no real reason to brave the pouring rain to visit a housekeeper with fears of her own. Especially when there was a microwave oven and a well-stocked minirefrigerator right there in the turret.

Lindsey started a novel, but she never made it past the first chapter. She couldn't shake the conversation with Ruby and Garon, not even after she'd explained it to Graham in detail. Jerome, dressed in a khaki uniform, his dark hair a striking contrast to the beautiful blonde he held in his arms. Was that the picture she'd seen the night of the parade?

His dark hair. That was the catch. His hair wasn't dark. He could have worn a wig that night, but why would he have? Even if he'd planned the murder, he certainly hadn't planned to have a witness.

She pictured his face and hair in her mind, just the way she remembered them from that first day at Ruby's house. His hair was short, bleached by the sun. His face had been bruised and swollen from the accident, and dark stubble had dotted his chin.

Blast it! How could she have been so stupid? Of course it had been Jerome. His face was injured, but not from a wrecked Harley. He'd probably fallen while trying to get Roxy down the inside staircase. That was how her dress had gotten ripped from waist to hem, and how his pants had left strings of khaki cloth wound around the nail that stuck from the ledge inside the turret door.

Dark hairs on his chin. Bleached hair on his head. But not from the sun. From a bottle of peroxide purchased at the corner drugstore.

The answers had been there all the time, locked away in her memory. But she'd ignored them, instead spending all her energy trying to prove Garon could not be the killer. She'd simply failed to home in on the truth.

It had taken Garon's confessions to do that.

Lindsey rested her head on the pillow. It was almost dark, and she was so tired. She closed her eyes and let the incessant dripping of the rain lull her to sleep.

WHEN Lindsey opened her eyes again, the gray light of day had dimmed into the eerie glow of streetlights glimmering through the rain. Impulsively she reached for the mike that was attached to her skin. It was still here, a tiny bit of plastic, all but hidden between her breasts. She breathed easier, knowing that lifeline to whoever stood guard was still intact.

"Graham."

"Is anything wrong?"

The response was instant, but it was Rooster's voice that answered.

"No. I just thought Graham might be there. If he was, I wanted to talk to him."

"He just left. He would have told you he was leaving, but you were sleeping soundly."

"How would you know that?"

"Your deep breathing, and that cute little snore."

"Did he say where he was going?"

"He sure did, and he said to let you know as soon as you woke. He got a call from the hospital."

"Not about Brigit. I mean, she's not…"

"Good news this time. She's not out of the woods yet, but she's awake and asking for Graham."

"What about Jerome? Have they found him?"

"No, but they will soon. Don't you worry. If he shows up here, I'll get him for you. I'd like to get the son of a— Anyway, I'd like to be the one to drop those cuffs around the murdering skunk, whoever it turns out to be.''

Lindsey eased from the bed and went to the bathroom for a big glass of water. She threw some cold drops in her face and finger-combed her hair into place.

''Do you want me to try to get Graham on the radio?''

''No. I'll wait. It's nothing important.''

''Okay. You take it easy up there, and don't worry a bit. I'm on duty down here, real close, and there's still a couple of other police cars cruising the area. All I have to do is radio them, and they'll be here in two shakes to help us. Not that we'll need them. If the Oleander boy or anyone else comes anywhere near here, it's *gotcha!*''

''Can you see the turret from where you're parked?''

''Clear as day. I'm watching the place like a hawk. I'll know if anyone sets foot on those back steps. And the way Graham has that house and balcony wired, no one can get past us.''

Reassured of her safety, Lindsey walked back through the turret. It was a lovely room. Too bad it had been the setting for such horror. She stopped at the window and stared out into the night. The turret was a world apart, the king's crown, the top hat, the diamond stud that jutted to the sky in clear view of everyone. Unless you had the drapes drawn tight, it was risky business to do anything up here you didn't want folks to see. So why in the world had Jerome, or someone else, chosen this very spot to commit a murder?

Unless, of course, the murderer hadn't chosen it.

A streak of lightning zigzagged across the sky. Something caught her eye, a darting movement in the shadows by the hedge. She watched and waited. But everything was still now.

Her nerves were on edge. Every shadow would be

sending her into a panic if she let them. But she wasn't going to. Rooster was on duty, and she was perfectly safe. Besides, even a killer would probably stay inside on a night like this. Rain pelted against the window, and lightning darted savagely across the stormy sky.

She moved back to the bed and slipped out of her shoes as a crash of thunder seemed to shake the house from its foundations. The lights blinked and then went out.

Her heart slammed against her chest, but she willed herself to speak calmly into the mike. "The electricity just went out, Rooster. But I'm fine."

"Stay put. I'm on my way. I don't want you up there alone in the dark."

Lindsey breathed deeply, telling herself over and over there was no reason to be afraid. Rooster was on his way. She relaxed even more as the door flew open and a large figure barged into the room.

"You made it, but you must be soaked," she said, jumping from the bed to help him out of his wet clothes.

"There's no time for talking. Just get your raincoat."

Blind panic clutched at Lindsey's lungs, stealing her breath away. The voice was not Rooster's.

She scooted to the back of the room. Her mike was still on, and Rooster would hear everything. She just had to stay alive until he made it to her door.

The man rushed across the room and wrapped his strong arms about her, half carrying her, half dragging her, toward the door.

"You won't get away with this," she whispered through clenched teeth. She felt it then, the small prick at the back of the neck, the cold blade of a knife on her skin.

"Don't fight me. We have to get out of here fast," he

whispered. He yanked her raincoat from the hook by the door and threw it over her shoulders. "Just run," he urged, "as fast as you can, and don't stop. If you do, you'll be dead. There'll be no screwups this time."

Rain pummeled Lindsey's face and cut through her clothes as her abductor forced her down the steps at a dizzying pace. But Rooster would show up any second. That was the plan. She would be safe, and the killer would be caught.

A bolt of lightning split the sky in half, turning the darkness to day. Lindsey twirled around and glimpsed the face of the man who held her captive.

Her breath caught in her throat, new terror squeezing her breath away. The face that had stared at her from the turret window was staring at her again. Only this time it didn't disappear. Horror clutched and clawed at her insides. The nightmare was no longer a dream.

"Don't do this, Jerome." She stifled a sob that tore at her throat. "I know you murdered the woman in the turret. I saw you."

He shoved her in front of him, the point of the knife like a needle on her skin.

"Give yourself up," she pleaded. "If not for you, then do it for your mother."

"Run, lady. Just run." His own voice was hoarse and shaky. "Everything's out of control." He hastened his pace, his feet and hers barely skimming the steps as they neared the bottom. "Don't slow down," he warned, the knife pressing against her skin. "Head for the bushes in the back of the house."

She grabbed the railing and prayed for the lightning to strike again. One blinding flash could illuminate her and, hopefully, alert someone driving by.

Strong hands pulled her fingers loose from the railing

and dragged her along, but her obstinacy slowed their pace. That was all it took.

A large figure jumped from the back door of the house. He stepped in front of Jerome, a shiny metal object in his hand. A quiet thud sounded in the night, and then Jerome fell at her feet.

"I never cared much for your choice of friends."

"Thomas!" She fell against him, relief turning her bones to liquid. "How did you find me?"

"It's a knack I have. Being in the right place at the right time. It's one you should have worked on."

Lindsey fell to her knees in the blinding rain and felt for Jerome's pulse.

"Don't waste your time. He's dead."

He took her hand and led her back toward the turret steps. She followed him gladly. Who would ever have thought she would be this happy to see Thomas LeBlanc?

THE TIRES on Graham's unmarked police car squealed as he rounded the corner by the hospital parking lot. Brigit was so weak she had barely been able to speak, but she had given Graham the information he needed. A positive identification.

He still didn't understand the alibi routine. But he would before it was all over. Brigit hadn't wavered for a second. She had seen the man up close, too close. She'd remember the face of her attacker for as long as she lived.

Hopefully, that would be for a great many years. And, hopefully, Thomas LeBlanc would spend all of them behind bars.

## Chapter Fifteen

Lindsey ran for shelter, her bare feet slipping on the rain-drenched steps. She had almost made it to the second-floor balcony before she realized Thomas was not behind her. She bent over the railing and tried to see why he had not followed her, but the rain and darkness made it impossible.

Finally Thomas rounded the corner of the house and raced up the steps behind her. Rain dripped from Lindsey's hair, trickling down her neck in icy rivers. She pulled the raincoat tighter and started back up the narrow steps that led to the turret.

One foot slipped on the metal, and she grabbed for the rail. The electricity was still out in the house and in the surrounding neighborhood. They were bathed in darkness, without even the glow from streetlights to illuminate their slippery path.

At last they reached the top step, and Thomas swung the door open wide, all but pushing her inside.

"Well, here we are, just the two of us."

A sinister tone colored his voice. Bewildering apprehension shot a surge of adrenaline through Lindsey's body as her mind tried to understand the sudden change in her savior. Impulsively she backed toward the door.

Thomas slammed it shut and turned a key in the dead bolt. "You wouldn't really want to go out in the storm again, now would you? Not when it's so cozy up here in the turret."

"No, why would I want to leave? You just saved me from a murderer." For some sick reason, he delighted in seeing her frightened, but she wouldn't play his games. Not now that she was finally safe. "There are two police cars cruising the area. They routinely check with Rooster." She eased past Thomas and stood in front of the window. "As soon as he fails to answer their call, they'll be in here to check on him and me."

"I wouldn't count on it." Thomas moved to her side.

"And why is that?" she questioned, suddenly afraid to hear his answer.

"Because Rooster must have told them he would be away from his post. When the lights went out, he headed up here to find you. Unfortunately, he found me first. He won't be finding anything else."

Thomas reached over and pulled Lindsey's raincoat from her shoulders, lowering it and slipping it off her arms. Her thin dress clung to her damp skin, and she hugged herself for warmth, and for cover. She knew Thomas couldn't see much in the dark, but her skin prickled from the memories of past encounters.

"What did you do to Rooster?" Her voice cracked, the inner trembling taking its toll.

"You needn't worry about him now. You have problems of your own. But at least *you* have a choice." He scooted closer, his muscled chest brushing against her back. "If you do what I ask, you won't have to die."

"I don't understand. Jerome murdered Roxanne and Danielle. Not you. You risked your life to save me from him."

He loosened his grip, letting his hands roam her arms possessively. Cold terror knotted in her stomach. She was standing in front of the turret window, in the very spot where Roxanne had crumpled to the floor, her blood flowing freely across the green velvet ball gown.

Now Lindsey was here with a new madman. She tried to jerk away, but Thomas's hands tightened on her arms.

He threw his head back, and his laugh filled the room, raucous and maddening. "You just don't get it, do you? You and your cop friend think you know everything. But you overlooked one costly little detail."

"What was that, Thomas?" She forced the words past the suffocating lump in her throat.

"You weren't the only one who witnessed the Mardi Gras murder. I saw it, too."

Her mind struggled to comprehend. "Then you know Jerome's guilty. No one will blame you for anything." Lindsey had to keep him talking. Words were far safer than deadly silence or the sound of his deranged laughter. "But how could you have seen the murder? You went straight from the airport to the party."

"Almost. I had planned to come by here first and freshen up, but your little parade got in my way. Too bad for you and Jerome. When I couldn't get through, I parked a few blocks away, planning to walk to the house and change."

"But instead you saw the light in the turret."

"You catch on fast."

"Apparently not fast enough."

"Once I saw the light," he continued, clearly enjoying bragging about his criminal prowess, "I had to get close enough to see who was nosing about in my apartment."

"So you stood and watched while Jerome killed Roxanne. You watched and then dashed off to party with your friends. I don't believe it. Not even you could be that heartless.''

Thomas jerked her toward the turret door. ''You're about to find out just how heartless I *can* be. Especially for half a million dollars that should have been mine anyway.''

''The jewels belonged to Katie,'' Lindsey reminded him through shivering lips.

Thomas held Lindsey's arm with one hand and swung open the inner turret door with the other, all the time dragging her closer to the dark inner passage.

''The money good old Uncle Dick used to buy his wife and her playthings should have been mine.'' Vengeance hardened his voice. ''Richard LeBlanc is a dirty cheat. He tricked my father out of his share of the LeBlanc business. My old man got a lousy quarter of a million in cash. Poor Uncle Dick kept this house, and total control of a multimillion-dollar business he claimed was going down the tubes. Generous of him, wasn't it?''

Lindsey dug her feet into the carpet, resisting Thomas's attempts to force her through the inner door. It led to the narrow passage and then the metal steps that dropped into the second-floor storage room. She feared whatever Thomas planned for her would not be pleasant.

''So you just came to Jerome and demanded he let you in on the heist?'' she questioned, stalling for precious time. ''Weren't you afraid Jerome would kill you as he did Roxanne?''

''Jerome? Ha! He's a wimp. A cowardly, sniveling wimp. He killed his girlfriend in a fit of rage, but he would never have gotten away with it on his own. He would have squealed his guts out the first time the police questioned him.''

Fear clogged Lindsey's lungs like poisonous smoke.

She struggled for air, and for her racing heart to calm. "I thought Roxanne was Garon's girlfriend."

"Then you're a lot stupider than you look. A babe like that would never fall for someone like Garon. Jerome set up that romance, got his gullible brother and Roxy together so she could talk Garon into bringing her to the LeBlanc house. It was the only way to find out how to get into the safe. Katie wouldn't even trust me with that bit of information."

"Imagine that," Lindsey quipped. She and Graham had missed the boat about Thomas's involvement, but apparently part of their theory was on target. Roxanne had taken the jewels, but she had not given them to Jerome. She had double-crossed her accomplice, hiding the jewels somewhere in the house before he arrived.

"You thought you could blackmail Jerome, make him share the take with you. But you still don't have the jewels, do you, Thomas? Because Roxy hid them a little too well."

"That's where you come in." Thomas's fingers dug into Lindsey's flesh as he pulled her through the door and into the narrow passageway. "You see, I *do* know where the jewels are. It took a while, since I've never been privy to family secrets, but I finally discovered the entry to the secret passage. It's no more than a rat hideaway now, but when the house was built it was a neat little pathway for hiding Great-grandfather LeBlanc's smuggled goods."

"So you're not the first LeBlanc to be a thief?"

"No. I'm only better at it."

Thomas shoved Lindsey through the passage, his own body pressing into hers, forcing her to keep walking. They had almost reached the end when he stopped. She pressed her body against the wall, the coolness wrapping around her like a ghostly shadow. Thomas leaned over her and circled his right hand about her neck before letting it slide to the flesh between her breasts.

Her body jerked in revulsion, and she filled the air with her screams. It didn't matter that there was no one in the house to hear, or that the wind and rain would drown out the sound. She just couldn't take any more.

Thomas's reaction was swift and brutal. One hand slammed across her face, while the other found the hidden microphone and ripped it from her skin. He let go of her mouth and grinned.

"You can kill me, Thomas, but you won't get away with it." She hurled the words like bullets. Fury mingled with her fear now, and she refused to continue in the role of frightened victim. It gave him too much pleasure.

"Wrong again. If I kill you, I *will* get away with it. The police are after Jerome. You said so yourself. They suspected me at first. In fact, your stinking detective longed to pin Roxanne's murder on me. But he couldn't. I was innocent of that one."

"And what about Danielle's? Are you innocent of her murder?" Lindsey spit the words contemptuously.

"I merely planned it. I only meant to plan the other girl's, too. You know, Brigit, the pretty one. But by then Jerome was losing the stomach for killing young women."

"But not you?"

"I do whatever it takes. It's a talent of mine. When Jerome lost the guts to get rid of possible witnesses, I had to step in. I couldn't let Jerome be identified and arrested before I had time to find the jewels and skip the country. He'd squeal loud and long and make sure I was thrown in the cooler with him."

"And once you had the jewels, you wouldn't have to worry. You planned all along to kill Jerome, too."

"Right again. Only I planned to do it here, in the privacy of the turret. He was supposed to be watching you while I took care of that cop. Instead, the fool tried to help you escape."

Thomas leaned into Lindsey again, and once more her stomach tied itself into a thousand knots. But he wasn't touching her with his creeping hands. He was fiddling with something above her head. And then the wall behind her began to move, swinging open to drop her into a new hell. She fell to the floor, the frigid dampness so thick it clogged her lungs.

Using her hands for support, she managed to pull herself to a standing position. The ceiling was higher here, and she no longer had to stoop. She spread her arms. The slimy feel of moist concrete met her fingertips. The passage was about two feet in diameter, wide enough for her to move her arms freely, narrow enough that she shuddered at the claustrophobic boundaries.

"Is this the passage Roxy persuaded Garon to show her?"

"One of them. Fortunately, she was thoughtful enough to leave it ajar in her rush to hide the jewels before Jerome arrived."

"Of course. Where else could he have hidden the body so conveniently?" Lindsey added, another piece of the puzzle suddenly falling into place.

Thomas followed her inside the narrow passage and prodded her along. "Don't stop yet. You have a job to do. I want the jewels in my hands, and you don't have a lot of time left to find them. If you don't get back quickly, I'll have no choice but to close this door and leave you inside. And it would be a shame to bury someone as lovely as you in such a primitive tomb. Especially since your heart will still beat, and your lungs will still struggle for air.''

Lindsey forced her trembling body to move forward. Thomas was so close behind her that the sound of his breathing hammered in her ears. ''Roxanne hid the jewels somewhere in the secret passage,'' Lindsey said, wanting to talk, to hear her own voice, strong and alive. ''That way she could disappear from the masquerade ball that was supposed to serve as alibi. She planned to retrieve them when Jerome was not around and hop a plane for some foreign port.''

''So you have done some of your homework. Too bad it's too little, too late.'' Thomas still pushed behind her, but his forward progress had slowed. The passage was growing narrower, and his body could barely squeeze between the walls.

''All you wanted were the jewels. But the longer it took to find them, the more likely it was that Garon or Jerome would talk and the real story might start to unfold.'' Lindsey was no longer able to keep the trembling from her voice. Each step increased the likelihood of Thomas's prophecy coming true. The concrete tomb she walked through might be her own. ''If you're sure the jewels are in here, Thomas, why haven't you already found them yourself? You could be long gone by now.''

''You'll find out soon enough.''

Lindsey took a longer step. Her toe slammed against a wooden wall. ''Looks like this is the end of the trail, Thomas.''

''For me, but not for you.''

Once more, he pushed against her, perspiration beading on his skin, in spite of the temperature, which seemed to dip closer to freezing with each step that led them deeper into the passage. His hands were above her now, fumbling with something she couldn't see. But then, she couldn't even see her own hands in the blackness that surrounded them.

This time she was prepared for the opening door. "And did Roxanne leave this door open for you, too?"

"No, this one I found all by myself. Of course, I would never have thought to search for it if she hadn't already been so helpful."

Lindsey's hips brushed against the wall as the passage grew tighter. She squeezed farther. It was almost impossible to move now, and she no longer heard Thomas's breathing.

"Keep going." Thomas's voice echoed down the chamber. "And don't even think about taking your time. If your boyfriend returns, I'll have to give up on you, slam the passage door and leave you for the rats. They'll be the only ones who can hear your screams then."

The laugh began again, only this time it was a thousand times worse. It tumbled through the narrow passage, bouncing and echoing off of every surface, like a legion of madmen chasing at her heels.

Lindsey pushed ahead. Thomas wouldn't be following her now. If he tried, he would become lodged between the rough surfaces and left to die with the rats himself. That was the reason he hadn't found the jewels. He needed her slender body to maneuver down the icy passage. It was the only reason she was still alive.

She inched her way forward and around a curve. The downward slant of the floor was much steeper here. The passage had to be leading from the turret to the second floor. Thomas was probably right. This was the most likely place for Roxanne to have hidden the jewels. She could have just opened the door to this passage and tossed them, letting them slide down the slope to the end of the passage.

Garon had probably shown her how to open the door, but he wouldn't have brought her down here. He couldn't have made it through himself. So Roxanne would have had no idea that she was hiding the jewels so well she might never be able to retrieve them. And she hadn't lived long enough to find out.

Lindsey tried to concentrate, but the fear and cold were numbing her senses. She struggled, pulling a large gulp of stale air into her lungs. She had to stay alert, to examine every possibility for her own escape. Passageways had to lead somewhere. If not…

No, she couldn't think of that. She crept along, determined to focus on outsmarting the psycho who temporarily ruled her life.

Her foot brushed against something, and panic shot through her body. She forced her heart to calm. Whatever was down there was not alive. It was clunky, a soft bag of some kind, filled with loose items and with some sort of cord.

She kneaded the bag with the sole of her right foot. The jewels. She couldn't be certain, but the chances were good she had just located the stolen treasures. There was no room to bend over and pick them up, but she wasn't leaving them behind. Dragging the bag with one foot, she squeezed forward, and then stopped.

Her heart pounded maddeningly in her chest. The walls pressed into her breasts like suffocating hands, robbing her of breath. She had reached the end of the line. A tear slid down her cheek. She couldn't even wipe it away. There was no room for her to lift her hand from her side.

A man's voice rang again from somewhere above her.

It must be Thomas, although she couldn't tell anymore. The words echoed in garbled fashion through the narrow tunnel.

Thomas would wait for her as long as he could. Then, when the police finally sensed something was wrong and appeared at the house, he would close and lock the door to the passageway and disappear into the night. He would do it without the jewels, but that was little consolation now.

She could make her way back through the dark and give him the jewels, or take her chances on being discovered by the police. If she returned, Thomas would kill her. If she didn't return, she would probably die here, frozen and alone in this dark tomb.

GRAHAM ROUNDED the corner at breakneck speed, his tires skidding dangerously on the rain-slick streets. Brigit had given him what he needed, a positive identification of the man who had tried to kill her. Now he would finally be able to convince Lindsey to give up her dangerous game.

Relief flowed through his body, letting his muscles begin to uncoil from the knots of anxiety that had tormented him since the first moment he had suspected Lindsey's life might be in danger. Protecting her had become an obsession, a driving force that had replaced the need for food or sleep, the need for everything except finding the killer.

He still didn't understand how Thomas had managed such a convincing alibi for the night of the Minerva parade, but the story would crack now that the police had a witness who could identify the killer. Brigit had been determined to give Graham what he needed, struggling through her pain to provide an unbelievably detailed description of the man who had attacked her so brutally.

And if Graham had held any doubts about the identity of Brigit's attacker, they had vanished the second he flashed the photograph of Thomas LeBlanc. The sudden trembling that had overcome Brigit's weak body and the sheer terror that had burned in her eyes were all the proof he needed.

Graham rounded a corner onto the avenue. The rain had lost some of its intensity now, but an eerie darkness encircled him. Apparently the electricity had not been restored. But at least he knew Lindsey was still safe. Rooster had radioed him the second the lightning knocked out the power, and Graham had backed his decision fully. Lindsey should not be left alone in total darkness.

He turned down the side street. There was Rooster's car, all right, parked in the shadows of a giant oak, on a street dotted with other parked cars. Graham slowed, but didn't stop. Rooster was obviously still in the turret with Lindsey.

Graham eased his unmarked car into a parking space at the back edge of the LeBlanc property. He could squeeze through the hedge and take the back steps directly to the turret. It would be a lot quicker that way, and the sooner he saw Lindsey, the better. She'd be thrilled with his latest discovery, and this time, when he took her in his arms, he wouldn't have to let go for a long, long time.

Rushing from the car, Graham headed straight for the bushes that formed a natural fence around the back yard. He pushed a branch of the hedge aside. A noise, a rustling of footsteps, stopped him in his tracks. It was probably Rooster, he assured himself, but his right hand instinctively dropped to the loaded pistol at his side.

He shifted, trying to peer between the leaves, but only darkness met his gaze. He reached for the compact flashlight that hung from his waist and aimed in the direction of the noise. He wouldn't use it unless he had to. He much preferred the element of surprise. If it wasn't Rooster behind the hedge, then chances were good it was Thomas LeBlanc, waiting for his chance to add one last victim to his list.

Graham's pulse quickened, but not with fear. It was pure anticipation that heightened his senses. He waited, scarcely daring to breathe, praying for just one quick strike of the lightning that had flashed across the skies like fireworks for the past half hour.

The rustling grew closer. A car rounded the corner behind Graham, its headlights briefly washing over the bushes. But that one brief moment was enough to bring the scene into view. There were two people on the other side of the fence. One crouched, his face hidden from the view. The other one was lying dead still on the wet ground. Graham felt a sickening lurch in the pit of his stomach. The crouched figure was not Rooster.

Silently he slipped the gun from the holster and charged through the bushes. "Don't make a move," he growled, the gun pointed squarely at the man's chest.

The dark figure turned slowly to face him, but didn't try to rise from his stooped position. "You've got this all wrong, Detective, as usual."

The deep voice of Thomas LeBlanc came as no surprise. "No," Graham shot back. "I finally have it all right." He flicked on the flashlight with his left hand, his right still busy holding the weapon that kept Thomas in place. He directed the beam at the ground near the edge of the bushes and into the dead stare of Jerome Oleander.

Instantly Graham dropped to one knee and felt for a pulse, his eyes and pistol still riveted on Thomas. Again there were no surprises, and Graham felt the cold, lifeless wrist fall from his hand.

"This is not what it looks like. I just found the body myself," Thomas offered. "I was driving by when I noticed all the lights were out. My first thought was that something might have happened to Miss Green. I was rushing up to check on her when I stumbled over Jerome here."

"Save your breath, LeBlanc. Your lies won't help you now."

"I know you're itching to pin the rap on me, Detective, but you're out of luck this time. I'm squeaky-clean."

"Sure you are," Graham quipped, barking his orders for backup into the police radio.

"Wait. Shine your light over here, on Jerome's left hand. I thought I saw something there when you waved that flashlight around."

Graham lowered the beam from the twisted face of the newest victim, past the bloodied chest to the right hand and then the left. A silver revolver was tucked into his right hand, its flickering glint a sinister contrast to the life that had been snuffed from the young man holding it. A crumpled scrap of paper rested against the left side of his body, kept in place by a limp hand. Thomas moved the hand and retrieved the note, holding it up to catch the flashlight's beam.

"Get to your feet, Thomas. We'll read it later. Right now, you're going to get your wish. We're heading up the stairs to check on Officer Green." Thomas hesitated, and Graham moved closer, poking the pistol into his ribs. "I said move it, if you ever want to move again."

Thomas thrust the note toward Graham and stepped back. "I'm sorry, Detective. But it looks like we're both too late. Miss Green is apparently as dead as poor Jerome. And according to this note, her body will never be found."

Fury mixed with unbelievable pain, coursing through Graham's body with the force of a freight train, robbing him of reason. Robbing him of everything that mattered.

He raised the pistol, pointing it at Thomas's right temple. "You no-good, lying..." Curses flew from his lips, mixing with the taste of gall that choked him and drove him on. "Start walking, Thomas. Take me to her now. If you don't, I'll pull this trigger and blow you into little pieces."

"You won't pull that trigger, Dufour, and you know it. You have nothing on me, and you're too much a cop to take the law in your own hands."

And then his laughter rang out, filling the night with a taunting madness that tore away Graham's last vestiges of control. He pressed the short barrel of the pistol into the flesh at Thomas's temple. Without a word, he slipped his hand over the cold metal hammer and cocked it.

A COLD SHUDDER shook Lindsey's body as new noises assaulted her senses. The frightening sounds of footsteps and voices rumbled and echoed down the dark passageway. She tried to scoot farther into the tunnel, but she had already wedged her body as far as she could go. She had waited in the darkness for hours—or was it only minutes?

"Lindsey!"

The deep voice blared through the tunnel. It was much

closer than before. She tilted her head as much as possible. A glare stung at her eyes, and she forced them open. She was staring straight ahead, but the darkness had washed away. Instead, she was looking into a light so strong, it all but blinded her.

"Lindsey!"

Squinting, she turned and stared into the light.

"Lindsey!"

Her heart pounded against her chest. Was it Graham's voice that was calling her back up the incline and to the light, or did she just want it to be? Was it really Thomas luring her back into his trap? Thomas the terrible, waiting to kill again. She slumped against the wall. She couldn't think anymore, couldn't make decisions.

"I can't come any farther, Lindsey. If you're down there, you'll have to come to me."

The voice rolled on a wave of ghostly echoes.

There was no way to be sure what lay behind the light. But she knew what waited for her in the frigid dampness of the concrete tomb. Slowly she backed toward the light and the entreating voice.

"Answer me, Lindsey. If you're down there, say something. Say anything."

"I'm coming, Graham. I'm coming." She moved faster. The passageway was wider here, and she could actually move her arms and stand straight. She filled her lungs with air. The light was still shining, but the voice had dissolved into whispers.

And then a strong hand curled around hers and pulled her the last two feet, wrapping her in arms so strong, she knew she was home.

"Are you all right?"

"I am now, Graham. I am now."

GRAHAM STOKED the logs in the fireplace, creating a blaze that warmed Lindsey from across the room. She snuggled under the quilt he'd wrapped around her and sipped the hot, milky concoction of liquors and hot chocolate he'd said would warm her tummy.

But she didn't need the fire, the quilt or the drink to warm her insides. Graham was all she needed. She scooted over and made room for him to nudge his way in beside her.

"The case is solved, and Katie has her jewels back, but are you sure Rooster is all right?"

"He's fine," Graham answered, wrapping an arm around her. "Or at least he will be. Except for a little pain and a severe case of wounded pride. Thomas was the first guy who'd ever gotten the better of him. Thankfully, the bullet missed its mark by a lifesaving inch."

"It would never have happened if the electricity hadn't gone out."

"True. But you know my partner. He never makes excuses for himself."

"He's lucky to be alive." Lindsey cuddled closer into Graham's arms. "It's a wonder Thomas didn't kill him the way he did Jerome. The way he tried to kill me."

Graham nestled his chin in her hair. "He tried, all right. He had already closed and bolted the hidden doors to the passageway when I found him planting the evidence on Jerome's body."

"Thomas's gun, and the fake suicide note that explained Jerome was responsible for all the murders, that he could no longer live with himself." She felt the icy tremor snake up her spine once more, and she snuggled all the closer. "If you hadn't caught Thomas planting the evidence, he'd never have told you how to find me."

"Even then he wouldn't have. It took a .38 propped

against his right temple to convince him it was time to come clean.''

Graham slid his lips across her ear. ''I was so afraid I had lost you again, Lins.''

His voice cracked and broke on the words, and Lindsey tilted her head toward his. His lips were drawn into tight lines, but his eyes were misty pools of love.

''I don't ever want to know that feeling again,'' he said. ''I don't think I could and still survive.''

Lindsey traced his lips with her finger, easing the tight set of his mouth. ''You won't have to, Graham. I love you. I always have.''

''And now we'll have our time.''

''And Brigit will have hers,'' Lindsey added, warmth finally melting away the last traces of icy fear. ''The doctors say it'll be a long battle, but they're expecting a full recovery. It's a miracle. That was the only way they could describe it.''

''A miracle. I finally believe in them myself. Now that I have you in my arms again.''

Graham lowered his mouth to hers. His lips were soft and coaxing, promising a time for healing and a lifetime of pleasures to come. Finally he drew away and placed his hand under her chin, easing it up to meet his smoky gaze.

''I hate to let you go back to Nashville.''

''I know, but we won't be apart for long. When the project I'm working on now is finished, I'll move back to New Orleans. My friend at Tulane has been after me for years to join her research staff.''

''You do whatever you have to do.'' He traced a finger down her neck, dipping it into the cleavage of her unbound breasts. ''Dammit, I'll miss you like crazy, but we'll work it out. Nashville is only a short flight away.''

"I was wrong about you, Graham. You have changed a lot in ten years. You're far more wonderful than I remembered, better even than all my years of dreaming."

He kissed her again, but this time the gentleness was lost in the passion her words had licked into a roaring blaze. "Just wait," he said temptingly, his hands once again working their magic. "You ain't seen nothin' yet. I'm going to show you more love than you ever dreamed of."

And this time she believed every word he said.

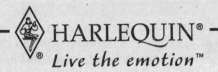

# HARLEQUIN®
# INTRIGUE®

## BREATHTAKING ROMANTIC SUSPENSE

Shared dangers and passions lead to electrifying
romance and heart-stopping suspense!

Every month, you'll meet six new heroes
who are guaranteed to make your spine tingle
and your pulse pound. With them you'll enter
into the exciting world of Harlequin Intrigue—
where your life is on the line
and so is your heart!

## THAT'S INTRIGUE—
## ROMANTIC SUSPENSE
## AT ITS BEST!

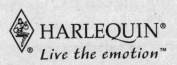

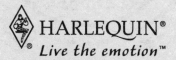

# Harlequin® Historical
### Historical Romantic Adventure!

*Imagine a time of chivalrous knights and unconventional ladies, roguish rakes and impetuous heiresses, rugged cowboys and spirited frontierswomen—these rich and vivid tales will capture your imagination!*

*Harlequin Historical . . . they're too good to miss!*

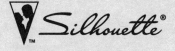

## SPECIAL EDITION™

Emotional, compelling stories that capture the intensity of living, loving and creating a family in today's world.

Modern, passionate reads that are powerful and provocative.

## nocturne

Dramatic and sensual tales of paranormal romance.

Romances that are sparked by danger and fueled by passion.

SDIR07